Other Titles By Deatri King-Bey

BEAUTY AND THE BEAST

CAUGHT UP

EBONY ANGEL

Whisper Something Sweet

Deatri King-Bey

Parker Publishing, LLC

Noire Passion is an imprint of Parker Publishing, LLC.

Published by Parker Publishing, LLC
12523 Limonite Avenue, Suite #440-245
Mira Loma, California 91752
www.parker-publishing.com

ISBN 978-1-60043-011-4

First Edition

Manufactured in the United States of America

Developmental Editing by Chesya Burke http://www.chesyaburke.com

Dedication

To my fellow sweet-a-holics out there!!!!

Acknowledgements

I thank…

God for the many blessings he bestows on me.

My family and friends for putting up with me (SMILE).

Angelique Justin for not allowing me to say, "I can't."

Carlos Jackson for being a beautiful person and for giving of his time to answer my questions about police procedures.

Chesya, my developmental editor, for her attention to detail and keeping me from going overboard. Brandi Green, my copy editor, and KB Mello, my proofreader, for working behind the scenes to make sure I don't take three lines to say what could be said in one and ensuring my "i" before "e" except after "c". I appreciate you ladies greatly.

My readers for asking for more.

CHAPTER ONE

The keys dropped from Sweetie's shaky hands. "I'm coming, Tess!" Her size fourteen double-pleated slacks didn't want to cooperate as she bent and snatched the keys off the floor. "Just two more seconds. Hold on, honey."

At the sound of her best friend's frantic voice over the phone, Sweetie had made the twenty-minute ride from the north side of Chicago in fifteen minutes flat, skipped the wait for the elevator and raced up five flights of stairs. She'd tried to call Tess several times as she weaved through traffic, to no avail.

Twice in as many months, Tess had explained suspicious bruises on her arms away to clumsiness. There were a lot of things folks could rightfully call Sweetie, but stupid wasn't one of them. The marks wrapped around her friend's arms couldn't have been made by bumping into anything, yet against her better judgment, Sweetie remained silent.

"If he touched her, I swear to God, I'll kill him!" She inserted the spare key Tess had given her into the lock. Door unlocked, she turned the knob, swung the door open and rushed into the apartment.

A hideous, pimp-daddy red, velvet sectional still dominated the living room. No blood stains were on the cluttered floor or tacky furniture. Dirty dishes and glasses littered the coffee table. A *Lost* rerun showed on the plasma screen. Clothes were strewn about. Everything was as usual, but there was no sign of Tess.

An anguished moan caught Sweetie's attention. She whipped her head toward the hallway that led to the bedroom.

"Please, Kevin, stop…" Tess whined.

Oh shit, he's killing her. Though a big girl, Sweetie knew better than to take on a man without a weapon to help level the playing field. She quickly scanned the room for an equalizer. The steak knife on the plate may give him a nasty cut and a bacterial infection, but didn't have the immediate stopping power she needed. She chastised herself for not speaking up about her concerns and for wearing open-toed sandals into battle.

"Kevin…please…stop…"

Frantic, Sweetie grabbed the knife and prayed for a miracle. She found her miracle in the form of Kevin's baseball bat, which was under a pile of clothes she'd stumbled over. He played for his company team, but thought he was better than Barry Bonds ever was. If he laid another hand on Tess, Sweetie would redefine "home run."

She crept down the hall for a surprise attack.

"You have to forgive me," Kevin said. "You can't live without this."

Back flush against the wall outside of the bedroom, Sweetie inhaled and exhaled deeply to calm her nerves, then tipped into the room. The sight before her eyes was unfathomable. Too stunned to move, she stared as Tess lay on the bed, dress hunched up and legs spread wide as Kevin milked her clit with his tongue.

"We can't do this, stop…" Tess squirmed slightly, but she didn't look to be in the type of distress Sweetie heard over the phone.

"You have to forgive me." He held her hips steady as he continued his oral assault.

A sucking, slurping noise Sweetie must have been to upset to notice before filled the room. Disgusted and pissed to the highest *pissivity* that her best friend had worried her so, Sweetie turned to leave.

"But Sweetie," Tess panted, "might be on her way…"

"Fuck that fat bitch."

"Aw, hell naw!" Sweetie cut in.

Eyes and mouth wide open, Tess jolted her body upright.

Kevin spun around. "What the—"

Sweetie wound up to hit a homerun. "This *fat bitch* is about to fuck—*you*—up!"

"Shit, Sweetie." He scrambled off the bed and backed away with his jeans unzipped, bulge shriveling and his hands up slightly. "I didn't mean it like that."

"You," she nodded at Tess, "close your legs and mouth and put some clothes on. You," she pointed the bat at Kevin, "have ten seconds to explain how you meant 'fat bitch.' If I don't like your answer, well…" She shrugged.

"Dammit, Tess, get your girl. She's crazy!"

"Shut up, Kevin!" Tess leapt out of the bed and stood between the two of them. There was a new bruise on her upper arm and shoulder her skimpy, black dress didn't cover.

"So now I'm a crazy, fat bitch. Wrong answer!" The fear she saw in his beady, black eyes almost made her laugh. Abusive men were such punks. Her mother had dated one or two abusive men and quickly kicked them to the curb. The one thing Sweetie and her mother agreed on was not to allow a man to put his hands on you. "Im'ma show you crazy. Tess, how did you get that bruise on your arm?"

Tess's gaze went from Sweetie to Kevin back to Sweetie. "I…I…must have bumped into something. You know how clumsy I can be. And I bruise so easily."

"You've only been clumsy since you've been living with Kevin. Now this is the *last* time I will ask. How did you get that bruise on your arm?"

Tess bit her bottom lip and shifted her weight from one bare foot to the other.

"Answer me, girl!"

"Kevin did it," Tess cried.

"You lying slut!" Kevin stepped forward, but retreated quickly when Sweetie reared back.

"So he's so good at sucking twat you'll allow him to cheat, beat your ass *and* call you out of your name. Now that's what I call crazy."

"What the hell you been telling her, Tess!" He tugged his sagging jeans up.

"Everything," Sweetie answered before Tess had a chance. "Now be quiet. Is this the life you want, Tess? If this is what you want, fine. I'm out of here, and don't call me for this mess again. If not, pack your shit, and let's go."

Kevin inched forward. "She's not leaving."

Full lips pursed, Sweetie calmly stated, "I don't like you. Take one step closer, and I'll show you how much. It's your *choice*, Tess. I'll support whatever *you* want."

"I…I wanna go, but…but…I don't have anywhere."

"I'll bet the this jag off has you believing that garbage. Girl, pack your stuff."

Tess hopped over the dirty clothes on the floor to the closet, tugged her bags off the top shelf and set them on the bed.

"Tess," he barked, "I'm not taking you back if you leave with this f…with Sweetie."

Smile wide enough to show all thirty-two pearly whites, Sweetie cooed, "Do you promise? Now strip."

He tossed the are-you-serious look at her.

"You said I was crazy, right?" Sweetie smashed the lamp on the nightstand next to Kevin. He just about jumped out of his pants. "Well, I'd hate to disappoint you." She glanced over at Tess who was throwing her clothes from the drawers to the suitcase.

"Sheeeet…" He jerked his jersey over his head.

"Hurry up, Tess." While Tess scurried about, Sweetie watched Kevin. *What on earth does she see in him?* The same height as Sweetie, he was average height for a man. She'd lay odds his light skin and "good hair" landed quite a few women in his bed. The puny package he carried between his legs didn't impress her either. A nice thick girth and extended length were her cup of tea.

"I knew you were freaky." A sneaky grin slid across his lips. "See, Tess, she's just angry we didn't include her in our fun."

Tess didn't spare a glance at the two, but continued packing. Sweetie laughed at his arrogance. She'd had him strip to give them time to reach their cars before he came after them, yet this jerk actually had the nerve to be growing hard and stroking himself for a taste of the sweet one—at least that's what her former fiancé had called her.

"Now that I see what you have to offer," she said, "I fully understand why you prefer to go the oral route."

Hate flickered in his marble eyes. "Bitch!" He rushed toward Sweetie. She easily sidestepped and kicked him in the butt with all her might. The force of the kick sent him flying, face first. He threw his arms out to catch himself, but hit with a loud thump and skidded.

That had to hurt. Rug burn wasn't too nice as it was, especially down in the nether regions with that hard-on he had.

Tess squealed. Kevin slowly pushed himself up on all fours. Sweetie reared the bat back in case he decided to throw another pitch. "Oops, looks like Kevin's the clumsy one now."

"I'm done, Sweetie." Tess struggled to zip the overstuffed luggage. "Let's just go."

"Excellent." Tess hadn't even packed half of her things, but Sweetie was grateful. They needed to make a break for it before someone ended up in the hospital or in jail. "Kevin, be a gentleman and carry the lady's bags out to the car."

He shook his head as he stood. Several abrasions adorned his body. "You really are crazy if you think I'm stepping out of my apartment like this."

"You should know. After all, you are the one who deemed me crazy." Bat still in hand, she crossed her arms over her ample chest. "Edgerton Trust is trying to clean up its image, isn't it?" Wide eyed, she innocently tapped her chin with her index finger. "I wonder what they'd think about one of their junior execs being arrested for domestic battery."

"Hell, woman, being arrested for indecent exposure is just as bad."

"Duh! You did call me a bitch, didn't you? Well, I aim to please."

"I can't be arrested over this stupid shit. Tess, do something."

"Sweetie, I think he's learned his lesson." She hefted one of the large leather bags off the bed. "He'll stay away from me, won't you, Kevin?"

"Yeah, of course."

"You'd better stay away," Sweetie warned. "Now be a good boy and carry those bags to the door. Sorry, but I don't trust your scrawny ass."

Freshly showered and dressed in a yellow satin night slip and matching panties, Sweetie watched her reflection in the bathroom mirror, as she parted her natural hair into sections and twisted row after row of her medium-length, black tresses. She'd decided to go the natural route with her hair two years ago when she gave up trying to be what others wanted her to be. No more starving herself to fit into a size eight, no more running around like a chicken with her head cut off to please others, no more putting up with shit from men to find a husband, no more sitting back at work waiting for others to realize her abilities, no more.

This wasn't to say she wouldn't be there to support others, but she wouldn't allow anyone to define who she was or should be. Since her change in disposition, she was much happier and quickly climbing the corporate ladder, yet wasn't fulfilled.

Twists completed, she realized she'd forgotten to oil her hair. She opened the jar of hair butter, scooped out two fingers full and dapped the paste onto her palm, then rubbed her palms together to warm the hair food. For the most part, she loved her life and was grateful for all she had. When honest with herself, she felt guilty for wanting more when there were so many out there with so little. She massaged the hair butter into several of the twists that kissed her neck, then continued the process until all of her hair had been cared for properly.

Cared for properly. Her ex-boyfriends and fiancé could use several lessons on how to care for a lady properly. She knew there were good men out there. Her uncles, cousins and brothers proved daily that there were plenty of good men out there, but for some unexplainable reason, she only drew the trifling men. So two years ago when she gave up trying to morph into what others wanted, she also gave up men. Since she wasn't attracted to women, the companionship one receives from having a special someone in her life was missing from hers, leaving her stooped in loneliness. The choice between loneliness and the oftentimes painful drama of relationships wasn't an easy one to come to, but she felt she'd made the correct decision.

A *tap, tap*...at the bathroom door knocked her out of her musing. "Come in."

Dressed in an oversized white T-shirt, Tess tipped into the room and stood beside Sweetie. The two were as different as sandpaper and lotion, but had been best friends since junior high school. *You remind me so much of Mama, it's scary*, thought Sweetie.

Tess slowly lifted her sad hazel gaze to Sweetie's warm brown one. "I'm so sorry you had to come save me..." her slender shoulders slouched, "...again." She picked the brush off the cream marble sink and absently brushed her long, straight, honey-blonde hair. "I'm so tired of this..."

"Your life won't change until you take the steps to change it." Sweetie took the brush from Tess and brushed her hair to the back. "I can't do it for you." She sectioned her best friend's hair and began oiling then braiding it into large plaits and fastened each one with a ponytail holder. For as long as Sweetie could remember, Tess had played on her beauty to use males to get what she wanted, just as Sweetie's mother had. Over the years, the tables turned in a way Tess hadn't expected, and now she was dependent on men.

"I'm not like you." Tess fidgeted with the jar of hair butter. "You are the definition of strong black woman."

Many complemented Sweetie for being a strong black woman because she had her "head on straight" and "takes care of business," yet there was a piece of the equation some seemed to forget. Two years ago she'd also cut loose many of her "strong black woman" friends. They actually believed if a woman wanted to be more than desired by a man but wanted to be loved by a man, she was defining herself by her man and therefore less of a woman or saying she needed a man to be complete. In Sweetie's opinion, they were the ones defining themselves by their "man" status. Either way, she had as much time for those women as she had for the trifling men who were so attracted to her.

She pulled the braids away from Tess's face. "Don't believe the hype." She nodded at the bandana on the counter. "I need to tie your hair back or you'll be one giant zit in the morning."

"Hype my foot!" She fastened the bandana while Sweetie held her braids back. "You have everything!" She giggled. "Hell, I wish I could be you when I grow up."

"You're a fool." Sweetie joined her friend in laughter as she turned on the tap, and they washed her hands.

"I'm serious. If I could just say no to dick, I'd be in there." Tess snatched the hand towel off the rack.

"And tongue." Totally tickled, Sweetie dried her hands on the opposite end of the hand towel. Though joking, Sweetie knew Tess's real problem was love of money—actually, the things money could buy her. Unfortunately, Tess's only criteria for dating a man was how much he could spend on her.

"Oh Lawd have mercy, Kevin can work that tongue!" Tess fanned herself. "I don't know how you do it, sista girl!"

"Open that drawer down there for me." She motioned toward the corner linen cabinet.

The way Tess timidly pulled the drawer open and peeked inside, you would have thought she expected a poisonous snake to jump out. "Oh snap!" She selected a rectangular box a little over seven inches long and an inch or so in width. Smile spread across her lovely face, she teasingly asked, "And what do we have here?"

"Welcome to Sweetie's toy box." She crouched beside Tess. "In here you will find everything from the G-spot tickler to the Lily Vibe," she continued in her best announcer voice. "Batteries not include."

"Daaayum, I knew your freaky butt couldn't give up sex." She sat on the floor with her legs crossed.

"Oh no. It's still one of my favorite pastimes." She tapped the boxed Classic Vibrator Tess had initially taken out of the drawer and was still holding. "This was going to be your birthday gift, but you might as well have it now." She shuffled through the drawer for the unopened bottle of anti-bacterial toy cleaner. "Here you go."

Accepting the cleanser, Tess's narrow shoulders bounced as she giggled. "You are such a mess."

"Humph, I don't see you turning down the gift. You act right, come Christmas you'll find a Champ dildo in your stocking." She winked and made a double click sound with the back of her tongue as if to tell a horse to giddy-up. "Come on. This tile is too hard to be sitting on." She pulled Tess along and grabbed a second bandana to tie her own hair back.

"Shoot, I ain't mad at you." Tess left her new toy on the dresser, then took the bandana from Sweetie and fastened her hair with it. "But don't you want a real man sometimes?"

"Real man—yes. The drama associated with him—no thanks."

"I hear you. I'm through with Kevin. I should have kicked him to the curb the first time he hit me. But I can't give up men all together. I wish to God I was strong enough."

Sweetie flicked off her slippers, then slid between the sateen sheets of her Camelot king-sized bed. The cherry wood finish of the head and footboard blended perfectly with the hardwood floor and muted copper tones used to decorate the room, but she'd grown to hate the bed. She'd pleasured herself in every way imaginable in her bed, but the closest she ever came to having a second body in it was when Tess would spend the night.

The first few months of celibacy were difficult, but the more she distanced herself from men outside of work, the easier it became. She'd thought she'd conquered the want for male companionship until…She sighed as she sunk into the bed and propped her head on a pillow. Everything was hunky dory until Gabriel Windahl. Six months ago she'd called to give him a status report on a project, and her life hadn't been the same since.

He was her firm's largest client and had seduced her with his voice. When and how he accomplished this feat, she didn't know. What she did know was that the mere though of his deep, sensual voice had her moist between the legs and wishing Tess would sleep in the spare room so she could have private playtime with her toys.

The sound of Tess laughing broke Sweetie out of her lustful trance.

"You're thinking about Mr. Sexy Voice again, aren't you?"

"Go to sleep, Tess." She turned away and switched off the lamp on the nightstand.

"You're not getting out of this so easily, young lady," Tess said playfully as she poked Sweetie's shoulder. "Come clean. What's up with you two?"

"Nothing."

"What about the phone calls?"

Sweetie sucked air through her teeth and rolled over to face Tess. "Those are strictly business. You know I'm on the short list for a VP position, he's just giving advice."

Lips pursed, the sliver of moonlight that escaped though the cracks between the shades did little to hide the disbelief on Tess's face. "Yeah right." She palmed her breasts. "And I didn't have a boob job. You two talk in code."

Sweetie stifled a giggle. "Code?"

"You know what I'm talking about. To the outside world it sounds like you guys are discussing facts and figures, but the current, the tone, the feel would make a phone sex operator blush."

This time Sweetie actually laughed, and laughed hard. There was no reasonable explanation, but Tess was correct. Anyone reading a transcript of the "business calls" between Sweetie and Gabriel wouldn't think anything out of the norm, but to actually witness one—as Tess had on several occasions—was a totally different story.

"So we both are passionate when we talk shop. It's no big deal."

"You actually said that with a straight face. He's been trying to get you to travel across the pond to see him for months, but you keep weaseling out."

His last attempt to get Sweetie to his home country, Sweden, was the cutest by far, but she'd outsmarted him, yet again. A financial analyst by trade, she broke down the financial feasibility of new and established businesses. She did everything from writing business plans for upstart companies to cost assessments to helping corporations decide on investment opportunities.

This time Gabriel hired her firm to conduct a financial analysis of a software development company in Stockholm, Sweden. He had expressly asked for Sweetie—actually Monica Fuller, the name placed on her birth certificate thirty-five years ago—to lead the project.

The higher-ups bent over backwards to keep Gabriel Windahl happy and his money in their firm, and since Monica was their best financial analyst, they quickly assigned the project to her. Over the last two or three weeks, she'd allowed Gabriel to assume she would be heading to Sweden with the rest of the team she'd assembled to conduct interviews and pour through documentation at the main site. A devilish smile tipped her lips. It had to be at least midnight her time, so pretty soon he'd discover he'd assumed wrongly.

"I don't get you, Sweetie. You and this guy spend half the day talking, then you end up working half the night so you don't get behind. I Googled him, so I know he's one fine chocolate-chip, dimple-cheeked, deep-pocket brotha."

Sweetie didn't have anything against white men; she just wasn't physically attracted to them. And though Gabriel sounded like a brotha, she'd checked to make sure her fantasy man was actually a brotha. Needless to say, she was not disappointed. And those hands of his…she released a drawn-out breath of longing…how she wanted those thick fingers to caress her body into compliance for anything he wanted.

"Snap out of it, girl!" Tess clapped her hands. "Talk to me. You've been acting so non-Sweetie lately. Why won't you go for Gabriel?"

There were too many reasons to number. The main reason—she'd seen the women who clung to his side when she'd Googled him. Thin, beautiful, so light they were almost white, long straight hair—Tess. Though Sweetie considered herself beautiful, she wasn't thin, loved the kink in her natural hair, and no one would ever come close to mistaking her for white. "I have the perfect fantasy man. Why would I want to ruin it?"

"Because your fantasy can become reality with Gabriel."

"I'm sorry, but there is no way the real Gabriel can compete with my fantasy Gabriel. I've built him up so much in my mind." The fantasy Gabriel desired her for her mind, body and soul. The fantasy Gabriel didn't complete her, but complemented her. She rolled onto her belly, stuffed the pillow under her arms and rested her cheek on her interlaced fingers. "Logically, I know no man can compete, but I can't stop my mind from comparing, finding flaws and holding them against him. I value my friendship with him too much to let some stupid horny hormones screw this up."

"I guess I see your point. I just…Well, it seems like the only reason you allowed him to get this close is because he's halfway across the world. With him so far away, you don't see him as a danger to this life you're living."

"I guess I can't call you a dumb blonde today."

Tess giggled as she motioned about the bed. "This is a no hate zone. Seriously though, are you sure about this?"

"I'm not trading in a great friendship for a bunch of drama. No, make that *international drama.* With his money and looks, that man has worldwide drama as his shadow."

"Yeah, I guess you're right. I'll bet he has a long trail of women following him."

The thought of Gabriel with other women sent jealousy-laced chills through Sweetie. "Girl, stop messin' in my fantasy and straighten out your own life. You need to stop falling for these shallow pretty boys with a little pocket change and get a real man. What about James from the office?"

Tess jerked back as if slapped. "That broke tailed janitor. You *are* out your mind!"

"First off, he is the maintenance man, not janitor. And even if he were, so what? He's a good man, has a steady job, fine as all get out and interested in you."

"Girl, please. I need a man who can afford me. For such a great catch, I don't see you going for him."

"He can't compete with my fantasy Gabriel, and he is interested in you, not me. You keep going after the same type of man and ending up in the same type of unfulfilling relationships. I think it's time to try something different."

"Humph. This from a woman who hasn't been touched by a man in years."

"By choice. Now what are your plans?"

Tess rolled onto her back and placed her hands behind her head. "You're right. Forget men. I gotta get my finances together. I don't understand where all the money goes. I have credit card bills out the yang!"

Sweetie wasn't shocked. Tess worked as her personal assistant and earned an excellent salary, but she didn't make convertible Mercedes-type money—of which Tess had just purchased a new one a year ago at a ridiculously high interest rate. "Bring in your statements tomorrow, and I'll see what I can do. You need a budget, to cut debt, join shop-a-holics anonymous and to start a savings plan. Did you know that many times you can call credit card companies and simply ask them to lower the interest rate?" she rambled on. Talking shop excited her almost as much as the thought of hopping on a flight to Sweden dressed only in a fur coat and surprising Gabriel.

"You lyin'."

"Nope, ask my brother, Charles. I had his rates dropped from eighteen to ten percent on most of his cards and set his butt up with a payment plan and budget. He is even investing monthly now." All three of her brothers had done well for themselves career-wise. Two were obstetricians and one was a contract lawyer. Though all four siblings had different fathers, their mother ensured each father paid heavy child support, so they all were raised in the best private schools and had no issues making tuition payments for college. Another lesson Sweetie's mother pounded into her head was: "Don't have no babies with no broke-ass man!"

If Sweetie had the choice of having her father or the money he sent monthly, she would have chosen her father. She didn't completely fault her mother for her father's absence. That was his choice. What she faulted her mother for was seeking men who wouldn't be more than paydays.

"Man, Sweetie. You brighten up whenever you talk business. You need to start your own firm."

"I love what I do. If I start my own, I'd have to give up the part I love and replace it with daily operations type stuff. No thanks." Guilt unexpectedly needled her. *I should have told Gabriel I wouldn't be traveling with the team.*

Hands stuffed in his front trouser pockets, Gabriel watched the runway. Soon, soon he'd finally meet the woman with the sensually seductive voice. The voice he had become addicted to from the moment she purred, "Good afternoon, Mr. Windahl. This is Monica Fuller." So businesslike, yet sweet and sexy. He found himself calling her daily and talking "business" about issues outside of the project her firm was assigned. But it was more than the voice. One second she would impress him with her knowledge, then the next, he would be laughing at something she'd said. How he wished he felt half as free as she did to express himself. And work...She could talk circles around him regarding the financial business world, and her instincts were right on point.

The women he tended to draw were quite beautiful physically but didn't have much more to offer. After his last failed relationship, he barricaded himself off, using work and indifference as brick and mortar. Quickly approaching forty years old, he wanted more than a showpiece on his arm, and he wanted to be more than a cash-filled wallet. He absently kicked at one of the seats. No more investing emotionally in hopes of finding something that obviously didn't exist. Yet, every time he spoke with Monica, he could see himself in a meaningful relationship with her. How she'd been able to weave her way through the barrier he had erected had him stumped.

A search on the Internet for her picture turned out to be fruitless. He leaned against the window. Though he had fought to keep from drawing an image of her in his mind, he had lost the battle. The fullness of her voice and freedom of her spirit brought forth images of a full-figured, passionate woman, nothing like the model types his parents routinely set him up with. Many a night's sleep was beyond his reach, pushed further away by fantasies of making love with his fantasy Monica. *Damn.* His manhood stiffened at the thought of tasting her, of delving so deep into her he lost himself.

He shoved the sleeve of his designer suit up and checked his watch. Almost 8 A.M.; to Monica and her team, it would feel like 1 A.M. Their flight would be landing any second, and he had everything prepared. They would go by limo to the pier. From there they would cruise on his yacht from central Stockholm to his villa, located on one of the many islands that made up Stockholm. He would allow everyone to take a nap, and hopefully by noon, the day would have warmed up to the promised fifty-seven degrees, and he could give Monica a personal tour of his private island. If things worked out properly, Monica would allow him to keep her warm and his months of self-imposed celibacy would be history.

He had wanted to purge himself of the women he had been involved with and clear his mind, then Monica's voice seduced him, and he wanted no other. Once he discovered she wasn't married and only a few years younger than him, the chase was on.

He saw his jet making its approach for landing. He snatched his lightweight leather jacket off the seat and headed for the runway. Showtime had finally arrived. He stopped mid-stride to compose himself. Yes, he throbbed for Monica in the most delightful ways, but he didn't want to run out there like some dog in heat. He strolled to the limo and waited for his guests. He'd had all flight traffic at his private airfield halted until a few hours after Monica's flight was to arrive. He knew it was a bit much, but he wanted to impress her. Unlike the other women he had dated, Monica had built her own wealth, so it would take more to impress her.

Twenty minutes later, a black and a white man—both average size and in their early forties—exited the building and headed for the limo, bags slung over their shoulders with an older white porter close behind them pulling a cart of luggage. Gabriel stepped out of the car. The porter tailed behind, rolling the luggage rack.

Uninterested in the men, Gabriel was tempted to ask where Monica was. "Hello, I'm Gabriel Windahl." He bowed slightly, then glanced around the luggage rack toward the entrance. No one walked through the door. He gulped the lump of disappointment down his throat, then plastered on a smile for the gentlemen. "And you must be Mr. Jordan Levy and Mr. Alex Daniels. Pleased to meet you both."

After exchanging pleasantries and handing their remaining luggage over to the chauffer, all three men settled in the limo. Frustrated beyond belief, Gabriel continued to be polite, but found it difficult. Monica had never said she would be accompanying her team, but he just knew she would jump at the chance to spend time with him. He gazed out the window at the lush trees that lined the road. Last time they spoke, she'd been excited about an upstart publishing company she might be assigned to write a business plan for. Granted, she wouldn't be needed in Sweden, but he had hoped she would choose to see him over this new case.

He laughed internally for his foolishness. Their conversations over the phone were all business, except for the undertone. *Or maybe I'm imagining*...He allowed the thought to slip away. He had never been insecure before, and he wouldn't start now. Monica would be his.

CHAPTER TWO

My foot is killing me." Sweetie pushed the revolving door forward and limped through into their office building. "My first stop after work is the shoe store." A few people's brows rose as they watched her hobble along, but Sweetie didn't care. If she could get away with walking to her office in stocking feet, she would go for it.

"You didn't try them both on, did you?" Tess flitted her hair behind her shoulder. They were almost late because Tess had insisted on straightening the wave in her hair from the braids five minutes before they were supposed to leave for work. "I'll bet that right shoe is a size too small."

"I didn't have time." She scanned the busy lobby for Sam, her favorite security guard. Sam reminded her of her cousins who lived in a low-income area of town. On weekends, Missy loved to travel with her men, so Sweetie and her brothers spent time with the only people Missy trusted with her babies, her family.

Sweetie needed a "fix" Sam claimed he could supply. She'd run out of her stash over the weekend and was *fiending* something awful. She hated frequenting the usual hangouts for her supply. Because of her specialized taste, they couldn't fill her order as she liked.

The slightly past middle age, lean guard spotted her and waved her over to the security desk. "Jill, Tyra!"

Sweetie laughed at his nicknames for them. He called Tess his "Bony Bootleg Tyra Banks" and Sweetie his "Perfect Piece of Jill Scott."

"I can't stand broke brothas," Tess hissed.

"There's nothing wrong with Sam." Hoping he would deliver on his promise today, she headed toward the security desk. "He's supposed to have that *special* package for me." There was an "extremely special package" she wanted that was a few thousand miles away. Since she couldn't allow herself to take a chance on Gabriel, this would have to do.

Tess grabbed her by the arm, pulled her close and spoke quietly so no one else could hear. "I thought you were giving that stuff up."

"Noooo. You said I should give it up. I never said I was quitting. Everyone needs at least one vice." Right foot ready to burst out of the too tight pump, Sweetie gently jerked her arm away. "Now go on if you gonna be all up in mine. I've got business to handle, and I want to get out of these shoes."

"Fine." Tess's three-inch heels clicked on the black marble as she weaved her way through the crowd toward the elevator bank.

Sam bobbed his head slightly as Sweetie approached. "Umm, umm, umm, you are entirely too fine, even with that limp." He winked.

"You are too much." She raked her fingers through her medium-length twists as she leaned on the desk. Unlike Tess, she planned on keeping her hair twisted for at least two days. Sam's eyes went from laughter to lust as he took in her ample breast.

Since she was a teen, many men spoke to her chest as if expecting it to answer. Lately her back had been hurting her more than usual, so she was seriously considering breast reduction surgery. Along with the reduction, she prayed the gawking would decrease. "Okay, enough oogling for today." She straightened her cream silk blouse. She always left the top two buttons unfastened, not to provide a peep show, but because she wanted comfort.

He snapped his head up. "Sorry. But damn, girl. How you gonna keep all of that from…?" he trailed off and shook his head. "Never mind."

In a hurry to get to her office and kick off her shoes, she checked to make sure no one was near, then whispered, "Were you able to get my package?"

A big grin spread across his caramel face. "Of course, baby girl."

Excitement surged through her veins. "The good stuff, right?"

"Don't insult me," he teased. "Only the best for you. Now if we were talking about that bony bootleg Tyra wannabe you be hanging out with, it would be a different story."

Anxious for a hit, she set her clutch purse on the counter. "How much do I owe you?"

"It's on me this time. Just spread the word to the right people."

She nodded. "Okay, that'll work." After finishing her business with Sam, she rushed to her office on the twenty-fifth floor. Actually, she shared an office with Tess, her personal assistant. The firm had hired Tess and created the position for her at Sweetie's request, but they stopped short of giving Tess an office of her own. With all the extra projects the department had taken on, having Tess around for support really helped. Tess couldn't handle her own checkbook, but she was a dependable, hard worker. She'd even taken the initiative to track all of the associates' projects and point out conflicts.

"Whew, girl, I'm not going to make it." Sweetie sat in her leather executive chair and opened her package. Even her aching foot would have to wait until she got her fix in.

"I can't believe you actually associate with Sam," Tess spat from her desk across the opulent office. "You were doing so well."

Sweetie glanced up from her goodie bag. "I'm still doing well." She made greedy fingers over her stash. "In a few seconds, I'll be doing even better." With a dramatic dip into the bag, she pulled out one of the cherry Tootsie Roll Pops. Obtaining an entire batch of the cherry flavored goodies was impossible. Impossible until Sam let it slip that he knew someone who worked at the plant. A true sweet-a-holic, when Sweetie gave up her other vices, she refused to give up these. Cherry Tootsie Roll Pops were her favorite.

"You'll get diabetes if you keep eating all of those sweets."

Sweetie slowly unwrapped her treat. "You're just jealous because you'll never know how many licks it takes to get to the center of a Tootsie Roll Pop." She tossed the paper into the trashcan beside her desk, then licked the brim around the sucker. The sugar hit her senses in the sweetest ways. Gabriel came to her mind. *How many licks would it take to get to the center of his—*

"Sweetie! Snap out of it. You're thinking about that man again, aren't you? You need to hop your horny butt on a flight to Sweden and get you some. Celibacy isn't natural. You have needs. Stop denying yourself."

"Girl," Sweetie pointed the sucker at Tess with one hand and pulled off her right shoe with the other, "if you don't stop interrupting my wet dreams..." She laughed at how easily her mind transferred her delight in her candy to delighting Gabriel. She thanked God he was in Sweden. "Hand over your bank statements and bills so I can get an idea of what I'm dealing with before things get hectic around here."

"Aw, man, I'll be right back." Tess grabbed her keys out of her purse. "I left them in the car." She rushed out the office.

Sweetie put the sucker into her mouth, then lifted her foot up and around into her lap and massaged it gently. "I'm so sorry, baby," she cooed, sucker still in her mouth and distorting her speech. "I'll be sure to check the size of both shoes from now on." The phone rang. She lazily reached over and grabbed the phone with one hand and took the sucker out of her mouth with the other. The massage had felt so good and the cherry sucker tasted so succulent, she moaned her pleasure, sighed, then answered the phone.

"Good morning. Jamison and Drake Investments. Monica Fuller speaking. How may I help you?" The person on the other end didn't answer. "Hello, Monica Fuller speaking."

A few more seconds passed. "Am I interrupting anything?" he finally said. "You sound...busy."

The rich timbre of Gabriel's voice flooded her senses and left her panties damp. "Oh, no, not busy at all." She fumbled with the Tootsie Pop. "I just wanted to...Well..." Technically, she hadn't done anything wrong, yet she felt she owed him an apology.

"I was shocked when you didn't accompany your team."

She drew in a deep breath, then exhaled slowly. "What had happened was..." She sighed. "I'd wanted to come but..." She tossed her cherry delight into the trash along with delightful fantasies of Gabriel. "All reasonable thought just slipped out of my brain."

He chuckled. "It's all right, Monica. No explanation is necessary. But we need to have a serious discussion. Give me your private number."

"Are Jordan and Alex settled?"

"Yes, they are well settled. Did you get the account for that upstart publishing company?"

Grateful he'd allowed the none-to-subtle subject change, she gave him the *Spark Notes* update of her new account.

"Sounds like you're on the right track."

"Is Andersson still holding out on you?" Sweetie brushed the sleeve of her blouse up slightly and checked her watch. She had a meeting to attend in ten minutes and needed to prepare.

"Jesper Andersson is one of the most stubborn people I've ever met, but he finally agreed on the partnership with Electrolux."

"Wow, I'm impressed," she said truthfully. "When I have more time, you have to tell me about it. I'm putting you on speaker." She pressed the button, then rushed over to Tess's desk to see if she'd printed out the updated agenda and presentation.

"Monday morning status meeting....Oh how you love them," he teased.

She clicked the mouse to send the agenda and presentation to the printer. "Yep, they rank right up there with foot ache."

"If you were here with me, we could give Monday morning status meaning a whole new connotation."

This time it was Sweetie who didn't respond timely. The heat of his meaning hadn't worn off yet. Boy was she glad Tess wasn't in the room. Not even someone reading a transcript of this conversation would have misinterpreted him.

"When you answered the phone, what were you doing?" he asked, barely over a whisper.

The softness of his voice gently circled and caressed her breast. *Oh yeah, he needs to keep his butt in Sweden, and I'll stick to Chicago.* The printer kicked out copies of the agenda and broke her out of the lust-filled haze he'd trapped her in. "Umm, tell me more about the Electrolux deal." She shakily picked up the stack of agendas and tapped them on Tess's desk as the printer continued to work on the presentation.

"Determination," he answered, simply. "I always get what I want."

"Always?" Hard copy of the presentation finished printing, she checked her watch—five minutes until show time.

"Yes, always."

"Well, I'm almost late for a meeting." Copies of the agenda and presentation in hand, she returned to her desk. "So in one word, tell me what's next for determined, arrogant, always-gets-what-he-wants Gabriel Windahl?" she teased as she stuffed her foot into the confining pump.

"You."

Tess couldn't believe she'd forgotten the weekly status meeting. Sweetie could navigate Tess's workspace easily, but that wasn't the point. Tess's one source of pride was how well she performed her job. She longed to be intelligent, respected, confident—Sweetie. She reached to unfasten the already unfastened top buttons of her blouse. At times her jealousy was so palpable, she was sure her complexion had a green undertone. But the jealousy was tempered by her true love and admiration for Sweetie.

Unlike Tess's family and the majority of her friends, Sweetie believed Tess could be more than a pretty face pampered and cared for by men—not that Tess didn't like being pampered. It felt good to have someone believe in her abilities. She quickened her step as she approached the car. Last year one of Tess's modeling friends was in a car accident. Until the accident, Tess thought Mariah had everything going for her. Mariah had her own money, but didn't have to spend a dime of it because men lined up to spend time with this beauty.

Mariah survived the accident, but was burned over seventy percent of her body and paralyzed from the waist down. Tess leaned on her Mercedes and said a silent prayer for her friend. The only people outside of family and health care providers who visited Mariah now were Tess and Sweetie. *At least Mariah had money to fall back on. I have nothing.*

She took her bill statements out of the glove compartment. Deep in her heart, Tess knew purchasing the car was a mistake, yet she couldn't stop herself. Just as she couldn't stop herself from entering relationships with men she knew weren't right for her. *What's wrong with me?*

After closing the door, she spun around to rush from the parking garage to the office, but bumped into someone. The bills fell from her hands. She glanced up as she stooped to retrieve the statements. "Kevin!"

"Hey, baby." He gently took her by the arm and helped her stand. "Sorry, I didn't mean to scare you."

"What are you doing here?" She shoved his hand away. "Never mind. I don't care."

"Of course you care." He playfully tapped her arm with his fist. "That's Sweetie talking, not you." He leaned forward to kiss her. Tess stepped back, but was stopped by the Mercedes. She turned her face away.

"No, Kevin. I'm just saying what I should have the first time you laid your hands on me."

To distance herself from him, she crossed her arms over her chest. "It's a shame I had to see some bitch going down on you before I saw the light." She held up her hand. "I take that back. I shouldn't disrespect that woman because your ass is trifling." Now that line she'd stolen from Sweetie, but it was true. How many times had she gone after the woman for screwing with the man who supposedly "loved" her? Well, no more. She'd had more than enough.

Tess had never noticed just how beady Kevin's eyes were. Now that she really looked at him, he resembled a rat. Repulsed she'd allowed him access to her most intimate places, she shivered.

He dipped his head slightly. "So it's like that, huh? One night with Sweetie, and you think you can talk shit to me. Is that fat bitch your *man* now? Is she the reason you're not answering my calls?"

Hands on her hips, she worked her neck in sista-girl fashion, as she said, "You wouldn't be talking shit if she was here. I'm late for a meeting. Bye, Kevin."

"Well she's not here now." He snatched her by the arms and yanked her close to his body. "I'm not through with you yet."

Engulfed in fear and heart racing, she drew in a sharp breath. "You're hurting me."

"Is there a problem here?"

Kevin loosened his grip on Tess as James stepped into their line of vision. Tess didn't know what to do. Kevin had never manhandled her in public and had never come to her job.

Dressed in his navy blue work clothes with his sleeves rolled over his bulging biceps, James folded his arms over his expansive chest. "Get over here, Tess."

Gladly, she scurried to James's side.

"This is between me and my girl. You need to step your ass out of shit you know nothing about."

For all the bravado in Kevin's voice, Tess noticed he didn't step up on James or look him in the eyes.

"If she's your girl, why is she by my side? Come on, baby."

James placed his hand at the small of Tess's back and guided her toward the exit. As she returned to the office building, escorted by Mr. Tall Dark Sexy as Hell and Handsome himself, she knew he'd called her baby to anger Kevin, but his words were so gentle, so reassuring, she wished he'd meant them.

She stumbled over her thoughts. No way did she want this broke maintenance man. He'd just been there in her time of need. These feelings for him were some sort of misplaced gratitude mixed with the attraction she'd always had for him.

At her office door, he hesitated before he followed her inside. "I'm not trying to tell you what to do, but—"

"I know, I know. I'm through with Kevin. We broke up, and he seems to be having a hard time letting go. He's been blowing up my cell. I'm thinking about changing the number," she rambled. The way James watched her every move unnerved her, but in a good way. Too good. She didn't want to be attracted to him. "Thanks for helping me out there."

"If you want, I'll walk you to your car at the end of the day."

The sweetness of his offer made her heart sigh. "You're too kind, but I'll be fine." The scent of his masculine cologne reached across the room and wrecked havoc on her libido. Perhaps he'd be interested in a strictly sexual relationship. He'd be something to hold her over until she found a man suitable for her. She shrugged off the thought. He would become attached, and then there would be a new boatload of issues she would have to deal with.

"I guess I should get on to work." He backed out slowly. She wanted to ask him to stay, but she was through with men who weren't right for her. She wanted—needed—a man with the means and desire to treat her as she should be treated—not a warm-blooded sex toy.

He stopped in the doorway. "Be careful, Tess. How did he know you'd be at your car? You're usually in the office by now."

She wondered the same thing, but couldn't figure out the how or why. They had only been living together a few months, and though she thought of herself as the ultimate catch, she knew he wasn't madly in love with her. "I'll be careful. Thanks again, James."

"I'm always here for you. As a matter of fact, I have an extra ticket to the Cubs game this weekend. If you go to the game with me, I'll take you wherever you want afterward. Or if you can't stand baseball, I can pick you up after the game, and we can still do whatever you want."

She laughed. "What if I want to do something with you during the baseball game that has nothing to do with baseball?"

"Don't play games when you don't know the rules, baby girl. I'll see you around." He nodded, then closed the door as he left.

"God that's one fine man! Sweetie, Sweetie, how could you give up men?" She fanned herself with her bills.

"Shit!" Kevin slammed his fists against the steering wheel of his Escalade. He'd gone to the parking garage, hoping she'd uncharacteristically left the car unlocked. He needed to take out the "spare tire" in Tess's Mercedes before someone discovered it wasn't filled with air. The car was locked, and the only way he knew to break in would be to bust a window and pop the trunk. That would draw too much attention and probably end in his arrest, so now he was stuck.

"I could strangle the life out of her!" Sweetie. He blamed this all on her man hatin' ass. Hell, Tess didn't give a damn what he did until Sweetie stuck her nose into their business. He had Tess well trained, then Sweetie hit the deprogram button. And that, that heifer had the audacity to disrespect him in his own home. Hell naw! She'd pay. But first, he had to get a handle on things.

"You just had to go showin' off, didn't you?" he chastised into the rearview mirror. On his pick up, he'd used Tess's car to impress this fine piece of ass he'd been after for a while. She'd been sniffing around his Escalade, but every other playa on the block had one. He switched to the car to stand out. It worked. He'd banged her long and hard in the back seat, front seat, in his apartment. Unfortunately, Tess came home from a shopping trip in New York a day early and caught his latest conquest sucking his dick.

Initially he had thought he would be able to convince Tess to try a threesome, but she totally flipped out and chased his new honey away. From what he could gather, she must have called Sweetie when she'd locked herself in the bathroom.

"Damn…" His head fell back onto the headrest. If only it were as easy to talk Sweetie out of her pants as it was Tess. He would venture to guess she would rock his world as it had never been rocked before. He grinned. The fun would be in breaking Sweetie, the prize would be in dominating her. Maybe instead of kicking her ass he would kiss it and see just how sweet she could be.

"What time does he usually arrive home from work?" Sweetie dropped two storage boxes on the bedroom floor of Kevin's condo.

"We have at least two hours. And since he was harassing my tail this morning, he'll probably have to work late." Tess entered the walk in closet.

"Do you have any house shoes in there? My foot is killing me." She kicked off her pumps and sat on the bed. As soon as they finished gathering Tess's things, Sweetie planned on hitting the shoe store. "I'm still tripping from him walking up on you like that. I knew he was an ass, but didn't know he was crazy, too." She took a cherry Tootsie Roll Pop out the pocket of her slacks and unwrapped it.

"That makes two of us." Tess tossed out a pair of plush black slippers.

Sucker sticking out of her mouth, Sweetie mumbled, "I'm just glad James showed up when he did."

"I hate to admit it, but…" She leaned against the closet doorway. "Man how he makes my juices flow."

"Guuurl, you really need to give up your gold digging ways and take a good hard look at James."

Hands planted firmly on her hips, Tess said, "I know you did not just call me a gold digger."

Sweetie waved the slipper in the air, "If the shoe fits," then put it on, "wear it." She fell onto the bed dramatically. "Oh these feel wonderful."

"I am not a gold digger. I just happen to be attracted to men who like the things I like. I have expensive taste. A baseball game won't do it for me. And Kevin isn't rich, so that shoots that theory down."

"Not filthy rich, but he makes over two hundred grand a year and spends like there is no tomorrow." Sweetie rolled to the edge of the bed, leaned over, and checked underneath. "Did you guys ever clean under here?"

"Just because I don't want some broke brotha doesn't make me a gold digger."

"You are correct." Sweetie pulled a few boxes from under the bed. "What makes you a gold digger is your *only* qualification for a man is how much he can afford to spend on you."

"That's not true!"

"You know I love you, but once Kevin's bankroll is gone, so are you. And why aren't you going out with James this weekend?"

"Why do I let you do this to me?" She turned away and continued packing her items from the closet. "You're lucky I love you." She poked her head out. "And that I need you to buy my car."

"I love you, too, boo."

They worked quickly to retrieve Tess's belongings, then left Kevin's spare key on the kitchen counter. Sweetie knew she was hard on Tess, but she couldn't stand seeing Tess repeating the same mistakes. Tess's family was no help. They basically taught Tess that women like Tess were to be lavished upon and cared for; their contribution to society was just being.

What a bunch of malarkey.

They'd accused Sweetie of being jealous. In a way, she was, but she never allowed the rare bouts of jealousy to interfere with their friendship. It just didn't seem right that the people society deemed the "beautiful ones" didn't have to pull their weight, while folks like Sweetie worked their asses off. Then one day Tess's friend Mariah fell from the graces of society. Gone were the friends, men and social standing. Gone was any trace of Sweetie's jealousy.

She couldn't stand the thought of Tess falling. They weren't getting any younger, and eventually Tess wouldn't be able to compete with the new generation of "beautiful ones." Sweetie also noticed society rarely deemed forty-something-year-old, black women among the "beautiful ones." Then what was in store for Tess?

Now that Tess was supporting herself financially—well almost supporting herself—Sweetie hoped she would listen to her in the man department. Sweetie couldn't fathom her accepting celibacy as a way of life, but maybe she would give James a chance. *I may have to help it along—a little.*

CHAPTER THREE

Sweetie reached down to take off her shoes, but burst out in laughter at what she saw. Apparently, her feet were so grateful to be out of those pumps, they conspired with her brain to keep her from putting them back on. Thus, she still wore the slippers Tess had loaned her and forgotten her shoes behind and the shoe store. She set the house shoes under the edge of the bed. *I guess Kevin has a new pair of shoes.*

Tess would be taking the spare room, so Sweetie had reclaimed her bedroom. It was only seven, but she felt drained. After a nice hot shower, brushing her teeth and wrapping her hair, she slipped between the cool sheets with a romance novel and several cherry Tootsie Roll Pops. Tess had decided she needed to celebrate her freedom from Kevin and gone to some jazz club, so Sweetie was truly alone.

One sucker and three chapters into the romance book, she began to fall asleep. The melody of her cell phone startled her. She set the book on the nightstand and turned off the light. She wasn't in the mood to speak with anyone, but answered the phone anyway.

"Hello," she sighed more than said as she sank into the pillows.

"You sound as if you've had a hard day."

His voice sent her heart racing. "You have no idea." *What the?* "Gabriel?" She shot up. "Gabriel! How did you get my number?"

His hearty laugh filled the line. "Not exactly how I envisioned you calling out my name, but we can work on it. It's been a long day for me also."

"I'll bet." She scooted back into the pillows. "Obtaining private numbers mustn't be the easiest task in the world. So who ratted me out?" She reached over to the nightstand for a sucker, but knocked them onto the floor. They sounded like marble raindrops as they landed onto the hardwood. *Great.*

"My lips are sealed."

She bent down and fished on the floor for a sucker. "I all ready know it's someone from work. I just need to know which someone." *Gotcha!* She reeled in two of the suckers, set one on the nightstand and began to unwrap the other.

"What if I told you I obtained your number from your cell phone company? I know people in high places."

"I'd say you were a liar." She positioned herself between the pillows. In principle, she was angry he had obtained her personal number without her permission. She took a long pull of the sucker. She hated to admit it, but the thought that he'd go to such trouble to speak with her, to be with her, sent an ego-building, lust-filled rush through her that had her rethinking her decision not to go to Sweden. It seemed like everything led to her hopping on a flight to see her fantasy man. She constantly reminded herself that the person on the other end of the line attached to the sexy voice and smooth ways, was not her fantasy, but a real man—a real man who was physically attracted to women like Tess.

"You still with me, Monica?"

The soft sound of her name from his lips...Nice full lips she wanted to taste, to feel on her. She stifled a moan. "Stop doing that."

"What?" he said in an innocent way that stroked her in a way none too innocent.

"You know what." She took another pull of the sucker. "Back to this phone business."

"As you wish. Are you eating something?"

Oh God, please tell me I'm not slurping all up in this man's ear? "Wait a sec. I'm putting you on speaker." Eyes accustomed to the moonlight, she set the sucker on the wrapper and phone on the nightstand, pulled a pillow over her face and screamed, "Get it together, woman!" A few calming breaths later, she drew the pillow from her face. "I feel much better now."

"When we make love, I'll swallow your screams of ecstasy."

A needy aching beat between her legs. "Aw man..." She rolled onto her stomach and laid her head on a pillow. "How did this get so out of hand so quickly? Do you know how long it's been since I...Never mind. Can we *please* talk about the phone?"

"As you wish, but tonight I'm going to make you *cummm...*"

She drew in a sharp intake of air as the hum of his "*cummm...*" gently caressed the lobes of her ears with promises of what was ahead. "Umm, what were we talking about?" she shakily asked.

"How much I want to make love to you. If you were with me now, I would—"

"Noooo..." The ache between her legs demanded attention she refused to give. "We were talking about phones." She subconsciously ground her pelvis into the bed. "Yeah, phones." She hugged her pillow.

"Oh yes, phones." He paused, and she knew she should have changed the subject before he had a chance to continue, but the grinding had intensified and felt so good she couldn't think clearly enough to say or do anything. "Your voice has redefined oral pleasure and left me in quite a state. Don't leave me like this. Whisper something sweet to me, baby."

A weak, *umph*, was all she could manage.

"That's it, baby," he sighed. "I can taste you. Do you feel me?"

"Yes," she moaned, and did. The moist stroking she felt at the apex of her femininity was all Gabriel. The sound of his breathing growing as ragged as hers pushed her further toward the edge.

"Pull me in, baby."

She tightened her stomach and behind muscles and pulled him in. How it was possible to feel him entering her was beyond her comprehension or care. All she wanted was for him to keep the magic flowing. "Gabri..."

"Let go, baby. Umm, let go."

Gripped in the midst of an orgasm the likes she'd never felt before, she cried out.

"Oh Monica..."

"What the hell do you mean you can handle her? How did your girl get our shit?" Ronald slammed his beer onto the coffee table.

Kevin thought the glass bottle would shatter under the force of Ronald's anger, but like Kevin, the bottle stayed in tact. "We had a bit of a disagreement. I've got it covered. I just wanted to let you guys know there's a minor glitch in the plan. She's hiding out at Sweetie's."

Hands rubbing together in grubby need, Zack scooted his skinny behind to the edge of the pimp-daddy red velvet couch. "You mean that big, fine-assed bitch Tess be hangin' with? Are you tappin' both of they asses?"

Kevin stared at his whiter-than-Casper buddy who had attended the most prestigious private schools in the world and was now a lawyer in one of the city's most prestigious law firms, yet turned into a shabby imitation wigger whenever he wanted to seem *down with the crew.* "Hell, yeah!"

Zack fell to his hands and knees. "Aw, man, you my idol," he teased. "Did you do both at the same time?"

"Get your dumb ass up!" Ronald smacked Zack on the side of the head. "That was our seed money. Some of us don't have a rich daddy to bail our asses out." He trained his stormy brown eyes on Kevin.

Zack returned to the opposite end of the couch from Ronald. "My daddy don't give me shit!" He snatched his beer off the coffee table. "I'm a grown-ass man."

That was the problem. When they brought Zack into the fold, he was supposed to be the "safe" white boy with easily accessible backup cash. By the time they discovered Zack's family had disowned him, because of his preference for dark meat, he knew too much to be excluded. Of the three hundred grand seed money, Zack was only able to contribute twenty grand, which left Kevin and Ronald in the pinch for an additional forty grand each.

"This is my ass on the line!" Ronald said.

"I'm not rich," Zack defended. "Twenty grand is a hell of a lot more than a hundred and forty to you. I wish I had a hundred and forty to blow."

"I didn't." Ronald ran his thick hands over his shaved head. "Don't you get it? This is not some game. We don't have that kind of loot to throw away, and we sure as hell don't have rich parents to bail us out."

Their predicament was touchy, but Kevin didn't think it warranted the anxiety in Ronald's voice. In a few days, he'd be able to work his way back into Tess's panties. All he needed was for someone or something to distract Sweetie while he convinced Tess she was his one and only. "I told you I can handle Tess. What's really going on?" Kevin asked from the recliner.

"I…" Ronald shook his head and drug his hands over his face. "I had to borrow fifty grand from…from Marco."

"That dude who had your boy Dennis whacked?" Zack laughed nervously. "Damn, how you gonna borrow money from a shark to use for seed money? That was stupid as hell."

"Those bastards at my job inhale more coke than they do oxygen. I would have been able to pay him back within a week, but," he trained his angry gaze on Kevin, "someone screwed me in the behind without even the decency of a reach around."

"I'll get the coke back!" Kevin drew in a deep breath to calm himself. Ronald had a right to be worried. Marco didn't play when it came to his money. One of Ronald's work associates found out the hard way. He'd owed over a half million, but was murdered before he could repay. Marco was cleared legally, but people knew he had something to do with the hit. "I just need a little time."

"I don't have time. Hell, we don't have time. That is *our* loan, not just mine."

"Wha…wha…what you mean our loan?" Zack jerked toward Ronald.

"I didn't stutter. I had to tell Marco what we were up to for him to loan *us* the additional seed money. If you had held up your end of the deal, I wouldn't have had to borrow a damn dime."

"Aw hell naw!" Zack shook his blonde head. "Don't put that shit at my doorstep. I can add. You would have still been ten big ones short."

"I could have cooked the books at work for the additional ten, and I would have been able to pay it back and fix the books in a short time without anyone noticing. I couldn't do that with fifty grand."

Fear filled Zack's blue eyes. "What we gonna do, Kevin? I can't tell my dad I borrowed money from a hoodlum to fund my upcoming drug operation."

Zack sounded serious as hell, but Kevin couldn't help but laugh. Soon, Ronald and Zack joined in the nervous laughter.

"Okay, okay..." Kevin sat up in the recliner. "Let me tell you how we need to work this. Zack, I need for you to get Sweetie off my back while I get back in good graces with Tess—"

"News flash," Ronald cut in. "She *hates* men, even white ones. You would do better if you convinced your sister to come onto her."

Zack straightened on his end of the sofa. "Oh ye, of little faith. By the end of the week, I'll be her boo."

"You know you'll have to leave that wigger shit at the door with Sweetie, right?" Kevin asked.

"You just worry about Tess." He licked his lips. "I'll handle Sweetie."

"More like, you'll be handled. Just keep her out of my way for a few days. When's the first payment due?"

"A month," Ronald answered. "I'm not too sure about this. Maybe we can just hire someone to carjack the Mercedes."

Kevin really liked Ronald, but sometimes he worked his last nerve. "And who do you trust enough to pull the jacking, not take our coke, and not get caught and trick on our asses?"

"We could do it ourselves," Ronald defended. "Hell, they're only two women."

Drenched in embarrassment and shame, Kevin couldn't look his partners in the eyes. He could still see Sweetie coming after him with the bat. He had never been so scared in his life. She had the triple S on her side: size, strength and speed. He hated to admit it to himself, and there was no way he'd admit it to his friends, but he feared taking Sweetie on physically. She would probably end up kicking all three of their tails.

"What's wrong with you, dawg?" Zack asked.

"Nothing...nothing. It's just that Sweetie will fight back. Are you guys ready to shoot her fat ass? Murder is serious jail time."

"He's right," Zack said. "My big mama won't go down without a fight. Give me a week. In that time we can think of a backup plan. But we won't need it. She's as good as mine."

"Wow, Monica, that was fantastic. Wait until we're actually in the same room."

Heat quickly rose to her face. What they had just shared was incredible, but she couldn't allow more. Still on her stomach, she rested her head on the pillow. "We'll never be in the same room."

"Why not? It's what we both want."

She stared at her phone, which was on the nightstand. She didn't know how to express her feelings without sounding insecure. Eyes adjusted to the darkness, she spied a sucker. "Because I'm not what you want." Since she couldn't have Gabriel, she settled for a different type of treat.

"What do you mean by that?"

"I've seen pictures of you." She unwrapped her cherry delight and licked the brim.

"Did you like what you saw?" he asked huskily.

"Too much," she answered breathlessly.

"Then I don't see the problem."

She didn't want to lose what they had built, but she couldn't see a way to hold off his questions and advances any longer. She would just have to tell him the truth, and then once she lost the real Gabriel, she would adjust to having only the fantasy. "I also saw the women you had at your side. I'm not a fashion model. I don't look like a fashion model. And I have no desire to look like a fashion model."

A nervous chuckle replaced his usual jovial one. "Hell, they don't even look like fashion models. It's all paint and plastic, baby. And give me a little credit. I'm not shallow. I've fallen for you. I don't give a damn what you look like. Even if you are all plastic and paint," he added quickly.

She noticed he was trying to cover all of his bases. "But that's obviously what you like."

"Okay, I hate to admit this, but my parents usually pick my dates. They've been doing it for years. I don't have time to meet women."

"Didn't you tell them what type of women to fix you up with?"

"Oh yeah, like that would work."

"You have a meddling mom, don't you?" she asked as she rolled the sucker about her tongue. Boy, did she know about meddling moms. Missy Fuller, her mother, was head of the meddling mom's brigade.

"Boy, do I! And her meddling is *global!* Though she lives in Chicago, daughters of her best friends continually end up bumping into me."

She pulled the sucker out of her mouth. When she'd Googled him, he didn't seem to have any significant Chicago ties. "You have much family in Chicago?"

"Yep, my mother's side of the family is from Chicago. Now enough stalling. The type of woman I want is speaking to me right now. I don't need a picture to tell me that."

"But what about attraction?"

"You're kidding, right?" The sarcastic smirk behind his voice brought a smile to her lips. "I know I've made a horrible impression, but I've never brought a woman to completion over the phone, and lord knows one has never bought me to completion over the phone. Yet I need to take a shower right now. Because of you, I'm a mess." He paused. "By the way. Thank you for making a mess out of me. Feel free to do it again, anytime."

A giggle bubbled in her throat. She could use a little of that "anytime" about now, but had to settle things between them. She wasn't the type of person to lead a man on. "Yes, we're emotionally attracted to each other, but there also needs to be physical attraction."

"I'm physically a mess, does that count?"

The giggle worked its way into a full-fledged laugh. "Stop doing that."

"I like being the reason you laugh," he paused, "moan…Can I make you moan again?"

She wanted to do a lot more than moan, but there was no sense in dragging out the torture. She absently tapped her teeth with the sucker.

"What's that clicking?"

She froze.

"You there?"

"Yeah…I just…What type of woman are you physically attracted to?"

"That's a totally unfair question. If I say anything that doesn't fit you exactly, you'll say I just proved your point that you're not my kind of woman. Listen to me, Monica. I've already fallen for you. I'm hooked. There's nothing that will change that."

"Oh really?"

"Really."

She sat up in the bed and folded her arms over her chest. "No one would ever mistake me for white." The women she'd seen clinging to him in the pictures were so light they were almost white or actually white. Even Tess might be too dark for his taste, and she barely had any melanin.

"Me either. So?"

"What if I told you my size fourteen pants fit too tightly"

"I'd say, more cushin' for the pushin'. Can I do you from behind?"

His strong hands steadying her hips as he drove deep into her…She sighed. Oh yeah, she could work with that.

"I liked that image myself," he whispered. "Let me make it come true."

Her whole body ached for him. "Stop that."

"What? Wanting you? Sorry, but I can't and don't want to."

She absently took a pull of her sucker. "I'm trying to be serious here."

"I am serious. What are you eating? I want to taste your lips…both sets."

In need of a serious change of panties and freshening up, she shifted her weight from one butt cheek to the other. She had to stop the madness, and stop it now.

She twiddled a few twists from under her scarf between her fingers. She planned on taking them down in the morning and wearing her hair in a twist-out. The first time she'd worn the style, her coworkers shot strange looks her way, most likely uncomfortable with her hairstyle but unwilling to say how they actually felt. All day she'd heard comments such as, "interesting," "that's…a different look," "you sure are you." She smiled. The women in the photos had bone straight hair, and she was sure in Sweden he didn't come upon too many black women who wore their hair in natural styles. "How do you like naps? I haven't had a relaxer in years and don't plan on ever having another."

"I've always preferred cotton over silk."

All that mind power she'd used to stump him, and he had quick rebuttals. She could strangle him. "You have an answer for everything, don't you?"

"Yes."

"My breasts are so large it's hard to keep from tipping over."

"Lawd have mercy! You're not my fantasy, you're heaven!"

"I'm having a reduction."

"Do you need me to take you to the doctor? We could give a whole knew meaning to prep."

"You are incorrigible."

His deep laugh filled the room and her heart. "I'm just trying to make it clear that you're worrying for no reason. You sound perfect." He drew in a deep breath. "Even though you won't tell me what you're eating."

"If you must know, a cherry Tootsie Roll Pop. I'm addicted to them. And I hate to rush you off, but I need to shower and try this sleep thing again."

"Well, my sweet, I'll let you get your beauty rest."

She disconnected with him, took a quick shower, then dressed and readied her laptop. She needed to check the price for airline tickets to Stockholm. Now that she'd been straight with him and he'd sounded genuinely interested in her, she felt secure enough to meet.

"Sorry to call so late, Mom, but I was preoccupied." He adjusted his earpiece, then dropped the damp towel into the neighboring spare seat. A birdbath would have to do until they landed. He had never participated in phone sex. He had always considered it the act of the desperate. *I guess I am a little desperate. But soon…*

Monica had jokingly revealed her appearance, then rushed him off the phone in fear of his reaction. When he had said she sounded perfect, he meant it. She was just as he imagined. The only way to make her believe he was attracted to everything about her was to show her.

"It's alright, darling. Are you in town yet?"

"We're about fifteen minutes away. Did you have Karen drop by my place to open the windows and clean? After all of these years, I'm sure it smells stale in there." He fought off a yawn. He hadn't been to bed in over twenty-four hours. As soon as he learned Monica wasn't coming to Sweden, he decided to go to her. To force himself to adjust to the time difference, he had stayed awake. He knew as soon as he arrived in his condo, he would fall out from lack of sleep.

"You should stay here. I miss you, Gabriel."

"I miss you, too, Mom, but I need my own space."

She huffed. "Fine. Have it your way. It's just that Angelica, a fine young woman in my book club, is staying with me a few days while her condo is being painted. She's simply breathtaking and *single.* She would be perfect for you."

"Another reason why I want to stay at my place. Thanks, but no thanks. Stop trying to fix me up, please." He shut his weary eyes and stretched his long legs out. Since he was the only passenger on his private jet, he had more than enough legroom.

"Is there anything you need to tell me?"

The concern in her voice threw him. He drew his legs in and sat up. "What do you mean? Is something wrong?"

"That's what I'm trying to find out."

"What are you talking about?"

She blew out a long breath. "I was a model for years."

"Yes, I know. Did one of your little model friends fall off a runway or something?"

"You're not funny, Gabriel. I'm worried, and all you can do is crack *bad* jokes."

"I'm sorry, I'm just exhausted." The fasten seatbelts light came on. Since he left on such short notice, he hadn't had his flight attendant accompany him on the flight. "What's going on, Mom?"

"Are you gay?"

"What!" Instead of fastening the seatbelt, he jerked it. "No! What on earth would make you think I'm gay! Come on, Mom!"

"In my line of work, I've met many gay men. There's nothing to be ashamed of. I just need to know what I'm working with."

This is not happening to me. He massaged his temples. *When I open my eyes, I'll wake to find this has been a nightmare.* He slowly opened his eyes. The earpiece was still snug in his ear, and he could hear his mother fumbling with something on the other end of the line. "What on earth would make you think I'm gay?"

"You're almost forty and never been married and don't look to ever get married. Men of your position are working on their second or third wife by now. Ask your father."

"So because I'm not married, I'm gay. That makes perfect sense." He fastened his seatbelt.

"Stop being facetious. I've introduced you to dozens of lovely young ladies who would make suitable wives, yet you've dismissed them all."

"If I decide to marry, I will pick the bride myself. And yes the young ladies were quite lovely, but they weren't what I wanted." A full bodied, full lipped, dark skinned, natural haired beauty came to his mind. What he wanted was almost totally opposite of what his parents sent his way. No wonder Monica thought she wouldn't be his type.

"If you had told me you wanted a man, I would have sent you suitable young men."

"I'm not gay, Mom!" He allowed his head to drop back onto the seat. "This is past ridiculous. I'll call tomorrow, after I've gotten some rest."

"Why don't you come over for dinner, darling?" she asked entirely too sweetly. So sweet he knew she had something up her sleeve.

"Look, I already have someone. A woman," he added quickly.

Her breath caught. "Oh. I'm so excited. Why didn't you tell me? Who's her family? When's the wedding? Oh, this is why you've come home. You want me to meet your fiancée. Wait until I tell your auntie! It's May, perfect for a wedding..."

A few minutes later, she was still talking without allowing Gabriel to get a word in and the plane was landing. Actually, he was glad for the change in course on the conversation. He didn't feel like being grilled about his sexually. He chuckled. *Yeah, me gay.* If Monica's breasts were even a quarter of the size she bragged about, he would be in heaven. He couldn't stand implants and wanted to slap whoever invented them. He was a firm believer that a woman should not get them unless they were corrective surgery after cancer removal or for some other medical reason.

She's having a reduction. He prayed he didn't sound like some insensitive horny jerk. Yes, he was a breast man, but he wanted her to be comfortable with herself. Whatever the reason for her choice to reduce, he would support her.

"Gabriel, are you listening to me?"

"Of course."

"Then I'll see you and your fiancée at six sharp for dinner."

He choked on his mother's words. "What? No. I'm not engaged. What are you talking about?"

"You just told me you're engaged. You made the fiancée up, didn't you?"

Exasperated and exhausted, he said, "Look, Mom, we're landing, and I'm not even supposed to be on the phone. I love you."

"We will talk more about this later. I want grandbabies. They allow gay couples to adopt."

CHAPTER FOUR

Zack couldn't believe his good fortune. He had spent fifteen minutes in the lounge area of Sweetie's office building, searching for a believable "chance meeting" when she stepped off the elevator and headed straight for the security desk. Someone interrupted his view of her firm, round behind. He grumbled as the person walked by. She looked good in red, but she would look even better in the buff. He wanted to lift her skirt and…Another person obstructed his view. *Damn, don't these people have somewhere else to be?* He ran his slender fingers through his short blonde hair.

He couldn't believe what a mess he'd gotten himself into with Kevin and Ronald. Though he, Kevin and Ronald worked for separate firms, they were all located in the same office building. Initially he'd befriended Kevin in hopes of being introduced to Sweetie. He'd only seen her twice when she'd accompanied Kevin's girl for a visit. He didn't know her real name, where she worked, if she'd return to the building or anything else besides how much he wanted to bed her. After a few weeks, he discovered the fat bitch Kevin always ragged about was actually Sweetie. The next thing he knew, Kevin was talking about needing seed money, and Zack was playing along until he could figure an easy way out. Kevin and Ronald wouldn't just let him walk away, he knew too much. But this whole Marco situation would work to his advantage.

He had more than enough money to pay off the loan Ronald took from Marco, but wouldn't bail them out until he had his chance with Sweetie. *Let them sweat.* He knew Kevin had lied about sleeping with Sweetie. He smiled. Unlike the sluts Kevin preferred, Sweetie carried herself with class and was truly a kindhearted, intelligent woman. After Kevin revealed her real name, Zack had done his research on her. She was perfect. He would bet even his parents would accept her once she started having their grandchildren.

He also had no intention of selling drugs. The seed money he had contributed was part of his cash stash and couldn't be traced back to him. It would be Kevin and Ronald's word against his. He knew both of them would have to use less-than-legal ways to obtain the additional forty grand each. He knew their methods and would soon have proof to use against them in the future if they tried to come between him and Sweetie.

A *future with Sweetie*...He sighed. Thirty-seven years old, he was ready to settle down and have a real family. He wouldn't be shipping his children off to boarding school halfway around the world.

By the time the path was clear, Sweetie was leaning with an elbow on the desk with her hand loosely balled and rested on her cheek. *Damn, she's got to be at least an E cup!* Top in the field of *breastology*, he could spot a DD in a crowded room from two hundred paces. And the much sought after, but rarely found, natural E cup...He repositioned his leather briefcase in his lap to hide his hardness. Jealousy coursed through him as she threw her head back and shared a laugh with the security guard. Zack wanted to be the one to put a smile on her face.

Sweetie strolled toward the bank of elevators—so graceful, confident, and soon she would be his. He approached, then waited patiently at the appropriate distance from her for the elevator. Midmorning, the demand for the elevators was low. If his luck held out, they may be in the same car—alone.

He nodded and offered her a polite smile. "Good morning."

"And good morning to you," she said with a cheer that matched her bright brown eyes.

Two more people joined in waiting for the elevator. He didn't waste time speaking with them. They could ruin his chance of being alone with her. He had never made love on an elevator before. He could see her backed against the wall, legs wrapped around him, skirt hunched up and him driving deeply into her.

"Are you all right?" Sweetie asked, concern etched on her beautiful coffee, with just enough cream added, face. "You look flushed. I know it's May, but it's still cool outside. You had best take care of yourself."

He tried to shake off the lust-filled thoughts, but with her standing so close, looking so sexy, being so kind, and smelling so damn good, it was virtually impossible. "I'm fine, thank you."

The doors slid open. Three people exited, then the four of them entered. He pressed the button for the twenty-fifth floor—Sweetie's floor—then asked what floor the others wanted.

"We're headed to the same floor," Sweetie answered.

"Three please," said the others in unison.

Grateful his two unwelcome guests would be leaving him alone with Sweetie, relief washed over him. That would leave him twenty-two floors of privacy to complete his move.

"Since you've shown me your kindness, seems the least I can do is introduce myself." He held his hand out to her. "Zack Manson at your service." She had a firm grip without squeezing. He liked that.

"Monica Fuller, but everyone calls me Sweetie. Pleased to meet you."

"Sweetie? Nice. It fits perfectly."

The elevator stopped at the third floor. After the two interlopers exited and the elevator doors closed, he asked, "Are you married or dating anyone presently?"

Eyes wide and mouth open, she belted out a laugh and soon had him laughing.

"I'm sorry." Still giggling, she fanned at the moisture in her eyes. "You're…direct."

"I figure the best way to obtain what you want is to go for it. So are you married or dating anyone presently? I'm not."

She hesitated. "No," she said softly.

"Then how about lunch today?" The elevator stopped at the twenty-fifth floor. They exited and stood in the deserted hallway. To the left was the accounting firm, to the right an advertising firm.

"Thanks, but no thanks."

"What's wrong? Is it because I'm white?" he asked quietly as he gently pulled her closer to the wall opposite the elevators.

She *tsked.* "Of course not. I haven't dated in over two years because…It doesn't matter. You seem nice, but I'm interested in someone."

Brow raised, he folded his arms over his chest. Kevin had filled him in on Sweetie. There was no way she was "interested in someone." She was just trying to let him down easily. He could hug and strangle the person who had hurt her. Hug him because his stupidity left Sweetie free to be with Zack. Strangle him because he had hurt her so badly she wouldn't give Zack a chance.

He reached in his inner suit coat pocket. "I'm giving you my card. Call me, email me, fax me, drop by my office. No dating, just friendship."

"I'm sorry, but I can't take your card. I'm not trying to be rude or anything. I'm pursing someone else right now." She glanced at her watch. "I need to get going. It was nice meeting you, Zack."

He watched her *ass*ets as she rushed into the accounting firm. He was so hard for her he ached. He made his way to the restroom, closed the door to the stall and set his briefcase on the well-polished marble floor. There had to be a way to convince her to take a chance on him.

He lowered his pants and stroked himself. Soon, soon she would be taking him into her luscious body. He could feel her surrounding him with her heat as they made love. He stroked faster, harder. Oh how he longed to suckle her chocolate covered peaks. She would be all his, and he would be her everything. He stroked her harder, knowing he could make her forget her pain. He heard her scream out his name. He bit his lip to prevent from calling in answer as he hit his climax.

Breaths ragged, it took him a bit to come down. Sweetie was the only drug he wanted anything to do with. Slowly, he opened his eyes to the reality of what he had just done. The stall wall was not as pristine as when he had entered. He quickly snatched toilet paper to clean himself. He would shower at the office, but this would have to do for now.

As he cleaned the stall walls, he swore never to use a public restroom again. No telling what went on in them. He washed his hands in the sink, then headed to the accounting firm to leave his card at the front desk for Sweetie. She wouldn't be getting rid of him so easily.

Sweetie rounded the corner just in time to catch the back of a man's leather heel entering her office. She didn't recall a meeting. She sped up, then slowed. Tess was there and could handle anything.

"Oh no, don't stand on my account."

Sweetie's heart lurched. That strong, sexy voice could only belong to one man. Gabriel! He had actually flown across the world to see her. Smile wide, she stepped into her office. Tess was sitting at Sweetie's desk with a dumbfounded look on her face.

"I knew you were joking last night," he continued, his back to Sweetie. "You are truly the most beautiful woman I have ever seen. What ever were you worried about?"

Heart stopped and breaking apart, Sweetie did everything she could not to burst into tears. She thanked God she had business to clear up before she hopped that flight to make a fool of herself. Of course he seemed attracted last night. What could he say? You sound like a fat blob! He probably hopped a plane as soon as they had hung up to see what he was getting himself in to.

"Bu…but…" Tess stammered, eyes wide and hands to her chest. "I'm not…"

Sweetie shook her head and waved her hands no. *Don't tell him you're not me,* she mouthed and prayed with everything she had for Tess to be able to read her mind, feel her humiliation.

Tess cleared her throat and broke out in a weak smile. "Pleased to finally meet you, Gabriel."

Though Sweetie's nose burned and she felt tears threatening to fall, a laugh almost escaped her. No way could Tess simulate her voice. Tess's attempt at low and sultry sounded like someone strangling a sick frog.

Head tilted to the side, Gabriel said, "You sound so different over the phone."

"Something's going around."

"I'm sorry to hear that. I guess I'll have to give you some tender loving care."

No way would Sweetie stand by and listen to the man of her dreams put a move on her best friend. She tipped backwards, but bumped into the doorway.

Gabriel turned and stared at her.

Oh what a mess she knew she had to look. Eyes all puffy, nose running, and guilt written all over her face. Tess rushed around the desk. "Gabriel, this is my friend…Sweetie." She motioned for Sweetie to come in the office. "Sweetie, this is Gabriel, the gentleman I told you about from Sweden."

He held out his hand, but Sweetie hesitated. She didn't want to touch him. She wanted to run away, kicking and screaming like a big baby.

"Pleased to meet you." He reached forward and took her hands into his. A warm energy flowed between the two. Tess stared at the two.

Sweetie couldn't speak. She didn't want to give away her identity, plus she was afraid the pain in her voice would be evident. She wouldn't let him know he'd broken her heart. *He was just a dream*, she told herself. *Why does this hurt so much.* She gently pulled her hand away.

"Umm, Sweetie is battling laryngitis." Tess pat her own throat. "All of us have a touch of something or other it seems."

Sweetie bowed slightly, then rushed out of the room. She had to get away. Tears falling, she ran down the hall, rounded the corner and bumped into someone.

"Monica?" Zack grabbed her and balanced them both from falling. The tears trickling down her cheeks infuriated him. Whoever had made her cry would pay. "What's wrong, Sweetie?" He wiped the tears from under her eyes with the pad of his thumb.

All that came out were hiccups and sobs. He looked around, spotted a small empty conference room, then pulled her inside. He had talked the front office secretary into allowing him back to her office. He was on his way to drop off his business card personally when Sweetie bumped into him.

"It's alright." Arms wrapped around her, he held her close and rocked slowly.

A large black man in an expensive suite stalked by the conference room, but stopped upon seeing the two. Sweetie's head was rested on Zack's shoulder, and her eyes were closed. The man narrowed his eyes on the two. Zack wondered if this was the man who had broken Sweetie's heart. *Of course it is. Who else would be staring at us?* He hummed softly, and she relaxed in his arms.

The man stalked off, but Zack knew this wouldn't be the last he saw of him.

"What happened," he asked quietly.

"I hate men."

"Ouch," he teased, "that hurt."

He wanted to kiss the sly smile off her lips, but thought better of it. For now, he would just bask in the glory of having her in his arm. Her ample chest flush against his body. He backed his midsection up slightly, so she wouldn't feel his hardness.

"We're not all jerks. You just have to find the right one."

She sighed. "I'm tired of looking. I give up. It hurts too much." She pulled out one of the rolling armchairs from the conference table. "I'm sorry about..." She hunched her shoulders. "I don't usually go slobbering all over strangers."

He sat in the chair next to hers. "What are friends for?"

"I totally blew you off earlier...I'm sorry."

"No, you didn't." He took his hankie out of his breast pocket and wiped her tears away. "We're not all jerks," he repeated.

"No, you're not," she admitted.

Gabriel couldn't believe how stupid he had been. If he could strangle himself, he would. He resituated himself on one of the leather sofas in the lounge area of the lobby in Monica's office building. After all that smack he had talked last night about how looks didn't matter...He ran his powerful hands over his dark face. *I'm such an idiot!*

When he first stepped into the office, he thought he had the wrong room. That twig behind the desk with the water balloon boobs, pale skin and straw for hair couldn't have been his Monica. No way did that powerful voice and free spirit belong to her. But the name plate said Monica Fuller. Who else would be sitting behind her desk?

He had played off his disappointment like a pro and was doing a good job until her goddess of a friend, Sweetie, caught his attention. He'd never seen a more beautiful woman, even with her eyes all teary, she was breathtaking. He didn't know what ailed her, but he longed to be her cure.

Oh how he had wanted to lick her luscious red lips…He ran his hands over his close cut hair. A passerby narrowed his eyes on Gabriel, then quickened his steps. After the way he had gone on and on about how looks didn't matter, Monica must have started describing her friend as a joke, but then he had played into it. But for him it wasn't a game. He honestly wanted the woman she'd described. Then he had become full of himself. He just knew she was what he wanted, so he arrogantly dogged out the women his parents had chosen for him—the women who resembled Monica. Then there was no way she could tell him how she actually looked. A *complete idiot!*

What unnerved him most was that she'd been correct. He had pictured her in his mind one way, and now she didn't fit that image. Instead, her friend was an improved version of the image. *Shit!* How he would hide his attraction for Sweetie was beyond him. When he had taken her hand, he didn't want to let go. He couldn't stop staring. There was an unexplainable energy drawing them together. The fear he saw in Sweetie's eyes told him she felt it, too. At least she'd had the decency to pull her hand away. He had never been so rude or disrespectful to a woman in his life. He shook his head. Monica was his friend and would someday be his wife. He would have to figure out a way to fight this attraction for Sweetie and do right by Monica. He loved her and would cage the animal part of him that craved Sweetie.

Lust. This thing for Sweetie could only be lust. He couldn't lose what he had built with Monica over lust. Hell, he didn't know anything about Sweetie, hadn't even heard her voice—though he'd bet it was sultry and sexy, just like her. He shook his head. Lust, he could overcome. He wanted more out of a relationship.

Sweetie exited the elevator with that white guy she was all hugged up with. Her taste in men obviously didn't run Gabriel's way. Jealousy needled him. She'd withdrawn her hand from his, yet allowed that blue-eyed, pretty boy to paw her in the middle of the office for the world to see. No, he didn't want this loose woman. He wanted Monica. Looks weren't everything. They were perfect for each other.

The white man's hand rested possessively on Sweetie's lower back as they headed toward the revolving doors. Man, she had a butt that could stop traffic. The man glanced over his shoulder toward the lounge area at Gabriel as they walked through the doors. Jealousy pushed out by anger, all he knew was he wanted to wipe the smirk off that white dude's face. *This is ridiculous.*

Sweetie was none of his business. He had to figure out a way to get back in with Monica. She'd said she had a meeting and rushed him out of her office. Her shaky voice wasn't the only reason he knew she was lying. He'd had the same sources that gave him her private number check her electronic calendar.

She must have seen the disappointment in my eyes before I had a chance to cover it up. Then I had to act a fool when I saw Sweetie. What's wrong with me? I've never acted like this.

With long, confidant strides, Sweetie reentered the building and went to the security desk. Every fiber of his being yelled that this voluptuous beauty was Monica. He shook his head. His being was wrong and trying to steer him down a path he refused to go. Why would they lie about who was who? That made absolutely no sense. No. The caged animal was just attempting to break free. *I'm the one in control. I love, Monica.* He sighed. *Which is why I feel so guilty about wanting, Sweetie.*

Sweetie headed toward the elevator bank. One second he's watching the sway of her hips—the red of her skirt drew him like a bull to the matador's cape—the next thing he knows he's slipping onto the elevator just before the doors closed. They were alone, and she looked terrified.

Her lavender scent, powdery light yet potent enough to knock out his common sense, enveloped him. He internally jerked himself out of the wanton haze. "I'm sorry. I didn't mean to startle you."

He took her half smile and the slight dip of her head as an acceptance of his apology. Even that simple act had him hard and ready to strip. *Shit.* This was a huge mistake. He knew what he needed to do, but didn't look forward to it. Since he couldn't trap his lust for her, he would have to stop her lust for him. In order to salvage any relationship he may have with Monica, he would have to take the desire out of Sweetie's eyes for him and replace it with anger, repulsion, disgust—anything that would keep her from returning his feelings. Without the mutual attraction, it would be easier for him to resist her.

The elevator lurched to a halt and broke him out of his musings.

Sweetie rolled her eyes to the heavens as the stalled elevator bell rang. He couldn't help but chuckle. The Monica of his fantasy would have done the same thing.

"You would rather be anywhere than on this elevator with me, wouldn't you?"

Smoldering eyes trained on him. It took all of his love for Monica not to pull this woman into his arms and do what they both desired.

"Oh yeah, you've lost your voice." He shrugged. "I can see why you would be worried. Trapped on an elevator with a strange man," he said nervously. "But you don't have to worry about me. You're not my type."

The way her face jerked away from him, anyone would have sworn someone slapped her. He didn't see the problem. Yes, he saw definite mutual attraction in her eyes, but she already had a man. She liked bony, white men. He wasn't offended. Then he thought about the delicate feminine ego. They all wanted to believe they were the most beautiful creature in the world. In her case it was true, but he had just...he had just accomplished his goal, he thought sadly.

He heard her sniff quietly. He prayed it was her cold and not her actually crying, but his heart told him he had hurt her deeply. *I'm such an ass. To make this easier on me, I hurt her on purpose.*

"Look...I'm sorry." He rested his hand on her shoulder. "That came out all wrong. You're a beautiful woman."

She turned further into the corner, away from his touch.

"I'm truly sorry." At this moment, he hated himself. He backed to the opposite side of the elevator and watched this beautiful, proud woman crumble. She didn't fit the standard for beauty, so he was sure she'd heard negative remarks before, but for him to say something so cold without cause was flat out cruel. He shook his head. Yes he had mused he wanted to replace the desire in her eyes with anger or some other negative emotion, but he had panicked. Seeing her like this hurt his heart.

"Please forgive me."

She glared at him: eyes red and puffy, nose watering. The alarm stopped, and she pressed the button for the door to open. They were only on the seventh floor. As soon as the doors opened, she rushed off.

"What do you mean you're going home for the day?" Tess adjusted her earpiece and continued down the hall. She'd had everyone in the office building she knew on "Sweetie watch." James said he saw her rush off the elevators on the seventh floor, but that didn't make sense. Why would she be there?

"I've been worried sick about you." She spotted James near the elevator bank, surrounded by tools.

"I don't feel like talking about it right now," Sweetie snapped. "I'll see you when you get home."

The line went dead. "I know she didn't just hang up on me." The click of her heels on the marble floor sped up as she neared James. "Why didn't you stop her? You knew I was looking for her!"

He barely glanced from the mat his tools were on toward Tess. "I'm working. It's not like I expected her to come running off the elevator. You two have a fight or something?"

"No we didn't have a fight." She crossed her arms over her chest. From his position, James could have easily peeked up her miniskirt, but he didn't. He just continued gathering his tools. She *accidentally* nudged him with her knee. Surly he wanted to see if she'd chosen to wear panties or a thong today. "Oh, excuse me."

He didn't even almost take a gander, which enraged her. What was wrong with this man? She knew he wanted her, and here she was giving him a free peek at the goodies. Hell, just because he couldn't support her, didn't mean he couldn't rock her world in the bedroom until something better came along.

"So what is the 'or something?' " Finished gathering his tools, he rolled up the cloth.

"Men are so insensitive!"

He stood with the rolled cloth in one hand and his toolbox in the other. She wanted to lick the dark chocolate lines of his bulging forearm muscles. She reached forward and straightened the rolled sleeve of his shirt. The slightest touch of his skin sent a current through her that made her jerk her hand back.

Brow raised, he smirked. "You touched me, not the other way around."

"See, insensitive!"

"Sweetie doesn't even date, so I know you two aren't arguing over men. And of course we're insensitive. That's part of what makes us men. So what's really going on?"

Oh, she would make him sorry for blowing off her advances. Who did he think he was? She'd made love with senators, actors, athletes, and he had the audacity to act as if he weren't interested in her. "She's upset because the man she loves is lusting after me. Some men recognize beauty when they see it."

That wiped the smirk off his face. Big brown eyes narrowed and jaw clenched, he asked, "What man?"

"Why do you care?" Lips pursed, she pouted. This always worked.

"Because Sweetie is good people, and I'll jack up anyone who hurts her."

That wasn't the answer she expected. She literally felt the arrogance-filled, hot air seep out of her. Sweetie *was* good people and had been through more than enough. The last thing she needed was her best friend using her in some stupid game.

"I'm sorry I came at you like that, James. I'm just worried about her. She puts on the bravest front, but that's because she's been hurt so many times..." she trailed off. "I didn't mean to hurt her." Close to tears, she turned away and ran down the hall. Yet again, her beauty had proven to be a liability.

"How can you be angry at me for this?" Tess asked from her seat in the plush Cleopatra chair.

Sprawled out on the bed with the pillows propped under her arms, Sweetie glanced up from her latest stupid romance novel. Tess couldn't figure out what Sweetie saw in those things. Instead of reading about finding love, her best friend should be living it.

"What on earth would make you think I'm angry with you?"

Tess tossed her hair behind her shoulder with the flip of a hand. They both knew what the real issue was, and Tess refused to allow that issue to come between them. This was too important. "Of course Gabriel finds me attractive, but I don't want him."

"You're not serious are you?"

"You know I didn't do this on purpose. I'm a lot of things, but a skank isn't one of them."

"Do what, Tess?"

"Steal Gabriel from you. You're the one who refused to allow me to correct his mistake."

Sweetie calmly closed her book, then sat up and leaned against the headboard. She'd changed out of her red power suit to a dopey green sweat suit and wrapped her hair in one of those hideous scarves. The scarves were fine for sleeping in, but it wasn't even noon.

"First off, Gabriel was not mine to steal. Secondly, how can you call yourself my best friend when you honestly believe I'd be mad at you for his being attracted to your type? Am I that trifling? Thirdly, why must everything be about you?" She took a cherry Tootsie Roll Pop out of the new crystal bowl on her nightstand.

Tess bit her inner jaw and lowered her hazel gaze. How many times had she been told her arrogance drowned her common sense? Too many for her to count. "I'm sorry. I just didn't want you to think…I'd never…" Sweetie's last relationship ended when she found her fiancé in bed with one of her bridesmaids. Guilt washed over Tess. In a way she'd been gloating, proud that she was capable of getting the one thing Sweetie truly wanted. For once she'd beat her best friend, and it felt good.

"I know that." She took a pull of her sucker.

"This thing he has for me is only physical. He's in love with you. Tell him who you are and give him a chance to come around."

"Robert loved me, but that didn't keep him from screwing Veronica in what was to be our bed. I'm not Gabriel's type. Nothing I can do will change his desires, and I am not changing who I am. I like me."

Tess kicked off her stilettos, then crossed the hardwood floor and hopped into the bed with Sweetie. "Let's say two new guys come to work for the firm. With Gary, there are no sparks or any kind of attraction when you meet. With Devon, it takes all of your will power to keep from dropping your panties and sitting on his face."

Sweetie burst into laughter. "Does your horny butt think about anything besides oral sex?"

"Not on purpose." She winked. "Now for the next few months, Devon acts like a total ass while Gary is the most supportive and caring person you have ever met. You two just click. Next thing you know, you're wondering why you never noticed that one of Devon's eyes opens wider than the other. This unpleasant discovery leads you to many more. In the meantime, you find yourself seeking Gary out. There's something in his walk, in the way he talks, in everything he does that draws you to him. And for some unexplainable reason, he's getting more and more handsome by the second. I see this happen every day."

Sweetie twirled the sucker around in her mouth.

"Come on, Sweetie. You know full well I'm right. You are Gabriel's Gary."

"Oh Lawd, just what I need. A man on the down low." They both giggled.

Elated her best friend decided to crawl out of her funk, Tess nudged her. "Come on, Gary. Let's go out for lunch."

"I'm not hungry and…"

"And what?"

"And I don't want Gabriel."

Brows raised, Tess smirked. "Liar."

"I'm attracted to him, but he's Devon, not Gary. He went out of his way to…to…" She looked away. "It doesn't matter. I deserve to be treated with respect."

She turned Sweetie to face her. "What did he do to you? You saw him again, didn't you? That's why you came home." She shoved the covers off and swung her legs over the bed. "I'll kick his ass."

Sweetie giggled. "Get your narrow behind back in here."

"Oh no. He can't treat you any ol' way. Who the hell does he think he is?"

"Thank you for coming to my defense, but I'll be fine. Really."

From everything Sweetie had told her about Gabriel, it was difficult to picture him doing anything intentionally to hurt Sweetie. Tess had even heard many of his calls. He was a genuine good man. She narrowed her eyes on her friend. Sweetie had to be projecting her feelings about what happened with Robert onto Gabriel. *I'll get to the bottom of this.* She crawled back into bed with Sweetie.

"You're giving up too easily. You were in shock this morning. You are probably misinterpreting things."

Sweetie stared at her.

"What?"

"You just sound sooo, soooo, non-Tess today is all."

"You're always saving me, supporting me. It's my turn, and I won't let you down. Gabriel is in love with you. You are so beautiful," she said sincerely, "just give him a chance to see it. He's a man. You know he's going for the shiny box first. It won't take him long to figure out I'm not the package he wants." She grinned.

"What are you up to?"

"Nothing." *Just call me Devon.* "Absolutely nothing. I have a date with Gabriel tonight. I had planned on calling and canceling, but now

I've changed my mind. He'll be by around six to pick me up unless you stop this silliness and tell him you are actually the woman he's in love with."

"He's not in love with me. He made sure I understood I'm not his type. You have fun with *Devon.* I have a date of my own." She reopened her book.

"You have a date? With a man?"

Sweetie growled something incoherent under her breath.

"I didn't mean it like that. Who? When did this happen?"

"I can see I won't get any reading done today." She handed Tess Zack's business card, which she was using as a bookmark. "Since you plan on imitating my shadow today, let's head on over to the bank so I can pay off your car and have the title transferred to me."

Tess's gaze slowly traveled from the business card to her best friend. "Do you know what law firm this is?"

"Of course, it says it on the card."

"Stop being so damn difficult. This is one of the top firms in the *country!* I almost dated one of the partners there. How do you…" She *tsked.* "I know you aren't playing all wounded when you have," she flashed the card, "Mr. Zachary Manson chasing your behind. Hell, he's an associate partner. You know how much loot he has. Damn! You've won the lottery. No wonder you don't want Daily-double Gabriel anymore."

"I'm just going out to say thanks. Nothing more. Now put on some shoes so we can get out of here."

"What time is he coming by?"

"He isn't. I'm meeting him."

"Where?"

"Put on your shoes, Tess."

"Fine, be like that." She hopped out of bed and straightened her mini skirt. Since Sweetie was being so tight lipped, there was no way Tess and Gabriel could *accidentally* run into Sweetie and Mr. Zachary Manson.

CHAPTER FIVE

"You lyin' bastard!" Kevin bit out. "No way did Sweetie agree to go out with your white ass."

Zack glanced from his executive chair to his partners in crime who were seated in the leather armchairs in front of his desk. "I've handled my part, can you handle yours?"

"Yeah, can you handle your woman?" Ronald added. "We don't have time for playing games."

"You just keep her out of my way." Kevin walked out of the room.

"Was it something I said?" Zack laughed as he pushed away from his desk. "I have a date to ready for. Catch you later."

Monica sent Gabriel a text that said she'd lost her voice but still wanted to go to his mother's for dinner. She asked if he would pick her up thirty minutes early. They hadn't really connected in the office. He had been shocked when she agreed to the date, especially since it was to meet his mother. He wouldn't have asked had his mother not insisted on meeting this woman he had been keeping hidden from her. The way he saw it, he could either take Monica to meet his mother or his mother would show up on Monica's job and grill her.

So he agreed to the new time in hopes the awkwardness would dissipate quickly. Without Sweetie's deliciously distracting curves around, he would have his full concentration on the woman he loved.

He shook off thoughts of how much he wanted Sweetie. Monica was the one he loved, and that love was based on soul quenching sustenance, not physical satisfaction. Unlike his parents' love, which wasn't true love, but lust. Yes, they cared for each other, but what they had was too shallow to qualify as love in his opinion. Monica had opened the door dressed in a white designer pantsuit. His mother, a former model, would love everything about Monica. They could talk fashion, make up, hair, parties...He groaned. This was a side of Monica he hadn't imagined.

Frustrated and thirsty, he shoved his sleeve back and checked his watch. When he arrived, she let him in, then went to what he assumed was her bedroom without so much as a glance his way. He thought she would be right back. The leather sole of his shoe played an irritated rhythm on the hardwood floor as he tapped his foot. An hour had passed, and they were now thirty minutes late.

Sweetie stepped out of what he figured was another bedroom. Both stunned, they stared at each other.

Four long strides, three gulps, two headshakes and a reality check did nothing to subdue the throbbing ache behind Gabriel's pant zipper. He now stood in front of the one woman who made him want to say, "To hell with love."

The outfit she wore was totally innocent: royal blue, sleeveless dress, gold African-print emblems embroidered sparingly throughout, open-toed leather sandals, gold hoop earrings, and a gold crocheted headband that held her crinkly 'fro from her face. His thoughts of kissing her toes, lifting the skirt of her dress and continuing along her thighs, of suckling her breast, of weaving his fingers through her cottony soft hair, of plunging into her deeply were anything but innocent.

He forced himself to step away and all images of her riding him hard to the back of his mind. "I'm sorry about earlier."

A million and one questions flickered in her eyes. For a moment, he knew she felt the pull between them also, but she fought what she felt. She turned toward the kitchen.

The all-too-familiar guilt consumed him. The way she rushed off toward the kitchen, he was sure she felt it, too. Monica was obviously her best friend, and though they hadn't done anything inappropriate outside of their thoughts, this attraction could only lead to betrayal.

He slouched onto the sofa and lowered his face into his palms. *What am I going to do?*

The sound of footsteps caught his attention. Sweetie set a bottle of water and a soda on the coasters, nodded politely, then headed for her room. Just as she was stepping through the threshold, Monica came out of her room.

She spotted Sweetie, and a look of horror crossed her face. She rushed to her friend.

What was that about? Grateful for the water, he opened the bottle and quenched his thirst. Room temperature water, just the way he liked it.

"What on earth are you wearing?" he heard Monica say in an angry whisper. *I thought she lost her voice?* "Blue sheets are not sexy, Sweetie."

Monica dropped her clutch purse as she stumbled back out of Sweetie's room. The door slammed.

Good for you, Sweetie. He would have kicked her out also.

"I think we should leave now," he suggested. "We're running late."

Monica *tsked,* then banged on the door. A few seconds later, the door flew open. Sweetie held up all ten fingers.

"How could you?" Monica whispered.

Nine, eight…He could hardly wait to see what happened when Monica ran out of time.

"Why didn't you wear what I picked out for you?"

Five. Sweetie pointed to the front door with her free hand. Four, three…

"Stop being so—"

Sweetie calmly picked Monica's clutch purse off the floor, walked to the front door and tossed it out. She then stood in front of open-mouthed Monica.

"You wouldn't."

Three fingers. Two. One. Sweetie took her by the arm, escorted her out, and slammed the door closed. Whistling a happy tune, she turned and was seemingly shocked to see him still there. Big smile plastered on her adorable face, she hunched her shoulders.

"I like your style." He chuckled as he stood. "Thank you for the water. Have a good evening."

She bowed slightly.

What in the world could have happened to my Monica?

Gabriel nodded politely at the pod person who had replaced his Monica, then rang the doorbell. No way could this rude, snooty, arrogant bubblehead be the woman he had spoken to daily. *What kind of game is this?*

Man how he wished he could back out of taking this…this…woman to meet his mother, but until he figured out what was going on, he had to play along. On the limo ride over, she'd sat so far away from him that he'd tested himself for body odor. Not that she could smell anything besides the gallon of perfume she must have soaked her clothing in. The overbearing fumes burned his eyes and twisted his stomach into knots.

The door flew open, but instead of the maid who usually answered the door, it was his mother, dressed in a yellow silk jumpsuit, similar to Monica's. He sighed. *This is not happening.*

All smiles, Josephine hugged her baby boy, then pulled Monica into the penthouse. "She's so beautiful," she gushed. "Oh, and you're wearing Chaos Eau De Parfum. My favorite!" She took Monica's hand into hers, then turned to her son. "Fifteen hundred dollar parfum, my apologies. You *are* serious."

"I didn't." Oh yeah, this had to be a pod person from the old sci-fi movie *Invasion of the Body Snatchers*. No way would his Monica waste fifteen hundred dollars to smell like Pine Sol.

"You're just perfect." Josephine hugged Monica. "I'm sorry. I didn't raise my son in a barn." She released the now beaming Monica, and he knew there would be trouble. "I'm Josephine Miller."

"And this is…Monica Fuller." *At least that's who she claims to be.* "She isn't well and has lost her voice," Gabriel added. "We can't stay long."

"How could you drag this poor darling out when she isn't feeling well?"

Monica launched an irritated smirk his way, as if agreeing with his mother. These two women were a mess in the worse way. He had told his mother Monica wasn't feeling well and he didn't think tonight would be a good time to meet, yet she'd insisted he came or she would go to Monica's job to find out who his son had fallen so madly in love with.

Honestly, he didn't think Monica was very sick, he had just wanted a reasonable explanation to get out of the meeting. And Monica was the one who had contacted him, saying she wanted to go out even earlier than planned, then left him waiting.

The evening went from bad to worse. His mother took Monica on a tour of the penthouse. Initially, he thought the tour would be a good idea. It was a way to give him a break from this *Invasion of the Body Snatchers* pod Monica creature. She'd taken out a notepad and pen, he assumed to be able to communicate with his mother. When they returned, Monica tore off a few pages from the small pad and handed them to him.

I love you so much, Gabriel, he read, and his heart started pounding frantically. He had somehow misjudged Monica. Maybe the lack of sleep topped with the knowledge that he could never have Sweetie, kept him from seeing the true Monica.

I'll love you even more after you buy me the following items. Your mother was kind enough to give me prices and locations where the items can be found. Thanks. M.

He didn't want to look at the list, but couldn't resist—three pages totaling over a million dollars. This had to be a cruel joke. God's way of getting back at him for treating Sweetie so foully on the elevator. Next came dinner. Monica had often spoken of how she loved Moroccan cuisine. The chef had spent all day to prepare the meal, and she turned her nose up at everything from the chickpea soup to the Chermoula spiced Moroccan lamb barbecue. She didn't even try to hide her disgust. When his mother asked Monica what she'd like to have prepared, Monica wrote: ABSOLUTELY NOTHING THIS HACK OF A CHEF COOKS. I'D EAT PRISON FOOD FIRST.

"I believe it's time for us to leave." Gabriel had had more than enough. "Your behavior tonight has been abominable. What's happened to you?" he asked, but wanted to ask, "Who the hell are you?"

Monica pushed away from the table and sashayed her behind out of the dining room.

"I'm sorry, Mom."

Brows furrowed, Josephine dabbed the corners of her mouth with her napkin. "How could you bring that ghetto hoochie in here and try to pass her off as a sophisticated lady? I'm so disappointed in you, Gabriel."

At a total loss, he hunched his shoulders. "This day has been unbelievable, and I shouldn't have come here until I figured out what the hell is going on. I've never been so confused in my whole life."

"I don't know what's going on in your life, Gabriel. But you need to straighten out whatever it is. That woman in there is trouble with a capital T. Was this your way of getting back at me?"

"Of course not." He checked the doorway to see if Monica was anywhere near. He didn't see or hear her snooping around.

"You've always said I push my gold digging flunkies on you. Are you trying to make a point?"

"This has nothing to do with you, Mom. I really can't explain what's going on." He rounded the table and hugged her. None of this made sense. It was as if Monica were trying to make a bad impression. Well, if that were her goal, she accomplished the task. "I'm truly sorry about tonight."

The *tippidy-tap-tap* of Monica's acrylic nails on the armrest of the limo door would have pushed Gabriel over the edge if he hadn't already been shoved over. Long legs stretched out and eyes closed, he allowed his head to lull back onto the seat. The few times he'd heard this woman speak, the inflections, cadence and style weren't close to Monica's. Forget the "cold" she had. No cold could change a voice that much. Then there was the personality, the funky attitude and arrogant air. The Monica sitting beside him was nothing like the Monica he had grown to love over the months, but who was she and why was she pretending to be Monica? It wasn't like she'd known he was coming, so how could this imposter have planned this…this…whatever game she was playing.

I must be missing something. His mind's eye ventured back to when he had entered Monica's office. She'd glanced up from her desk and froze, obviously stunned, which was understandable. He had also been shocked she looked nothing like the woman she'd described over the phone, but covered up his disappointment with compliments. The way her cheeks flushed and the smile that danced in her light eyes told him she was genuinely flattered by his compliments. Then she suddenly put her hands out, as if to stop him, but he kept going. He'd had to reassure her looks didn't matter to him, but he was actually trying to convince himself he didn't care everything about her was fake from her weave to her acrylic toenails.

Then he heard Sweetie behind them. At the time he had been captivated by her beauty and could barely tear his eyes from her voluptuous perfection. But now that his mind wasn't clouded with lust and trying to cover his feeling from the woman he had thought was Monica, he could clearly see the pain in Sweetie's eyes, her slouched shoulders. His stomach churned angrily, and not because of the scent this "Monica" had decided to drench her clothing with.

Enraged at the deception, his eyes flew open, and he took in the woman who was perpetrating this hoax. *Who are you? Why didn't you say you weren't*...Then it hit him. She hadn't said she was Monica. He had assumed she was Monica and wouldn't let her speak. He had been so busy trying to prove to himself that her not fitting the image he had drawn in his mind of Monica didn't matter, he had ignored everything else—until Sweetie stepped in. *Shit! Sweetie is Monica and this must be...Tess!*

Finally, all the pieces were falling into place. Monica had never mentioned a Sweetie, but had mentioned Tess countless number of times. *Damn, damn, damn.* His Monica must have heard him fawning over this woman, then he had acted the complete jerk in the elevator and confirmed her fears.

"Son of a bitch," he bit out.

Mouth and eyes wide open, Tess jerked around toward him.

"I'm sorry. I wasn't speaking to you." Awkward silence filled the car. Now the hostility he sensed from the woman he thought was Monica made complete sense. He had hurt her best friend. The limo easily maneuvered through the evening traffic. He wished he could maneuver halfway as easily through the minefield that had become his life. The woman sitting beside him clearly had her mind set on making his life miserable, so he knew he couldn't count on her to help him out of this mess. Using "woman logic," this was entirely his fault. This time he actually agreed with the "woman logic."

How he would convince Sweetie he was actually attracted to her and not Tess was only the tip of the iceberg.

"I'm sorry…Tess."

She folded her arms over her imitation chest. "How could you hurt Sweetie like that? Yes, I'm a beautiful woman. But Sweetie is just as beautiful. What's wrong with you men?"

Stomach clutching laughter erupted out of him. He didn't mean to, but her arrogance was hilarious.

"You are such an ass. I don't know what she sees in you."

He stifled his laughter the best he could. "I'm sorry." The limo parked in front of Sweetie's condo complex.

"You should be." Tess didn't allow Gabriel to say another word. As the chauffer rounded the car, she shoved the door open, hopped out and headed for the entrance. Gabriel didn't particularly want to spend any additional time with Tess, but he needed to try and reason with her before he approached Sweetie. So he escorted her to their unit.

The night was young, so he was sure Sweetie would still be out. *Damn!* He only wanted her to go out with him. He wondered if the white guy he had seen her all cozy with was her date. Another image hit him. The way the man was holding Sweetie was more of conciliatory than anything else, and this had happened just after Sweetie had heard Gabriel espousing Tess's attributes. *Shit! I pushed her into the arms of that dude.*

Tess opened the door and marched into the condo. Gabriel followed. Both of them came to an abrupt stop upon seeing Sweetie with a sucker in her mouth. The sucker dangling out of her mouth clinched it for Gabriel. His eyes lowered. The lace trim along the V-shaped neckline of her yellow nightgown framed the crevice between her breasts perfectly.

"What are you doing here?" Tess stammered, then threw her hands in the air. "I don't care. I'm starved." She snatched keys off the entry table and walked out of the condo.

Gabriel could care less about Tess's sour mood. Falling into the real Monica's graces was all he cared about. After what Monica had heard him say this morning, he knew she wouldn't believe a word he said when he changed his story to being attracted to women with her body type. *I'll just have to show her.*

"I guess she didn't like the Moroccan feast my mother had the chef prepare," he nervously joked. The sorrow that clouded her eyes told him he had said the wrong thing, yet again. Moroccan cuisine was Monica's favorite, and he had just introduced her best friend as his intended to his mother.

Foot in mouth, he shook his head. "I'm sorry…about everything." He took off his charcoal suit coat and draped it over the plush arm of the salmon colored chair, just inside of the entryway. Finally, her not speaking to him would work in his advantage. She couldn't ask him to leave.

"I'm starving." He walked past her toward the back of the condo to the kitchen.

What in the world does he think he's doing? Sweetie quickened her pace into the kitchen. Gabriel rolled the sleeves of his white dress shirt to above his forearms, then washed his hands in the sink. Dumbfounded, she remained silent as he searched through the lower cabinets until he found a skillet. The way his slacks outlined the firm cheeks of his butt made her wish she'd also placed the plates and eating utensils in the bottom cabinets. *Yummy.*

Skillet in hand, he glanced over his shoulder and caught her checking out his butt. Face heated with embarrassment, she wanted to die on the spot. To make matters worse, he winked.

"I can only prepare one meal to perfection. And it's just what the doctor ordered. Grab a seat." He nodded toward the table, then set the skillet on the stove. Oh how she loved Alpha males.

If there were a way to rewind a day, she would definitely rewind this one and delete it permanently. She settled at the table while he made himself at home in her kitchen. This morning when she'd begged Tess not to correct his mistake, she'd been hurt and in panic mode and couldn't think beyond the moment. All that went through her at the time was the renewed pain of seeing one of her "friends" with the man she loved. *I can't…won't go through that again. If I have a man, he will want all of who I am.*

She toppled the tiny ceramic iron toothpick holder, then sorted through the toothpicks. She knew he wasn't stupid. If he hadn't figured out Tess wasn't her by now, he would shortly. Then what? Would he try to convince her physical attraction didn't matter? Or worse yet, would he try to convince her that she was actually his type? In desperate need of another day's reprieve, she wished she hadn't cancelled her date with Zack.

How did I get into this mess? Over two years of celibacy celebrated, and she still ended up with man trouble. The man she loved lusted for her best friend and Zack…Well, he seemed nice—really nice—but he just didn't do it for her. They could be friends, but she couldn't see anything more between them. For breaking their date tonight, she promised to skip work and spend the day with him tomorrow.

Gabriel glanced over his shoulder at her a few times while he prepared dinner. The desire she saw in his eyes called to her. *Well, I'm barely dressed. Of course he's attracted now.* She flicked the tiny bow at the base of her V-neck. She would have put on a robe, but everything happened so quickly. *Oh my God. What if Tess told him? That's why he's here!* Tess hadn't even tried to disguise her voice, and why else would she leave them alone? *No, no, no, no, no, this is not happening. This is not happening.*

Gabriel set a tray with two bowls of tomato soup and two grilled cheeses on the small table. The delicious smell brought pleasant memories of her childhood. Memories she'd shared with Gabriel. Missy Fuller was allergic to cooking. The only time Sweetie and her siblings had home-cooked meals from their mother was when they were sick. If one of Missy's babies were sick, she would give her baby her undivided attention, including preparing the one meal she could without filling the house with smoke—grilled cheese and tomato soup. *Mama has some serious good points.*

He led her to the sink. She wanted to jerk away from his touch and the emotions he stirred within her, but the surreal state she was in kept her body from cooperating. Instead, she allowed him to wrap his arms around her and guide her hands under the warm water. He had such powerful hands. She glanced over her shoulder into his eyes and saw something deeper than desire. Something she feared to lose—love and admiration. *He does know who I am.*

After drying their hands, they returned to the table where he said blessing.

"Your friend is…" he trailed off and cut the grilled cheeses in half, then quarters.

With him sitting so close that his thigh touched hers, she could barely concentrate on more than him touching her in a lot more intimate ways. For now she knew he wanted her, but what about the long haul. Once the uniqueness of what they shared wore off, would he crave women such as Tess. Unsure how to proceed, she slowly twirled her finger in the air next to her temple.

"Yes, crazy she is. Monica Fuller, she is not."

The mere thought of Tess trying to pretend to be her was hilarious. To keep him from seeing the amusement she knew was on her face, Sweetie watched herself stir her soup.

"I'm not my mother's favorite person right now," he said with a bit of laughter behind his own voice. "I take it that was Tess?"

Playing mute was fun and gave her time to figure out if she should risk her heart. She bit into one of the grilled cheese pieces. *Just as good as Mama makes.* She tapped his plate lightly to remind him they were supposed to be eating.

"Still not talking to me, huh?" As he ate, he watched her every move. "No problem. I have lots to say."

I'll bet you do. She blew off a spoonful of soup and tasted, though what she really wanted to taste was Gabriel. To her surprise, they ate in silence. By the end of the meal, the awkwardness had disappeared, but her desire for him had intensified. The man sitting beside her was her fantasy man, and she couldn't figure out a way to turn off her feelings for him.

He took their dishes to the sink, then returned. The devilment in his eyes put a smile on her face. They'd had so much fun over the phone, she couldn't wait to see what he had to offer in person.

"Time for dessert." He knelt before her and pulled a cherry Tootsie Roll Pop out of his pocket. She laughed so hard tears fell from her eyes. He was even better than her fantasy man. Perfect in every way. The passion in his eyes reassured her that he wanted her as much as she wanted him.

"I only have one," he said as he unwrapped it, "so we'll have to share." He placed the sucker into her mouth, then rested his hands on her bare thighs. Just as in her office, when his flesh touched hers, she felt an energy flow between them. Tess often teased her for reading romance books, but this was…this was actually better than any romance book Sweetie had ever read.

"You know what my favorite dessert is?"

Feeling unusually shy, she slowly shook her head no.

"You." He took the sucker out of her mouth and descended on her lips.

She opened freely, and soon found herself on the floor with him, her arms wrapped around his neck as their tongues mated. It had been years since she'd been kissed, and never had she been kissed like this.

He weaved his fingers through her hair and deepened the kiss as if she were his breath of life. He broke away long enough to moan, "Monica." Without loosing contact with her mouth, he helped her stand, then backed them out of the kitchen and toward her room.

She was so weak with need, she wasn't sure she would make it to her room without ripping both of their clothes off and making love were they stood. He gripped her behind and pulled her along his body, encouraging her to wrap her legs around him. As he carried her to the room, she could feel how thick, long, and hard he had become.

He stepped through the threshold, and she was flooded with an ice shower of memories. Instead of seeing her bed, she saw her fiancé screwing one of her bridesmaids. She gasped.

"What's wrong?" Gabriel asked as he lowered her.

She looked from the bed to Gabriel back to the bed. How many times had she caught Robert sneaking peeks at other women? She'd thought all men look at beautiful women. That was only normal. Heck, a cute guy or two or three had caught her eye also, but had she ignored the signs? "I…I…" She pushed away from Gabriel. "I'm sorry." She could hear Gabriel telling Tess she was truly the most beautiful woman he had ever seen. How long before she found him in bed with another woman.

"What's wrong?" he asked again, passion in his voice replaced with concern.

It hurt too much to think about Gabriel betraying her. "You should leave."

He wrapped his arms around her. Though she wanted to push him away and tell him never to touch her again, she rested her head on his chest and was comforted by the steady beat of his heart.

"What did he do to you, baby?" he asked softly.

"You should go back to Sweden. I'm not your 'type.' "

"You are exactly 'my type,' and why would I go to Sweden when what I want is here?" He lifted her chin with the tip if his finger. "I always get what I want, Sweetie—always."

"Not this time." She forced herself to take a step back.

He walked over to the bed. "Come, sit with me. We need to talk."

She folded her arms over her chest.

"Scaredy-cat," he teased.

"Reverse psychology will not work on me."

He took his cell phone off his belt clip and speed dialed someone. A few seconds later, her cell phone rang.

Smiling, she said, "I know you aren't calling me." She checked the caller ID. "You are crazy!"

"About you, yes I am. Now answer."

Showing just about all of her thirty-two pearly whites, she answered, "You are entirely too ridiculous."

"Well, the only time you open up is when we're on the phone. No matter what, we are friends. Now tell me what scared you."

"You're always so bossy. But this time, you're right. I'm being childish." She disconnected, then climbed onto the bed and rested her back on the headboard. "Did I ever tell you I was engaged before?"

"No." He kicked off his shoes and settled in beside her. "But I'm glad you didn't go through with it."

"That makes two of us. When we broke up, I was so angry and hurt. With you…" She leaned her head on his shoulder. "I don't do insecure well."

"So what happened between you and this guy? Why the breakup?"

"He was always trying to change me. Yes, I'm heavyset. I'm also healthier than most folks, and love how I look. Why should I have to change?"

"You shouldn't."

"I saw the women you had on your arm. They looked a heck of a lot more like Tess than me…"

He took her hand into his. She could never get enough of his hands. She wanted to feel them on her, in her.

"I was wrong the other night," he said softly. "I was so arrogant. I didn't realize until I saw Tess and she wasn't what I'd pictured, that attraction does play a large role." She withdrew her hand, but he pulled it to his lips. "The woman of my fantasies looked like her best friend. I had to cover up, but it didn't work."

"You're lying."

"Every time I even think of you, this happens." He placed her hand on his hardness. Tempted to squeeze gently and stoke, she licked her lips.

"You are exactly my type. And I apologize for hurting you."

Recalling when he had introduced himself to Tess, he did sound awkward. And now she acknowledged the passion she saw in his eyes when he had turned to her. At the time, she'd been to hurt to believe it. "All is forgiven. We both jumped to conclusions."

"So was your fiancé trying to get you to lose weight?"

"Society is so crazy. For your being attracted to me, they consider you some sort of freak."

"Well, I am a freak, but that's a discussion for later." He bounced his eyebrows. "I'm just grateful you realize that you are what I'm attracted to. All of you," he ran his hand along her cheek, "as is."

A love-filled rush went through her body. "You keep this up, and I'll have to jump your bones. But seriously, the last straw was when I caught him in bed with one of my bridesmaids."

"Daaaaaaaymmmm, no wonder you put a halt to my good lovin' when we came in here." He brushed off the comforter. "Not in this bed, right?"

"No, not in this bed." She liked that he could always bring a smile to her face.

"I have never cheated on a woman, and never will." He hesitated before asking, "Who did you have a date with tonight?"

"His name is Zack. I was kind of distraught this morning, and he was there when I needed someone."

"So this was a thank-you date?"

"Yes, but since I cancelled on him, I promised to spend tomorrow with him."

"You need to cancel. I saw how he was looking at you. Tell him sorry, but you have a man."

Jealousy usually annoyed her, but her ego had been so bruised today that it felt good. "I'm not canceling. I'll explain that I'm in a relationship to him tomorrow." She giggled.

"What?" he snapped.

She ignored his sour mood. "I can't believe we're actually doing this."

"Are we?" he asked, his voice low and husky.

"Yes."

"Then I give you permission to see this guy tomorrow," he said with a touch of tease in his voice.

Brow raised, she crossed her arms over her ample chest in feigned outrage. "You *give* me permission?"

"You are my woman, and I don't share." She squealed as he pulled her over so she would straddle him. He held onto her hips, rocked her gently over his hardness and rubbed his cheek against hers, whispering, "I saw the way you kept looking at my hands." He slipped one of his thick fingers into her, a second. "Umm, all ready hot and wet."

A soft *umph,* was all she could manage. It had been too long, and her emotions for him were too strong to play like this.

"I want more dessert," Gabriel said. He claimed her mouth, still working his magic fingers.

She gyrated and pressed against the palm of his hand, but she wanted—needed—more. She loved Gabriel and would give her all. His mouth traveled along her neck to her breast, soaking the thin material of her nightshirt.

She lifted her nightie over her head and threw it to the side.

"Oh, please don't change your mind," he uttered as he gently took the tip of her hardened nipple into his mouth, then drew in more and suckled.

Ready to drown happily in the pool of ecstasy he soaked her in, she unfastened his belt buckle.

"Let me help with that." He removed his hand from pleasuring her and readied himself to *pleasure* her. She watched him strip and slip on a condom. She moved to take off her panties, but he interrupted her, saying, "Don't you dare."

She was tempted to nickname him "rush" because he had the uncanny ability to send a sensually charged rush through her that flowed from her toes, swirled around her center and reached to the tips of her hair.

He encouraged her to lie on the bed as he brushed his lips over her chest and worked his way down. How such a light touch could be so potent she would have to figure out later. For now she was busy being taken away to new isles of pleasure. His fingers latched into her panties and pulled them down as he continued his descent.

It had been so long since she'd taken a man into her body, but that wasn't why she was nervous. She was nervous because she worried that she couldn't measure up to the fantasy woman he had imagined. He had all ready surpassed her fantasy man. She closed her eyes and prayed she was what his heart desired.

He returned to her lips, nibbling the bottom until it tingled. She could feel him throbbing on her belly. She also throbbed—with need. She loved foreplay as well as the next guy, but she was tired of the games. Voice lost, she pressed her hand against his shoulder. To her surprise, he understood that she wanted him to roll them over.

She lowered herself onto him. Her walls expanded to accommodate his girth.

His eyes rolled back. "Umm, that's it, baby." He held onto her hips, but allowed her to take in inch after glorious inch at her own pace.

They began to stroke. Slowly at first, until neither could take the sweet torture any longer. He held tighter with one hand and pulled her down with the other. He took one of her breasts into his mouth as they continued their mating dance.

Sweetie was falling to pieces. This was way more intense than what she'd given up two years ago. "Oh Gabri…"

Without losing contact, he flipped them both over and plunged into her depths. Moans and the rhythmic slapping of their flesh filled the room with the most beautiful music Sweetie had ever heard. The bed creaked out a complementary tune. A powerful orgasm gripped her. She could barely breathe, but didn't care. "Oh God," she sang out.

With a final thrust, Gabriel joined the chorus. His body quaked, sending tingly residual shivers through her.

It took a few moments for both of them to calm. He brushed his lips over hers. "God made you for me."

"I was just thinking the same thing about you."

"Hold on to me."

She held tight, and they rolled, him still inside her. At peace, she rested her head on his shoulder. Her ex-fiancé had never wanted her to lay on him. He had acted as if she would flatten him or something. A smile tipped her lips.

"What's so funny?"

"I was just thinking I'll never have inhibitions about joining you in the bedroom again."

He chuckled. “Umm, next I’ll remove your inhibitions about joining me on the elevator.”

“What?”

“You’ll see.”

CHAPTER SIX

Unable to fall back to sleep, Tess stared at the clock—5 A.M. She still had a few hours before she needed to leave for work. She had arrived home shortly after midnight to the sounds of Sweetie and Gabriel consummating their relationship. On one hand, she was overjoyed her best friend had found her Mr. Right, on the other, she was jealous. Sweetie already had everything going for her, and now had a rich man in love with her, while Tess…Thoughts of James warmed her heart. *What's wrong with me?*

The way he'd come to her rescue and how he was always respectful and compassionate to her had not escaped her notice—neither had his sexy walk, talk and manner. She'd pretended Kevin was James too many times to count. James was perfect except for one major flaw—his wallet. She knew if they started a relationship it would be great at first, but after the newness wore off she'd start resenting him because he couldn't afford to give her the things she deserved, and he'd start resenting her because she wasn't content with what he could afford. *Why can't the real James measure up to my fantasy James? It worked for Sweetie.*

She kicked off the blankets, slipped on her house shoes and headed for the living room to watch a DVD or do anything else besides think about how much she wanted James. She could see a dim light through the crack in the door. She didn't hear any moaning or any other activity, so she peeked in to see if Sweetie was trying to catch up on the work she'd missed yesterday. Sure enough, Sweetie was at her desk with the lamp turned down low.

Sweetie looked up at Tess and waved her in, but put her finger to her lips. Tess tipped into the room, careful not to wake the hunk of a man snoring in Sweetie's bed.

"Do we need to have a birth control discussion, young lady?" she teasingly whispered as she knelt beside her best friend.

"Silly. What are you doing up so early?"

"I couldn't sleep." She pulled Sweetie to the living room couch with her. "I'm so glad you came back to your senses. You were acting crazy yesterday."

"Like you've never panicked. Thanks for playing along with my lunacy."

"Hey what are friends for?" She waved Sweetie off. "What happened with that lawyer guy you were supposed to go out with?"

"I'm spending the morning with him."

"What? No way is Gabriel allowing you to go out with another man."

"You're right. He's not. I have my own mind and have been making it up for myself for years now."

"Umm-hmm, yeah right. Now what's the real story?"

Sweetie grabbed one of the throw pillows and popped Tess with it. "Stop being mean to me. I had already cancelled out on him once. Even yesterday it was a thank-you date. I'm still grateful, so I am still going out with him."

"And…"

"And I'm telling him I'm dating the most wonderful man in the universe!" She squealed.

"Damn, girl, you're actually glowing. He must have really known how to lay that pipe right." They both laughed and giggled.

"Next we need to get you and James together."

"Oh no, I don't want no broke ass man."

"What makes you think James is broke? And money isn't everything."

"That's easy to say when your man's filthy rich."

"I said the same thing when I didn't have a man."

"Does Gabriel have a brother?"

"He's an only child."

"I know he has a rich friend he can hook me up with."

Sweetie rolled her eyes. "Woman, you need to stop this nonsense before you blow it. I've seen the way you and James watch each other."

"That's nothing but a healthy dose of lust."

"It goes a hell of a lot deeper than lust, and you know it. You'd best wake up before you oversleep and miss out on love."

Mouth and eyes open wide, Tess fought against the truth in Sweetie's words. "I am not falling in love with James."

"Of course you're not." Sweetie stood. "I have a lot to do before Zack comes. Have a nice day at work. You can use the Mercedes today, but I expect you to have a car by the end of the week. And stay in the price range I gave you."

"Yes, Mama Sweetie."

I can't believe I'm doing this. Tess pulled the top right drawer of her oak L-shaped desk open. *It's too late to go back now.* She straddled the open drawer and leaned her body weight onto it. She then pulled the drawer up with all of her strength. She couldn't believe she'd sunk so low, but she couldn't think of another way to have a little one on one time with James. She yanked the drawer from side to side. Her fingers hurt from gripping it so tightly.

Why she wanted to see him so badly unnerved her. She wished the "why" were only a healthy dose of lust instead of wanting to hear his voice, see his dimpled smile, ask him how his day was going. *I have to stop this. Sex is fine. This will be nothing more than sex.*

Someone knocked at the door.

She straightened her short black skirt and sat in her office chair. "Come in."

James opened the door and poked his head in. "Good morning, Tess. I got your text message. What did you need?"

As usual, his voice sent her heartbeat racing, and his sexy grin would have left her panties moist if she'd been wearing any. "Come on over here, and close the door please. I need your help with this drawer." She nudged the drawer with her bare leg. To her chagrin, it closed easily. "I don't know what's wrong with this stupid thing."

He crossed over to the desk and crouched to the offending drawer. "You do realize that I do maintenance on the building, not office equipment or furniture? You probably know more about this than I do." He winked at her, then pulled the drawer out all the way.

She rolled the chair close and *accidentally* bumped his shoulder with her knee. "Oh, I'm sorry." She leaned forward. If he turned his head, they'd practically be kissing. "I just wanted to see so that next time I can fix it myself," she said softly as she inhaled his heady masculine scent.

He stared at her a few seconds. The desire she saw in his eyes told her she'd be getting what she wanted soon.

He shook his head, then returned to fiddling with the drawer. "You are a trip."

"What?"

"There's nothing wrong with this drawer that you didn't purposely do."

She gasped. "How could you—?"

"Hold that thought." He touched the metal tracking on the inside of the unit. "What did you do, sit on the drawer?"

Too stunned to speak, she remained quiet.

"Listen, Tess. This desk cost around fourteen hundred dollars—"

"No way!"

"I gave you my number because I want to get to know you better, not to play games." Still crouched, he faced his body toward Tess and held onto the arms of the chair. "Now what do you actually want?"

"For you to make love to me," she said softly.

"Is that all you want from me?" He rested his hands on her bare thighs.

No! "Yes."

"Liar." As he rose, he moved his hands to the arms of the chair, leaned forward and kissed her.

Bingo! She knew she'd get her way, but something in his kiss was different from when she'd kissed others. His was claiming, yet freeing; lusty, yet loving.

He pulled away.

"What's wrong?" she asked breathlessly. "We both want this."

"We both want it all, and I'm not willing to settle for less." He backed away. "I respect myself and you too much."

"You're not serious are you?" She inched her skirt up and slid her index finger into her heat. No man could resist easy access into the land of good and plenty.

He licked his lips, but didn't move from his spot.

She spread her legs. "See what you've done to me, James. You have to finish what you've started."

He drew in several deep breaths and seemingly forced his eyes to her face. "You may be willing to settle for less, but I'm not."

Heated and embarrassed, she lowered her skirt. "I know you aren't turning me down."

"I'm not turning you down. I'm saying I want to give you my all and that I want all of you."

She stomped as she stood. "Well this is all your broke ass can afford." She snatched a tissue out of the box on her desk and wiped her fingers. "I don't know what I was thinking when I asked you to come."

"That makes two of us. Yeah, I'm attracted to you physically, but beautiful women are a dime a dozen and sluts—"

"I'm not a slut!"

"Then stop acting like one. Where the hell are your panties?"

Ashamed of her behavior, she blinked wildly to keep from tearing up. "If you think I'm a slut, then why are you here?"

"Because when you aren't throwing yourself at men, I admire you."

"You…admire me?"

"Why is that so hard to believe? When you first started here, everyone except Sweetie thought you were just eye candy. Even I had my doubts. But you took the little job she gave you and grew it into a viable position within the company."

Pride straightened her posture. Associates, such as Sweetie, worked on several projects at once. The project manager made assignments and kept a high-level view of who was doing what, where and when. This kept conflicts in time lines to a minimum. The project manager had quit a few months before Tess was hired and projects where beginning to clash. To keep Sweetie's projects from hitting bumps in the road, Tess started tracking everyone's projects and pointing out conflicts.

Tess didn't assign projects, but the managers counted on her tracking when they made decisions on whom to assign to what. As Tess's job description expanded, Sweetie ensured her pay expanded. Sweetie had fought to have Tess hired as the new project manager, but Tess had asked her to back off. She knew that without a degree, management would never consider her to be qualified for the position.

"You have some serious skills, baby. How can I not admire a woman who would take on anyone who she thought had harmed her friend? I see the way you protect Sweetie. I thought whoever had upset her yesterday was a goner for sure. You have real heart, you just hide it behind all of that makeup," he teased.

She giggled. "I'm…I'm so flattered, I don't know what to say."

He reached into his back pocket and pulled out a flyer. "Have you considered returning to school? There's a degree fair going on at Navy Pier in a few weeks. Colleges from all over the state will be there. If you want, I'll go with you." He handed over the flyer.

Now she did want to cry. Sweetie was correct, yet again. James was one of the good guys, but Tess knew herself. Yes she was falling—had fallen—hard for James. She didn't care how much money he didn't have. All she cared about was the faith he had in her and the genuine love she saw in his eyes. She only wished she had half as much faith in herself.

Someone knocked at the door.

"Come in." She tossed the tissue at the trashcan, then looked up. "Kevin?"

James spun around.

"Hey, baby." He smirked at James as he strutted into her office with a rectangular jewelry box in his had. "I've missed you so much."

"What do you want, Kevin?"

"Come on, baby. How can you bite off my head when I come bearing gifts." He opened the box and showed her what was inside.

"Oh my God!" Tess didn't know squat about the cost of furniture, but she had recognized the diamond Tiffany rose pendant before he fully opened the box. She glared at James. *Why can't you be the one giving me gifts?* Angry with herself for falling for James, she forced a gracious smile. "Thank you, Kevin." What scared her most was she didn't care that James couldn't afford such an extravagant gift. *But for how long?* And how long would James be happy with just a pretty package? Since he was showing her degree fair flyers, she figured not for long.

"Are you're going to settle?" James asked.

"I'm not the woman you think I am, James."

Tess lay back on Kevin's bed in a dream state. Walking away from James hurt her more than all the hurts she'd had in her life combined. In truth, she didn't feel she was good enough for him. He saw her as who she wanted to be instead of who she was—the slut who had thrown herself at him and was now allowing Kevin access to her body.

Kevin parted her legs and inched her skirt up. "Umm, someone forgot to wear panties today." He licked and suckled along her inner thighs, and she retched.

"Just relax," he said.

Is this the life you want, Tess? Sweetie had asked.

"Kevin." She tried to move back, but he held her hips steady.

"I know, baby, just let it flow."

"No, you don't understand. I can't do this anymore."

His hands firmly on her thighs, he poked his head up from between her legs. "I haven't even gotten to the good part yet."

"I'm serious."

"So am I." He lowered his mouth to her crotch, but she pushed his shoulders with all of her strength.

"Stop it, Kevin. We're through. I shouldn't have come here with you. I'm leaving."

A momentary flash of panic sparked in his black eyes and left her confused.

"Come on, baby, I'm so sorry about before." He crawled fully onto the bed and straddled her. "Let me make it up to you."

"I'm not playing. Get off me, Kevin. I need to get back to work."

He rested his full weight on her waist. "I know you aren't running back to that janitor. Not with all I have to offer."

"What he has to offer is priceless." She pushed at his knees.

He grabbed her hands and forced her arms above her head. "So you were using my ass to make that broke nigga jealous?"

The crazed tone of his voice scared her more than the tight grip he held her in.

"N-no," she stammered. "I apologize for leading you on."

"So you think you can just walk out on me?" He backhanded her.

Ronald rushed into the parking garage of Kevin's building and made a beeline for Tess's Mercedes. He'd hidden in the entry closet until Kevin and Tess went into the bedroom. Then he crept out and took Tess's keys out of her purse. For all the shit Kevin talked about how easy Tess was, he sure had a hell of a time convincing her to go with him. Ronald would be surprised if she allowed him to do anything besides go down on her. She seemed like the selfish type that would do a brotha like that.

He slipped on a pair of latex gloves, popped open the trunk, dropped the keys into his front jeans pocket and set his backpack beside the spare tire. A young woman parked a few spaces down. He nodded politely at her, and she was on her way. They didn't want to draw suspicion by switching tires in the parking garage, and with the way Tess was acting, he knew he wouldn't have time to follow the plan and drive the car five minutes to his private garage at his condo complex. He tapped around the tire with his fist until a flap sank in. An incredulous smile tipped his lips. Only Kevin would buy such an asinine thing.

He scanned the area. No one was around. He took out one of the freezer bags that were filled with small vials of cocaine. *Yes!* He heard the door to the parking garage open, and stuffed the cocaine into a backpack he'd found in his backseat. *Let me stop fucking around before someone walks up.* The man who entered the garage walked in the opposite direction. Ronald snatched the pint-sized freezer bags from the tire and transferred them to his backpack. He didn't care about what would happen when Tess discovered her tire was fake, all he cared about was getting their merchandise. As he grabbed the final bag, it opened and vials spread all over the trunk of the car.

"Shit." He quickly gathered the vials and put them into his bag.

Kevin leaned against the bathroom door. "Please, Tess, I'm so sorry. You know how I get. I love you. I didn't mean to hurt you. Please, baby, can't you see I'm afraid of losing you."

Ronald tipped into the condo. "What the hell happened?" he whispered.

Kevin went to him. "I fucked up man," he said softly. "She pissed me the hell off, and I…" He shook his head. "Shit, she's probably calling the cops on my ass right now. You need to get out of here." He took the keys from Ronald.

"I'm out, man. I'll let Zack know."

"Don't tell him shit. I'll handle this."

"Don't be stupid. Zack is one of the best defense attorneys around."

"Do whatever the hell you want." Kevin returned to the bathroom door. "I'm ready to go for help, Tess. But I can't do it without you. I love you so much." He shot Ronald the what-the-hell-are-you-waiting-for look. "Go," he mouthed.

"Thank you for lunch, Zack. Actually, thank you for the lovely day. I've had a great time." Sweetie continued eating her slice of hot apple pie with vanilla ice cream and caramel to top.

The joy displayed on her face as she ate had him wanting to put joy on her face for purely carnal reasons. Instead of her licking the caramel off the ice cream, he could practically feel her licking the pre-cum off the tip of his hardness. He had to have her. "A great enough time for you to dump this Gabriel dude for me?"

"I'm sorry, Zack. You're a great guy, but I'm in love with Gabriel."

"You were crying on a stranger's shoulder yesterday because of him. I'd never make you cry."

"That was a misunderstanding." Her cell phone played the old Kanye West song "Gold Digger." She took the phone off her belt clip. "I'm sorry, but that's Tess. She must need something at work."

He nodded his understanding. Since he couldn't eat her, he settled for the edge of her apple pie.

"What's wrong, Tess?...What do you mean? Why are you at Kevin's?"

Zack's cell phone rang, but he couldn't tear his eyes from Sweetie. Whatever Tess was saying had upset her.

"Aw, hell naw! Stay put. I'm calling the cops."

Sweetie's conversation held him captive. He didn't even try to answer his phone. A few seconds later, the phone beeped with a message.

Her shoulders rose and fell as her breathing became heavy. "What are you, crazy? We need the cops!" She slammed her hand down on the table. Several of the other patrons in the restaurant looked at their table, others snuck glances.

He couldn't tell if Sweetie didn't care or notice the attention she was drawing. He set out enough cash for their meal and a sizable tip on the table, then led Sweetie out to his car.

By the time she was seated, her face was damp from tears. "Please, Tess, please don't ask me to do this."

His cell rang again. He turned it off.

"Fine! I'll be there as soon as I can."

He watched as Sweetie fought to regain her composure.

"I'm so sorry, Zack." She dropped the phone into her lap, then lowered her face into the palms of her hands. "I don't know what to do."

"What's wrong? I want to help."

She looked over at him and offered the saddest smile he'd ever seen. "Thanks, but I can't get you involved in this drama."

"I'm very capable of making decisions for myself. We are friends. Tell me what's wrong. If I can help, I will. If I can't, I'll help you find someone who can."

She sniffed and wiped at her face. "My best friend was just beat by her boyfriend, again. She won't let me call the police. I don't even know why she was over there. They broke up."

Oh shit! Now he wished he'd answered his phone when it sounded with the ring tone he'd assigned Kevin and Ronald. He'd thought they were just being jerks and cock blocking after they'd finished their parts. He couldn't allow Sweetie to call the police. He'd handle Kevin in his own way.

"I'll go over there with you. Cowards who beat women won't usually stand up to a man."

"You're right, but I won't allow it." She picked up her phone. "Tess is family to me. This is family business." She proceeded to call all three of her brothers, but all three were busy and couldn't leave immediately.

"Come on, Sweetie, let me do this."

"I won't risk your career on this nonsense. We are family; we have to do stupid stuff to save each other."

He chuckled. She was right. How many times had he done something he knew was stupid to help his siblings out? "I'm a grown man and capable of making an informed decision."

"No." She blew out a long breath, then dialed another number. He could tell she didn't want to call whomever she expected to answer. "Hey, Ray. Tess is in trouble, and I need someone to have my back. You down?…I knew you would be." She sounded more disappointed than grateful. "Thanks." She gave him the information. "I'll meet you there."

"Who was that?"

"My last resort, I mean my cousin."

"I'm coming."

"No. I'll take the train over there."

"I'll follow you. You don't have a choice in this."

She grumbled something under her breath he was glad he couldn't understand.

"What's the address?"

❧

Backs flush to the wall, Sweetie and Zack flanked either side of the door.

Ray knocked, but no one answered. He knocked again. "I've been sent by condo management for the three month extermination treatment."

Last month Tess had called Sweetie complaining that some strange man just walked into Kevin's condo. He'd knocked a few times, but she didn't feel like answering. He'd even said he was an exterminator. Once he entered, she discovered that they treated the condo every three months during the day and didn't need the resident's permission to enter.

Sweetie heard someone stomping. The door swung open and Kevin barked, "Damn, man, they just sprayed last— "

Ray pushed Kevin into the unit.

"What the fu…" Kevin tumbled back.

"I'll tell you what." Ray grabbed Kevin by the front of his dress shirt. "You think you can hit on my cousin, and I'm gonna let that shit ride? Hell, naw!"

Tess was considered part of the family. She fit in perfectly. Initially when Missy asked Tess to call her Mama, Sweetie had been hurt and jealous. She often felt that Missy held Tess up as the example of what she wanted in a daughter. When honest with herself, Missy's comparisons were still hurtful.

Sweetie closed the door behind them, but couldn't close the door on her feelings. Now wasn't the time to delve into her relationship with her mother. She had to save Tess from herself, again. "Don't hurt him—yet—Ray."

Zack stood off to the side. For a second, she saw shock and recognition in Kevin's eyes when he saw Zack. At first she was thrown, but then again, their offices were in the same building. It would make sense that they'd seen each other before.

"Aw come on, cuz, let me teach this ass hole what happens when he disrespects the ladies." Ray shoved Kevin onto the pimp daddy red sofa and dared him to move.

Sweetie rushed to the bathroom. Ray was the one cousin she'd known would be home. The majority of her family were everyday working folks, but Ray…He spent most of his days hanging out on the corners talking shit with his boys all day or vying for a fight.

She tapped on the door. "Tess, it's Sweetie. Open the door."

"I…I don't want for you to see me. Just keep Kevin away until I can get to my car."

"Stop being ridiculous and open the door." Sweetie could scream. *How can anyone be so vain?*

"Please, Sweetie, please…"

Sweetie swore under her breath, went into Kevin's bedroom, then returned with one of the many bobby pins Tess had left behind.

"Are you going to open this door today, or what?"

Silence.

She straightened the bobby pen, quickly stuck it into the hole in the doorknob, popped the lock and walked into the bathroom.

The shock on Tess's face as she looked up from her seat on the tub wasn't what stopped Sweetie. The showstopper was the bloodied nose, black eye and bruises on Tess's swollen face. She wrapped her arms around Tess. "Thank you, Lord. Thank you for saving my friend's life." Her tears mixed with Tess's.

"I'm okay." Tess drew in a ragged breath. "It isn't as bad as it looks. You know how easily I bruise."

"Baby, please. We have to call the police. I'll be with you every step of the way."

"Don't make me go to the police. They'll take pictures." She lifted her shaky hands to her battered face. "Please, Sweetie, please. I can't…" she sniffed, "…I can't go through a trial."

Torn, Sweetie didn't know what to do. "How did this happen? Why were you here?"

"I know I shouldn't have come, but I..." She lowered head. "I was running from James, running away from my feelings for him."

"James isn't the one who would hurt you."

"I...I know. It's me. I don't want to hurt him."

"What in the world are you talking about?"

Tess fiddled with her fingers. "I'm not like you. I need a man who can take care of me financially. I'm scared that once the newness of James wears off, I'll...I'll stop loving him. I'm afraid of hurting him."

"You're in love."

"Yes. I'm truly in love with him." An eerie laugh escaped her. "I love him so much I told Kevin I wouldn't sleep with him."

"So he got mad and beat you?" Though Sweetie was proud of Tess for choosing James over Kevin, she was enraged that Tess had put herself in the position—yet again—to be abused by this man. But now was not the time to chastise her.

"Basically," Tess said barely above a whisper. "Please, Sweetie, I swear to God I am through with Kevin. Just take me home."

Sweetie knelt before Tess and took her by the hands. "I love you so much, Tess. I wish..." She glanced out the door toward the living area. Thoughts of Kevin lurking around the parking garage and now this fresh beating shored up her resolve. "I wish I could give you what you want. He could have killed you."

"No!" Tess clung to Sweetie. "Please don't do this to me."

"I'm not doing anything to you. I'm doing this for you." She turned away from her friend. "Zack, call the police."

CHAPTER SEVEN

Three Tootsie Roll Pops down, and Sweetie still didn't know what to do outside of calling in reinforcements for help with Tess. On one hand, she wanted to support Tess, on the other, she wanted to strangle the life out of her for being stuck on stupid. After the police took Tess's statement and photos, Sweetie forced her to go to the hospital for an examination. Now Tess was in her room pouting.

How she'd explain this mess to Gabriel was another of her worries. He was already skeptical of Tess. He thought her performance at his mother's house was too good to be a complete act. So he was correct; it wasn't that much of a stretch for Tess, but Sweetie still loved her best friend and wanted Gabriel to see that Tess had a good side.

What are you doing now, Gabriel? The fourth sucker rolled over her tongue. He'd told her he wanted to spend the evening smoothing things over with his mother. If his mother was even half as upset as he'd said she was, Sweetie doubted she'd be seeing him tonight. *I miss you.* All Sweetie wanted was to relax in Gabriel's arms and forget about Tess, Kevin and James.

The doorbell rang. She dragged herself from the couch to the front door. The bell rang again. Sweetie knew whom the impatient person on the other side was and was starting to regret calling her, but she didn't know who else to call.

"Hello, Mama," she said as she opened the door for the most beautiful woman she'd ever seen. Sixty-plus years old, tall, lean, with short cropped silver hair and flawless caramel skin, Missy Fuller still turned the heads of men all ages and races.

Missy kissed her on the cheek and took the sucker out of her hand as she entered. "Hello, Monica." She hugged her baby girl. "You know I love you, but you'd be so much more beautiful if you'd lose a few pounds." She bobbed the sucker at her. "These aren't helping, darling." She set her purse on the entry table.

"I'm glad to see you also," Sweetie said dryly.

"Oh stop being like that." She pulled Sweetie into the living room and settled on the couch with her. "I'm just telling you how to go from getting your pick of most men to any man. That is when you stop this celibacy foolishness." She winked at her, eliciting a smile.

"You are too much, Mama."

"You're my baby. You deserve the best." She placed the sucker on the wrapper on the coffee table. "Now tell me what and who had my baby in tears."

"I wasn't in tears. I was upset. Angry and upset. You see, Tess has been…" Now she knew calling in her mother was a bad idea. At the time she'd thought of the similarities between Missy and Tess and hoped Missy could talk some sense into Tess. But now she realized she may be adding more drama into an already over drama infused situation. "Kevin's been beating her."

"What?" Missy snapped. "What do you mean 'been?' How long has this been going on?"

"A few months," she answered softly.

"And how long have you known?"

"Mama, she wouldn't admit to anything. She kept claiming to be clumsy. But this time…" Knowing she skipped a few steps, she tried to un-jumble her thoughts. "Well she broke things off with him, and she's been staying with me, but he's been lurking around her. For some reason she went to his place, and he…" Images of Tess's swollen and battered face filled her mind's eye. "He really beat her bad this time, Mama." She quickly filled her mother in on what had happened.

"Let me get this straight," Missy said stiffly. "You called your brothers, and they didn't help."

"You know how busy they are. I don't know what I was thinking. I shouldn't have called them. Ray was just what I needed."

"Ray! I've told you to stay away from that thug."

"That 'thug' is your nephew. Family. We stick together." Which was true. No matter what, they were always a close-knit family. "Now I don't know what to do about Tess. She's angry with me for calling the police, and I'm angry with her for putting herself in this situation. That's why I called you. Tess needs somewhere to stay until we both cool off."

"Don't worry, darling. Tess will stay with me until I think she is ready to act like she has the good sense God gave her."

Additional drama averted, Sweetie relaxed considerably and was glad she'd followed her first mind. She knew she could count on her mom. Though they didn't agree on their outlooks on life, her mom had always been there for her. It also didn't hurt that Missy loved Tess like a daughter.

"Let me use your phone. I have something else I need to handle."

"What are you up to, Mama?" She took her cell phone off her belt clip and handed it over to her mother.

"You just be quiet for a minute." She dialed, then held the phone to her ear. "Get your bothers on the phone *neow!*"

Oh shit! Missy was raised in "the hood" and easily went "ghetto" when angered. "Mama, please don't." Sweetie reached for the phone; her mother turned away. "Aw, man, they'll think I told on them. Mama, I was wrong. I shouldn't have called them."

Missy walked away from her daughter with the phone snug on her ear. "Tell me how the hell three strong men could stand by while their baby sister goes in to battle a psycho?" She tapped her heeled foot on the wood floor. "What makes you think I give a damn about your clients and patients? Family comes first. Your job is to protect your baby sister. The next time she calls for help, your asses had better be on the way before she can disconnect from the line. You here me?" She nodded. "That's better…I love you all, too." She disconnected.

"I love you, Mama, but you were wrong for that." She held her hand out for the phone.

"I had three boys who I raised to be real men. It's their job to protect their women. Until you are married, you are their responsibility to protect. After your married, they'd better still be there when you call." She handed over the phone. "And I'd better not hear about you taking on a man in a fight again."

"Mama," she drawled, "I'm not stupid. I knew not to go in there alone. Ray was with me. There was no need for you to go off on them like that. I called you for help with Tess."

"There was definitely a need. You are a vivacious *woman*. Stop trying to outman the men. Now where's Tess?"

Missy had left with Tess over an hour ago, yet Sweetie was still sulking. Even Gabriel coming in hadn't knocked her out of her funk. After she explained to him what happened, he was upset that she hadn't called him immediately. For a while, he sounded as if he were cut from the same overprotective cloth as her mother. *I'm not trying to outman anyone.*

He cupped her body into his as they rested on the sofa. "You know I love you, don't you?" he asked.

"Yeah, I know."

"I'm not trying to dominate you. We're a couple, a team."

The word "dominate" struck her. She feared being dominated by anyone. Maybe that was the reason she hadn't considered calling Gabriel for help. Knowing him, he would have taken charge of the situation. Maybe deep down inside she worried someday he'd dominate her. As contradictory as it was, his domineering personality was one of his most attractive features to her. *I'm one confused nut.*

"I'm sorry I didn't call you. To be honest, I didn't even think of you at first." His grip tightened around her. She rolled over. "Come on, Gabriel. We've only been a couple for a few hours. When the drama broke out, I did what I'm used to doing—I called my brothers. Even during the first call I knew I was making a mistake. I shouldn't bring them into this mess. And when you crossed my mind, I wanted you there, but…but I didn't want to bring you into the mess either. At least they are used to it."

"In the future…"

"You have been promoted to number two on my speed dial."

"I know this goes deeper than Tess. Tell me what's wrong."

She thought for a few moments to pinpoint exactly what was wrong. "Tess is a parasite, and I've been enabling her. I see all of this potential in her, but when…when will she put it to use?"

"When she has to."

"I just can't understand why anyone would want to be so dependent on others. When I was a child, our livelihood depended on the man Mama had in her life at the time. And you'd best believe when she wasn't around, they'd be sure to point out to us how we'd have nothing if not for them. How they'd paid for Mama like she was some sort of high-priced whore."

"That's jacked up."

"Real jacked up."

"So what about your father?"

"All four of us have a different father. Mama grew up poor and wanted more for her children, so she literally picked each of our fathers according to how well he could provide for his child financially. My dad is little more than a paycheck to me." The truth in her words hurt.

"Do you want more?"

"What I want doesn't matter."

"It matters to me."

She gazed into his warm brown eyes. "I have everything I want right here." She nibbled on his bottom lip.

"Umm, you lead me to distraction, woman." He ran his hands along her back. "But it won't work."

She slid her hand between their bodies, slipped it into his pants and wrapped it around his hardness. "Feels like my distraction skills are working pretty good to me." She'd started this to stop his prying into painful areas of her life, but with him pulsating in her hand her sorrowful thoughts quickly retreated to the dark recesses of her mind. "Make that very good," she purred.

He closed his eyes as she stroked him. "Very, very good," he said.

"You wanna see what else I'm good at?" Before he had a chance to answer, she latched her hands to the inside of his pants and briefs, then pulled them down.

"I want to finish our..." he trailed off the moment she began to gently suckle around the underside of the head of his now fully erect shaft. "I want to...to finish...this."

She knelt on the floor and continued her assault. Many a time she'd imagined the brim of her Tootsie Pop was Gabriel. Today she intended to see just how many licks it took to get to his center. She held him firmly while she worked her tongue along the line from the tip his hardness to the base back to the tip. They both loved control so much that she could hardly wait to see him lose his.

Breathing ragged, he weaved his fingers though her hair to her scalp with one hand and eased his other hand into her panties to her heat. As one finger then a second entered her, he massaged her mound with the palm of his hand. She knew he wouldn't be the only one to lose control, but with Gabriel, she didn't care.

"Take off your clothes," he told her.

She stripped off her Capri set as he milked himself. There was something about watching this powerful man stoke himself that sent the sensually charged rushes through her. She wanted to take him into her body and never let go. She dropped her panties and bra on the floor and tried to kneel back at the couch, but he pulled at her hips.

"I want a taste also," he said.

Fully understanding his meaning, there was no doubt in her mind they'd never have problems in the bedroom—or any other place they decide to make love. She propped herself up on her arms, then she straddled his face and took his hardness into her mouth.

He suckled along her inner thighs, then blew lightly.

"Umm," she cooed. It had become virtually impossible to concentrate on giving pleasure when she was receiving so much. She massaged his sac and returned to suckling the sensitive line of his pulsating manhood. Her reward—his large hands cupped her butt and pulled her down to his mouth. The feel of him parting her lower lips with his tongue, of him feeding off her, just about sent her over the edge.

Her lower body seemed to have a mind of its own and began pumping his tongue. Her abdomen tightened to pull him in deeper. They were lost in thrusts, ecstasy and lust until...

She could feel his seed shooting up his shaft as she came harder than she'd ever imagined possible. She couldn't cry out, she couldn't stop, she couldn't do anything but freefall over the edge.

Gabriel lowered the sheet so he could see Sweetie's body. The way her mocha skin glistened in the moonlight had him ready to wake her for another round of love making. *Will I ever be sated?* He ran his index finger from the base of her neck, along her spine to her lower back.

That she'd called everyone in her family tree without giving him a thought bothered him to no end. He wanted to be the one she phoned first. He wanted to be her support, her protector, her lover, her beginning and end.

Hearing how she had been raised, he understood why she had become so independent. Her independent way was one of her most attractive features to him, but it also drove him insane. How he'd get her to fully accept his love without suffocating her independence would be a challenge.

"Why won't you believe in me," he whispered.

"I do," she answered groggily, surprising him.

"Then marry me tomorrow."

She coughed. "Tomorrow?" She fanned her watery eyes.

"Yes. Tomorrow."

"I'll marry you because I'm in love with you, but not tomorrow." She snuggled in close. "What's the hurry? Are you pregnant?" she teased. "We haven't even met each other's families yet."

"It doesn't matter what my family thinks. We're getting married."

"Same here, but we still need to do things correctly. We should at least introduce ourselves first, and my mother has been looking forward to my wedding day since before I was born. There's no way I can't involve her in the plans."

"What will your brothers say?" Her mother didn't worry him. From the little he'd hard about her, he could tell his hefty bank account was all that mattered to her.

"Oh, they'll hate you on general principle. What about your family?"

"My father is still in Sweden. As long as I'm bringing money into the company, he'll be happy."

"Not your dad, too?"

"Oh no, baby. He's nothing like your father..." As he was trying to snatch the words out of the air and shove them down his throat, she pushed away from him. "I'm sorry. I didn't mean it like that."

"How exactly did you mean it?" She pulled the sheets up and covered her body.

He knew saying, "My father actually loves me," wouldn't quite work, and he didn't want to hurt her. "I meant the money is important to him, but he realizes I have a life outside of the business. He allows me to live my life."

"Umm-hmm," she grumbled. "And what about your mother?"

"We're having dinner with her tomorrow. I want her to meet my real fiancée."

"Oh really?"

"Yes, really. She's a snob. Just hold your pinky out when you drink your tea, and you'll be fine."

Her deep belly laugh with an added snort at the end confirmed she was definitely the one for him. She was so free. He patted his chest, and she laid her head on it with her body half on him. The light scent of lavender would always remind him of his Sweetie.

"I don't look anything like the women your mother chose for you."

"And I never considered asking any of those women to marry me. You're the one I love."

"How you gonna send that ass wipe for me, Zack?" Kevin raged as he stormed into Ronald's place. "You could have had me out hours ago." He punched his fist into his hand. "I can't believe that fat bitch had me arrested. Her ass is gonna pay for this shit."

Zack gnashed his teeth. No way would he allow Kevin to blame this fiasco on Sweetie. "You were arrested because *you* couldn't hold your temper. And how was I supposed to represent you? I was busy having my date with Sweetie ruined by you at the time. We can't have any ties, and after the way you beat Tess, your ass is lucky I called anyone. What in the hell is wrong with you?"

"She's screwing around on me with that broke nigga at her job."

"Newsflash! You two are not a couple. If anything, she was about to screw around on him."

Chest heaving angrily, Kevin stepped up on Zack. "I will kick your ass, white boy."

"I'm not some woman. You will get your assed kicked."

Ronald shoved the two apart. "Stop this nonsense. Zack's right. He shouldn't have represented you, and you were a dumb ass for being arrested in the first place." He set his duffle on the coffee table while Kevin and Zack continued to stare each other down. "We have business to conduct."

"You know." Zack backed away. This was just the opportunity he'd been looking for. "I'm through. This wannabe Casanova is going to get us all caught. Y'all can have my portion. I'm done." He walked out of the room.

CHAPTER EIGHT

Sam barely made it to his post behind the security desk before Sweetie entered the office building. He couldn't believe he was playing a key role—heck, any role—in setting up his girl, but the money was too good to pass on and this was for her own good. At least that's what he kept telling himself.

She'd talked his ear off when she first arrived at work this morning. It was Gabriel this and Gabriel that. Initially, Sam was jealous, but the love infused in every word she spoke about Gabriel was truly beautiful. He was happy she'd finally found someone.

"Hey, Sam," she said as she approached. Her silk floral skirt was a treat. He'd kill to have those thick legs of hers around him as he drove into her.

"You okay, Sam?" She held out his car keys.

"Oh, I'm sorry. You caught me daydreaming." He took the keys from her. "So do you think that anorexic Tyra wannabe will like it? I'm giving her a serious deal." He'd only had his Grand Am a year and took excellent care of it. He loved his car, but with the money Gabriel had given him, he could pay off the Grand Am and buy a Grand Prix. Plus, he needed a way to get Sweetie out of the building for a while.

"She won't like it, but she can afford it. How do you keep it looking showroom perfect?"

"That's a playa secret." He glanced at his watch; everyone should be in place.

"Then why do you know it?" She giggled.

"Got jokes today, huh?"

"I come up with a good one every now and again. Let me get on back to work. I'll catch you later."

He rounded the desk and joined her.

"Ooooo, I get an escort," she teased. "I feel so special."

"Well, don't. I'm just tired of standing behind that desk." He winked, and they both laughed.

The right-center set of elevator doors opened, but he held Sweetie back. "Don't go on that one," he whispered as people exited. "They were having trouble with it earlier."

"Maybe you should put up a sign?"

"Nah, it'll be fine. You were already stuck on there the other day. Let someone else have their turn today." The far right set of elevator doors opened. He held out his hand. "There you go, my sweet. Have a great day."

"You, too." She stepped onto the elevator.

A man rushed toward the now closing doors, but Sam stopped them. "This one's out of order. She's doing a test run." The man nodded his thanks and stood to the side for the next elevator.

As soon as the door closed fully, Sam took out his cell phone and called James. "She's on her way." He picked up the magnetic "Out Of Order" sign that was lying on the floor next to the elevator bank and affixed it to the elevator Sweetie had gotten on, just as he had the rest of that set in the building.

The elevator stopped on the seventh floor, and the doors opened. Sweetie moved to the side for whoever would be boarding, but no one stepped on.

"Hey, Sweetie." James poked his head in from the side control panel. "Sorry I had to stop you, but I'm testing something."

"Should I switch?"

"Nah, this will be fine."

Gabriel stepped onto the elevator with a leather book bag slung over his shoulder, startling her.

A wickedly seductive grin spread across his face and sent her heart rate racing. "I thought you'd be glad to see me," he said as the doors closed, and he dropped the bag in the corner.

"I am. I'm also shocked."

Devilment burned in his eyes. She was tempted to ask him what he was up to, but decided to wait and see. Instead of standing beside her, he pulled her into his arms and descended on her mouth. He tugged her blouse out of her skirt. Though her mind said, "stop him," her body was unwilling to cooperate. He had her so hot and flustered she could do little more than moan.

The elevator stopped, bringing her close to her senses. She quickly pushed him away. "We can't do this here." She straightened her clothes.

"Of course we can." He reached for her again.

She swatted at his hands and walked around him to the control panel. "The elevator must be stuck again."

He wrapped his arms around her from behind and ground his hardness into her. Oh how she wanted to give in. The excitement of being caught added a nice touch of adrenalin to the rush he sent through her, but the thought of being caught and her losing her job sobered her. Her firm was extremely conservative, and being found in the elevator in a "compromising position" would definitely be career suicide.

She turned and stole one blazing kiss, then said, "You're killing me. We have to stop."

He chuckled. "Your hand is stroking me. How can you expect me to stop?" He suckled along her neck.

Hand conveniently wrapped around his engorged flesh, she giggled. *How did that get in there?* When her hands started acting on her own, she had no idea. "You're going to get me fired."

"I've made arrangements." He hiked up her skirt. "Stop worrying. This elevator won't move until I've shown you what type of woman I'm attracted to."

Sam's odd behavior and James just happening to stop her elevator car replayed in her mind. "What were you doing on the seventh floor?"

He backed her to the rear wall, then yanked her panties to the floor, and she stepped out of them. Seeing him at her feet sent a different type of rush through her—one of dominance. That she had this powerful man at her feet...She fanned herself.

He suckled along her inner leg to her thigh as he rose. The sensual play of his tongue had her liquid passion flowing. Still stooped, he held her waist steady and took a taste. His mouth making love to her was almost too much for her to bear. She massaged his head and shoulders. Even her fingers felt tingly.

He released her waist, but continued his oral assault. She heard him rip a foil package. She would have helped him protect them both, but she could do little more than grip at his shoulders.

As he stood, he grabbed her butt and held her still while he penetrated her. Sweetie knew she was a big girl and was impressed by his strength. She wrapped her legs around him, drew his face to hers and their lips connected. She tasted every succulent inch of his mouth to keep from screaming in ecstasy as he moved in and out of her. The pain from being smashed against the slick wall was nothing compared to the pleasure building inside of her. Their grunts intensified with each stroke.

Ready to burst, she licked her lips. He took her bottom lip into his mouth, and that was her undoing. A massive orgasm ripped through her. Her nails dug into his arms, and her whole body quaked. She pulled him in, wanting every drop of him, but was blocked because of the condom.

"That's it, baby," he said breathlessly. "Umm, that's..." His powerful legs thrust his hips into her harder. "Oh, shit!" He grit his teeth and his body tensed. "Umph..." A few staggered breaths later, he leaned his head back and laughed. Not a ha-ha-that-was-funny laugh, but an I-can't-believe-what-just-happened kind of laugh.

After his breathing returned to normal, he lowered her. "I love you so much, Sweetie." He pecked her lips gently. "And not just because you're the sexiest woman I've ever met. You're my only kind of woman. You do more than complete me. You complement me."

She'd read the saying "her heart smiled" so many times she couldn't count them, but now she understood what it felt like.

He held her close. "I came to Chicago for you because I'm in love with you. I made my decision before I boarded the flight. I don't need more time to think, and I sure as hell don't want to wait months to plan a 'proper' wedding. I'm ready to start our family. Marry me—today."

"I love you. Yes. I'll marry you today."

"I want a divorce," Sweetie said as the limo pulled out of the courthouse parking lot.

"No," Gabriel whispered and suckled along her neck. "We're in love."

"What's love got to do with it?" She pushed him away, but he drew her back into his arms—right where she wanted to be—and continued where he'd left off. "My mom is going to kill me, and my brothers are going to kill you." Too tired to fight back, too in love to deny her feelings, too whipped to stop his kisses, she rested her head on his shoulder. "How did I let you talk me into this?"

"Sweetie, we're married. All I care about right now is making love to you. I want to *feel* you like I never have before." He lifted her skirt and brushed his hand along her inner thigh. "I want to *fill* you like I never have before." He nudged her panties to the side and slipped a finger inside her.

This felt too good to stop, but she didn't have a choice. One of them had to be sensible. She nodded toward the partition that separated the passenger compartment from the front seat. "What if he sees us?"

"He can't see or hear what's going on back here unless we press these two little buttons." He tapped the remote with his free hand. "Wanna give him a show?" He massaged the nub of her passion with his thumb, sending tiny heat waves though her.

The car made its way through the city traffic toward her condo. The passenger windows were tented so darkly, she knew no one would see them, and she wanted to give in, but she couldn't. "You're killing me," she signed as she closed her legs on his hand and rotated her hips.

"I'm loving you. Come for me, baby. I want to hear you—"

His commands were so sweet to her hears. "Noooooo…." She rotated her hips, then forced herself to remain still. "No coming, no hearing anything, you devil."

A sinister edge accompanied his chuckle. "As you wish, my sweet." He removed his hands, licked his fingers clean, then straightened her skirt.

"I have to figure out how to tell my family I lost my mind in lust somewhere and got married."

"Why thank you," he teased. "But you know we have more than lust. Don't worry about your mother. From everything I've heard about her, she'll love me."

He was right on both counts. This was much more than lust and her mother would love him, but she was still worried about her family's reaction to her uncharacteristic behavior. She'd never been impulsive in her life. She'd known she would be a financial analyst before she knew the correct title for the position. She'd picked the undergraduate and graduate programs she'd attend by the time she was eight. She'd chosen the firm she'd work for when she was in high school and started internships there her first summer after graduating.

How could she explain to her family that this wasn't on impulse? That she'd known Gabriel for months and had fallen in love with him, yet neglected to mention him? That this was the natural progression of things? How could she explain their relationship?

She looked at her fine specimen of a husband. How could she explain to him that she was afraid people would misinterpret her love for him as weakness?

She sighed. "I might as well get this over with." She took her cell phone out of her purse, dialed her mother, then leaned on Gabriel's shoulder.

"Hello, darling, what a pleasant surprise."

"Hey, Mama. It's so good to hear your voice." And it was. Though Sweetie didn't like her mother's materialistic ways, one thing Sweetie never doubted was her mother's love for her and her brothers. They were number one in her life.

"Is something wrong?"

"Umm, how's Tess?"

"She slept most of the day. What's really bothering you?"

Sweetie smiled. "How do you do that?"

"You're my baby. Now tell me what's wrong."

She took Gabriel's hand into hers. "I don't know how to say this but..." *I met a man over the phone a few months ago and saw him for the first time the day before yesterday. Today he sexed me up so well in the elevator I'm still feeling after shocks hours later. Oh and by the way, we got married.*

"Just say it."

"I…I'm…," she held Gabriel's hand close to her heart, "…engaged."

He mouthed, "It's alright," and caressed her face, but the way her mother was ranting and raving told her things were anything but alright. She pressed speaker, then set the phone in her lap. Gabriel might as well hear what he'd gotten himself in to.

"This is unbelievable! How can you get engaged—*engaged*—without me even knowing you were dating? What's going on?"

"I'm in love, Mama."

"Yeah, right."

Now that hurt. "I'm capable of loving and being loved."

"Of course you are, but you refuse to let outsiders in. And you'll never attract men worthy of you carrying that extra weight and trying to outman them."

"Not again…" Sweetie drawled. As much as Sweetie knew her mother loved her, she also knew she was a disappointment to her. How many times had she suggested she be more like Tess? *Too many to count.*

"Oh God, please tell me he isn't some mail-order groom. Look, honey, you want some male companionship. That's only natural, but there are other ways."

"There is nothing wrong with my weight, and I'm not trying to outman anyone. I'm being myself. I've found a man who loves me for me."

"You didn't say he wasn't some sort of mail-order groom."

Sweetie laughed at the absurdity as the limo neared her condo complex. "He's from Sweden, Mama. Does that count?" She winked at Gabriel.

"He's only after a green card."

"I was born in Chicago, ma'am," Gabriel stated calmly. "My birth certificate is more than sufficient."

Missy's hacking and choking came through loud and clear.

Sweetie could imagine how confusion had marred her mother's beautiful face. Gabriel hunched his shoulders in a was-it-something-I-said way.

She mouthed, "You are the devil."

"I don't know what type of games you're playing, Monica, but I expect them to stop this instant. Who is that with you?"

"Mama, I'd like to introduce you to my fiancé, Gabriel Windahl. I thought we could have a family dinner at my place on Saturday."

"But you haven't even been dating. How could you have a fiancé? Oh Lord in heaven help me. She's met a man off the Internet. And I don't care that you're listening Gabriel Windham or whatever the hell your name is. If you think I'm going to let you hurt my baby, you are mistaken. Monica, I'm too upset to speak right now. I expect to see you first thing tomorrow morning."

"I have to go into work tomorrow. I'm already a little behind, and with Tess out, things are hectic. I can come there Saturday or you can come to my place."

"Oh, I'll be there alright. With the boys." The line went dead just as the limo stopped in front of her building.

"Well, that went better than I expected," she said.

"By the boys, she means your brothers?"

"I'm afraid so. So what will be your mother's reaction?"

"After the way Tess cut up the other day...there's no telling."

The café across the street from Sweetie's building provided the perfect spot for Kevin to watch as some big black dude helped her out of a stretch limo. The way she was all hugged up on the guy confused Kevin. First her man-hating butt went on a date with Zack, and now she was flirting and allowing some man to paw all over her. Something was not right, but he didn't have time to figure out what.

Because of her, he'd been suspended from his job for breeching the code of conduct. The suspension was with pay until further investigation, but how long would that last? He cursed under his breath as she entered the building. First she'd taken Tess from him and now she was trying to get him fired, and what had he done to her? Absolutely nothing. He was so angry he could strangle her.

He tapped on his cup of coffee. He didn't give a damn about the job. The customer base for his extracurricular activities he would be losing is what he cared about. Several of his faithful customers had already called and said he was too hot to deal with. He'd assured them this would blow over, but their punk asses had bailed out. *Shit!*

After the firm handed down his suspension, he'd hightailed it to Sweetie's office, but she wasn't there. His next stop was the café. Now that he'd had a few hours to cool off, he realized confronting her would have been a mistake. Right now he had to take care of his own affairs, but he'd get revenge on Sweetie. He'd just wait for the perfect opportunity.

CHAPTER NINE

Sweetie glanced over her shoulder down the hallway, but saw no one. She'd felt as if someone had been watching them since they had arrived at her condo. She grinned and held on tighter to Gabriel's arm. Of course people had been watching the free peep show they'd almost given. She was shocked they had been able to keep their hands off each other long enough for her to take a shower—alone—wash her hair and fix it into an Afro held back with a crimson crochet headband. After they were both showered and ready to go, they'd had to rush out the door. There was no time to make love. She didn't want to be late and make a bad impression on his mother.

Instead of pressing the doorbell to his mother's home, Gabriel asked, "You okay?"

Getting to the place in her life where she had truly accepted herself as a beautiful, confident, intelligent woman wasn't easy. It wasn't that she didn't care what others thought, but she'd come to realize she was a good person inside and out. So when people—even her mother—didn't approve of her appearance or her outlook on life, she wasn't affected to the point to where she'd try to change her self to meet their approval. Yet, here she stood, wanting to do whatever it took to make his mother like her.

The love in his eyes and warmth of his smile comforted her. "Yeah, I'm just a little worried. You don't think the earrings are too much do you?" She tapped the gold hoop, in hoop, in hoops that dangled down her long, thick neck. "I know you asked me to wear them, but maybe I should take them off. Be a little more conservative this first meeting."

"You're beautiful. Stop worrying."

Logically, she knew she was being ridiculous. If his mother didn't like her because of her choice of earrings, or even the crimson kulak outfit she wore, then the woman was so shallow she shouldn't care what she thought. But she couldn't stop her heart from caring. She wanted to impress his mother. And it angered her that she wanted to be accepted by his family—as he would be into hers. Even her brothers would accept him after the initial shock wore off.

"I'm good," she told herself more than him. "Just don't tell her we're married. I can't hurt my mom like this. We can never tell her our real anniversary."

"I understand. I don't want to hurt my mother either. But I'm not waiting on making babies." He brushed his lips over hers. "If you don't mind walking down the aisle with a swollen belly, I'll be right beside you."

Babies...Oh, how she wanted children, but with her increasing age and lack of a husband, she'd given up her dream. Yes, she knew that plenty of single women out there raised perfectly great children, but she didn't want to go that route. She missed not having her father play an active role in her life too much to do that to her children.

"Umm, that's my sweet." He drew her into his arms.

"What?"

"You're smiling at the thought of having my babies. Do you know how good that makes me feel?" He rested his forehead on hers. "Don't worry about Mom. Once she gets over me bringing two different fiancées over in three days named Monica Fuller, she'll be fine."

Giggling, she backed away. "Aw, man, I forgot about that."

"That's also why I don't think we should spring our marriage on her. She'll think I've lost my mind."

When Gabriel was six, he saw a teen ride a skateboard off the walkway over the stairwell. Gabriel was sure the teen had made a mistake and would fall onto the cement stairs. Instead, the young man held his arms out, surfed the air, then landed on the ground below—skateboard wheels down and his feet planted firmly on the skateboard. Josephine, Gabriel's mother, had pulled Gabriel along, fussing about how that hoodlum could have hurt someone. Gabriel had never seen a skateboard before, and did not know you could fly through the air with one!

As his mother dragged him away, Gabriel continued to watch the teen perform several tricks with his board. At that moment he knew exactly what he wanted to be when he grew up—a skateboard hoodlum. When he told his parents, they had explained to him there was no such career, but he knew they had to be wrong. He asked his mother for a skateboard, and she told him "no," because he'd break his neck. He continued to harass her until she finally gave in and said if he still wanted one when he was twelve, she would buy him one.

Six long years he waited. The closer to turning twelve he became, the more excited he became, and the slower time seemed to move. He'd swear to God that the last month of his eleventh year took three years to finish. The day before his birthday, he just about lost his mind. The day he'd been waiting for so long had finally arrived! At midnight, he ran to his mother's favorite toy hiding spot and tore through the packages until he came upon his skateboard. At the time he believed that heaven couldn't possibly be better than this. Over that weekend, he got a total of eight hours sleep—tops—and a sandwich here and there. Otherwise, he was out practicing.

He'd asked his mother if he could skip school the following Monday, but she wasn't having it. He made the best of his school day and bragged about his skateboard to anyone within earshot—earning a referral in each of his classes for disrupting the class and two detentions for acquiring so many referrals. Very few of the children at his private school knew much about skateboards, but they all wanted one by the end of the day.

That evening after he finished practicing popping a wheelie while doing a 360° on his skateboard, he cleaned and polished his baby. Tomorrow he'd show it off to his friends at school and earn at least three more detentions! Oh yeah, he'd be the envy of all.

He glanced at Sweetie as he pressed the doorbell button. The excitement and pride he'd felt as a child was nothing compared to how he felt now. Sweetie was perfect, and he knew his mother would love her. He couldn't understand why Sweetie was so worried. Though the switch in fiancées would throw his mother, she would be grateful once she met the real Monica Fuller. And he thanked God he'd been able to convince Sweetie to wear the bold, beautiful reds instead of the coco colored suit she'd wanted to wear. His mother loved color, and his Sweetie had too dynamic a personality to be trapped in that drab outfit.

He took her hand and intertwined their fingers. The way her luscious lips curled into an innocent smile had him thinking thoughts that were none too innocent and his body reacting. "Tonight I'm going to make love to you until we both faint from orgasmic overload."

As always, her laugh freed him. The door opened just as she snorted.

He hugged his mother. "Let me apologize again about the other night, Mom." He kissed her cheek, then took Sweetie by the hand and pulled her fully into the penthouse. "This is the real Monica Fuller, my fiancée." Beaming with pride, he cupped Sweetie's hand to his heart. "The love of my life."

Instead of greeting them, his mother slowly scrutinized Sweetie from her beaded thong sandals to the top of her Afro. Josephine's lip hitched up on one side and nose scrunched as if she caught a whiff of an offensive odor. "I don't know what type of games you're playing, but I'm not in the mood for them tonight."

He didn't need to see Sweetie's reaction to know his mother's words and tone had hurt her deeply. He protectively wrapped his arms around Sweetie and drew her into his body. Her back against his chest, he said, "I'm sorry, baby." Once she relaxed, he repeated, "Mom, this is Monica Fuller, my fiancée." He begged with his eyes for his mother to see Sweetie as he saw her or at least see that this was not some game and her words could hurt.

"You don't expect me to believe you're actually engaged to this…this…bohemian. What did I do to—?"

"Stop, Mom," he interrupted before she could cause more damage.

Sweetie took a deep breath and held out her hand. "Hello, Ms. Miller." He noticed a slight tremor to her hand, but her voice was as powerful as ever. "Gabriel has told me so much about you. My mother was a model for a short time. You two may even know some of the same people."

He could kiss Sweetie. This show of strength reaffirmed she was definitely the one for him. His mother stared at her hand a long while before shaking.

"You two are actually engaged?" Josephine asked slowly.

"Yes, ma'am."

The apology he expected to hear from his mother didn't come. He didn't know what to do. He'd never seen her act this rude before.

"I'm sure you must be starving." Josephine stalked into the dining room.

He turned Sweetie to face him. The pain on her face tore at his heart. "I'm sorry, baby. I don't know what's gotten into her. Tess did act a fool, but Mom is taking this overboard. We can leave."

"I think it's best we get this over with. My mother will want to meet your mother soon."

"Are you sure?"

"She's my mother-in-law. I might as well start getting used to her now."

After he and Sweetie washed their hands, they were seated at the dining table with his mother.

Sweetie ate every drop of her lobster bisque, though he knew she hated lobster. She'd tried engaging in conversation with his mother several times, but Josephine gave short, snappy answers.

Lasagna and snow peas were served as the main course. Snow peas were his favorite, but today they just didn't do it for him.

"So, Monica, how long have you known Gabriel?"

Shocked his mother actually said a complete sentence without being prompted, he almost shouted halleluiah.

"A little over six months. He's one of my firm's clients."

"They don't have some sort of fraternization rule at your firm?"

"Mom!" In the midst of another pod person switch-a-roo, he did his best to hold onto his composure. The mean-spirited woman across from him couldn't be his mother. His mother had more class than this...this...person.

"Not that you'd do this," she nodded her head toward Sweetie, "but you'd be shocked at how women throw themselves at men with money."

"I can only imagine," Sweetie calmly said, then took a sip of tea—her pinky held out. "And no, ma'am, there is not a fraternization rule at the firm regarding clients and employees."

"What a pity. What do your parents do?"

"My mom gave up modeling when she got pregnant with my brother and became a full-time mom and socialite. Now she spends most of her time trying to figure out how to get on my nerve, and my father is too busy to realize I have nerves to get on."

Gabriel laughed. "Boy can I relate."

Twenty agonizing minutes later, Bailey's Irish crème mousse cake was being served and Josephine was still going out of her way to insult Sweetie. Gabriel had had more than enough, but Sweetie appeared to be taking it all in stride.

"While you're here," Josephine tapped Maria's hand, "you might as well give Ms. Fuller a double serving."

"That's it!" Gabriel slammed the table with his fists, popping the place settings up. Josephine's look of disgust quickly turned to one of fear and worry.

Sweetie grabbed onto his arm. "It's alright."

"The hell it is!"

"Let me make a quick run to the powder room, then let's call it a night, okay?"

The pleading in Sweetie's eyes and voice were the only things that kept him from lighting into his mother. "Whatever you want, baby."

As soon as Sweetie was out of earshot, he bit out, "When did you lose your damn mind?" He'd never cursed at or even around his mother before, but he'd also never been so hurt, disappointed, disgusted and angry with her.

"Who do you think you're talking to?"

"I don't know." He hunched his shoulders. "You tell me. You look like my mother, sound like my mother, but my mother would never be so rude and downright nasty." He pointed in the direction Sweetie went. "That's the woman I love. That's the woman I choose to spend the rest of my life with."

Josephine angrily tossed her linen napkin onto her plate. "Why on earth would you want to marry that mammoth-sized tar baby when you can have any choice of beautiful women? You have an image to uphold."

"Oh, so people thinking I'm sucking some man's dick or taking it up the ass is better than me falling in love with a dark-skinned woman!" Gabriel had never heard his mother say anything that indicated she was color struck. The women she sent to him were always of the lighter variety, but since her former-model friends were light or white and all quite skinny, it made sense their daughters were the same. That's just how the modeling industry was back when his mother made her connections.

"You know that's not what I meant."

"I'm not going to argue with you about this, Mom. I'm in love with Monica. If you cannot treat her with respect and make her feel welcome, I will not bring her around. If she doesn't come around, neither will I."

Sweetie's legs felt as if they would give out on her at any second. No one had ever taken such an instant dislike of her as Josephine had. And the woman blatantly attacked her…All the stereotypes of the evil mother-in-law had nothing on Josephine. And poor Gabriel appeared shell shocked.

The deflated woman on the brink of tears she saw in the mirror looked nothing like the confident woman who had marched into the Justice of the Peace office ready to marry her fantasy man. That Josephine's barbs had hurt so much stunned her. That anyone would treat a stranger—or anyone—so horribly was beyond her comprehension.

A soft *tap, tap, tap* at the door broke her out of her musings. "Sweetie, I'm coming in."

"N…" Before she could finish saying "no" or lock the door, Gabriel stepped in and drew her into his arms.

She didn't think she wanted to see anyone, but having his arms around her made her feel wanted and secure enough to let go. She sobbed quietly as a lifetime of painful memories resurfaced. The most painful being her father's absence. Her brothers' fathers all took active roles in their sons' lives. When she was younger, she thought that if she'd been born a male her daddy would want her, too. By the time she was a teen, she could outplay her brothers in any game—physical or logical. She also made straight A's, unlike her brothers. Yet, she'd bet her father wouldn't had recognized her if she had walked into his office. After she graduated from high school at the age of sixteen and entered college, she thought that if she were prettier, more like her mom, then her father would want her. Oh, guys hit on her. Well, her breasts actually. She went on diet after diet and sent her father pictures to show the new Monica, but she was never thin enough for her father to take interest. At least that's how she saw things. And then there was her mother…

Once she calmed, Gabriel said, "Please believe me when I say I had no idea my mother would react so…so…I don't even know how to explain this."

"There's no need for you to explain. It wasn't your fault."

"I've never been so ashamed in my life."

"I'm so tired. I feel like I've run a marathon."

He sat on the commode with her across his lap, then pressed her head onto his shoulder. "You know what I could use about know," he whispered.

"What?" If he said sex, she'd slap him and *really* seek a divorce.

"A cherry Tootsie Roll Pop."

A giggle bubbled through her sorrow. "Make that two."

"If you want to stay here forever, just let me know. I have my cell phone. We can order delivery if we get hungry. We have a shower and somewhere to relieve ourselves. But most importantly, I have you."

"What about when your phone needs to be charged?" she said, feeling better by the second.

"Hmm…I'll have the delivery man bring me a new charger."

"Though I want to spend forever with you, I don't want to spend forever in the bathroom—especially your mother's bathroom. I think it's time to go home."

"Your wish is my command, Mrs. Windahl." He Eskimo kissed her, and her favorite rush reappeared.

"I like the sound of that, Mr. Windahl. Thank you for loving me for being me." She tasted his lips but wanted much more. "Oh yeah, we need to leave. Someone promised to make me faint."

"Let me make sure the coast is clear." As he stood he set her on the floor.

"I'm not running from your mother. I just needed some time to regroup. We didn't sneak in, and we aren't sneaking out. Just let me wash my face."

Josephine tapped her fork on the plate. Now that she had time to reflect, she realized she had acted abysmally with that moose Gabriel planned to marry. She'd just been taken by such surprise she'd lashed out without thinking. Lashed out at her lost dream.

One of the few chocolate complexioned models of her time, she'd taken a major risk having Gabriel. But his father, Johan Windahl, sole heir to over a hundred million dollars, refused to marry her unless she agreed to have his child and promised to divorce her if she didn't have the child by their third year of marriage.

Stretch marks and extra poundage from pregnancy would definitely hurt her modeling career, but she also realized she wasn't getting any younger, so her career would end soon anyway. She agreed to the arrangement and prayed for a daughter. She just knew her daughter would be the envy of all. She'd be fair skinned and have good hair like her father, but have her mother's bone structure and charisma. Her daughter would someday be the highest paid and most sought-after model ever!

Then she went and had a chocolate chip, nappy-headed son.

She loved her son more than she imagined possible, but he wasn't a daughter. When she approached Johan about having a second child, he'd said the deal was one child. He had his heir, so he was finished. To ensure she knew he meant business, he had a vasectomy. Crushed, she eventually adjusted her dreams. Someday her son would marry the woman who would become the daughter she never had. They would give her beautiful little granddaughters who would look up to their grandmother and want to be just like her when they were older. All of her friends would be envious.

She dropped the fork onto the plate. How could she show off that firetruck of a woman to her friends? She could imagine the rollie-pollie grandbabies that woman would pump out. Josephine would be a laughing stock. That oversized, kinky-haired heifer had to go, but Josephine would have to tread lightly until Gabriel got over this infatuation with the beast.

Why couldn't he be gay? At least then he could adopt the perfect grandbabies for her and break all sorts of prejudicial barriers.

Gabriel and Monica rounded the corner. The passion she saw in his eyes for Monica made her sick. She forced the snarl off her face and replaced it with a humble half-smile she hoped didn't appear fake.

"I owe you an apology." She dropped her napkin onto the table and rushed around to the couple. "I've just been under so much stress lately, then he brought that…that…gold digging hoochie over here. I'm so sorry. I truly thought you were his way of teaching me a lesson for butting into his love life."

Neither Gabriel nor Monica seemed moved by her proclamation. She took Gabriel's hands into hers. "You know I'm not like that. I was playing along. Trying to get you before you got me."

"Please stop. I'm not stupid. Sweetie is a beautiful, intelligent woman. What possible game could I have been playing?"

She'd give him intelligent, but boy was he off on the beautiful. "Look, I wasn't thinking clearly. I've been upset and took it out on Monica." She bowed her head slightly. "I truly apologize, Monica. How about we try this again—without me in bitch mode? We're going to be family. Let me make this up to you. I'll take you both out to dinner Saturday, and we can get to know each other better."

"Actually," Sweetie said, "we're having dinner with my family on Saturday. I guess you could come and meet everyone."

"Are you sure that's wise?" Gabriel asked.

"I'm sure I want to get all of the family drama over with. I don't do drama well. Why do you think I sent Tess to stay with Mama?"

"You have a child?" Josephine asked with a sharp edge to her voice she hadn't had time to cover.

"No, ma'am. Tess is my best friend. Why don't we all just meet at my place—"

"Our place," he interrupted. "I'm moving into her place."

To Josephine's dismay, Monica seemed pleased with Gabriel's announcement. "I don't think it's good to rush things, Gabriel. After all, you two have just met. Give Monica a little breathing room. You don't want to chase her away."

"Like I'd let her get away," he said. "I'll call you with details tomorrow. Right now I promised someone to make them faint."

Josephine plastered on a smile. *Oh yes, this heifer has to go!*

CHAPTER TEN

The elevator was too small for Sweetie to escape Gabriel's clutches, not that she actually wanted to. The limo ride from his mother's to *their* condo was almost as torturous as the visit with his mother, but for an entirely different reason. She wanted him so badly she could rip off their clothes and go at it, but she wouldn't cheat them out of their wedding night by rutting like out of control animals. Their first time as a married couple would be something special.

She playfully swatted at his hands. "Get on your side."

"Whatever side you are on is my side." He wrapped his arms around her and ground his erection into her butt. "Who do I call to have an elevator malfunction?"

She pressed against him and soaked in the love and want from him. "I'll never look at elevators the same. You've corrupted me."

"Why thank you."

The doors opened on their floor. They barely made it into the unit before Gabriel began unbuttoning his dress shirt. Sweetie calmly placed her keys and clutch purse on the entry table, then walked into her bedroom and locked the door. She heard the doorknob turn.

"Umm, baby?"

"Yes," she replied coyly as she sorted through her lingerie drawer.

"I think this would go better if I were locked in there with you."

"It's my wedding night. I refuse to be ravaged…at least not right away. Go take a nice cold shower in the spare room."

"I know you aren't serious, are you?"

She pulled out her favorite sexy nighties. "What color do you like best: royal blue, dark purple, or red?"

"You know I can knock down this door at any time, right?"

"Royal blue, dark purple or red were your only choices. Stop being difficult, answer the question and go take a shower. You promised to make me faint, and I'm holding you to it."

"Red. Can I come in now?"

"After we've both had a shower. Love you." She put the blue and purple negligees away and headed for the shower.

She was still in shock over actually marrying Gabriel. This was so uncharacteristic for both of them, but felt more right than anything she'd ever done. She hadn't even taken into consideration where they would live. While the shower water heated, she stripped. Him moving to Chicago was the most logical solution. She loved her work environment, and the years of hard work and dedication were finally starting to return rewards. Whereas Gabriel owned his company and had an office in Chicago. He was reasonable, so she didn't see an issue. And if he did have an issue, she knew they could find a compromise. Maybe her firm would let her head a European branch. Sweetie had won several oversees accounts for the firm in the last several months.

She put on her shower cap, then stepped into the shower and closed the stall door. The thought of Gabriel in the spare room preparing to "make her faint" had her turning the temperature ten degrees below too damn cold, yet she was still too damn hot. She reached for the lavender shower gel and squeezed a small amount onto the mesh sponge.

A soft, sweet floral scent filled the stall as she worked the lather over her body. She took extra time on her breast. Truthfully, they felt a little neglected. Over the phone he'd sounded like a die hard breast man, yet he barely touched them. She wasn't complaining. She'd just noted an area for improvement and knew that if she didn't tell him her needs, she couldn't fault him for not meeting them.

She turned off the shower and opened the frosted door to see the most handsome naked man God had ever made. Her breast instantly tightened and moisture accumulated between her legs that had nothing to do with the shower. "Gabriel…how…how did you get in here?" She pulled off her shower cap.

"Tess has at least a million hair pens in the spare room. Being the dutiful husband I am, after I finished my shower, I thought I'd help you along." He picked up the negligee she'd chosen to wear. "This is really nice, but I like what you have on now better. Can I dry you?"

She held the towel out to him, but instead of taking it, he took her hand and pulled her close. "I'm sorry, baby," he whispered as he slowly rocked them, his erection pressed against her belly. "I was acting like some sort of horny, sex-deprived maniac. Amazing what a little ice cold water can do."

"The cold water didn't seem to help me very much." She wrapped her arms around him and allowed the towel and shower cap to fall to the floor as he backed them out of the bathroom into the bedroom. "Gabriel…" she trailed off.

"Hmm, baby."

"Is there some reason you avoid my breasts?"

The pause between them went on too long, and she began to think he wouldn't answer.

"I don't want to hurt you."

She pulled back slightly. The only light in the bedroom came from the bathroom, but she could still see concern in his eyes. "Why would you think you'd hurt me?"

"You told me about the breast reduction surgery. I know your breasts hurt you. I love you too much to allow my sexual desires to harm you."

"Awww, you are perfect." She rested her head on his shoulder. "I'm having the surgery because my back hurts. I love to have my breasts suckled and caressed and given plenty of attention."

"You have no idea how happy you've just made me."

"I aim to please." They bumped into the edge of the bed. When she'd left this morning, she was a single woman. She glanced over her shoulder at the neatly made bed. Now the bed that had become a show of what she didn't have would be her marital bed. And she couldn't help but find ironic that the male approval she'd been fighting for so hard her entire life had come once she stopped fighting and accepted herself for who she was.

Gabriel suckled along her neck as he lowered her onto the bed. "I want to spend eternity with you, Sweetie." He cupped her breast, and his mouth found its way to one of her taut nipples, then expertly suckled. His hands were large, but she still spilled over his fingers. She longed to tell him she wanted to spend eternity with him also, but the pleasure she felt jumbled her mind and misplaced her ability to speak.

"Two breasts, one mouth," he said huskily. "What's a man to do?" He gently pressed her breast together and took both nipples into his mouth.

Oh yeah, this was what she needed. She ran her hands along his back to his head, and he added just the right amount of pressure. One thing she knew for sure was she'd never accuse him of neglecting her breasts again.

She reached down and began stroking him with her hand. His throbbing was the answer to the throb between her legs. Now that he was taking such good care of her breasts, she felt awkward to ask him to leave them alone to take care of other matters. As if reading her mind, he nudged her legs apart and entered her with one swift, harsh, yet glorious, stroke. Talk about being filled completely! She hadn't known this level of completion existed. She latched onto his butt and met each of his thrust, upping the ante by tightening her stomach muscles to draw him in.

He grunted something she was too far-gone to understand, bent her knee, then trapped her leg under his arm as they continued to pump, harder, faster.

She could feel herself slipping away. "Gabriel…" She wrapped her free leg around his thigh and gripped his butt to draw him in further, but the only place either of them could go was…

She clawed into the bedspread to keep from hurting him. "Oh, sheee…" The sounds of their bodies slapping together and moans became muted. All that was left were the wondrous sensations shooting through her body and the love she had for this man.

She watched his face contort into a strange, agonized, pleasured mix of emotions. He descended on her mouth as his body quaked, and his seed filled her. She contracted her muscles, wanting every drop and then some.

"Oh yes, baby, take me. Take it all."

She slowly released the bedspread and embraced him as she returned to herself.

He brushed his lips over hers, then rolled them over with him still buried deep inside of her. “I could stay in you forever.”

“Promise?”

“Yes, and I always keep my promises.” He pulled out of her—leaving her with an empty feeling—flipped her over and re-entered her before she had time to figure out what was happening.

As he fondled her clit with his fingers, he drove into her over and over, taking them to impossible heights. Sweetie was so exhausted she could faint, but his loving was too good to put an end to. She pressed her behind into him as she hit another climax. His hands moved up to her breast, and he yelled.

Sweetie’s body still tingled from a full night of lovemaking. True to his word, Gabriel had made her faint from orgasmic overload—the less common term for exhaustion by way of sex. Seven hours of workday lay ahead of her. She closed her eyes and leaned her head back on her executive chair.

“I’m not going to make it.”

Taking the day off wasn’t an option. She was already behind on her new project, and between spending quality time with Gabriel and refereeing the battle of the mothers she saw coming her way, actually accomplishing any work this weekend would be impossible.

“Sleeping on the job?” James teased.

Eyes half-mast, she slowly lifted her head. “Kill me. Please just kill me.”

“Late night?”

“I’m running on one hour sleep here.” She pushed herself upright. “Have a seat. We need to talk about Tess.” Tess had refused to come to the dinner to introduce Gabriel to the family because she wasn’t ready to leave the house yet. But that didn’t mean Sweetie couldn’t give Cupid a helping hand and send a special visitor to see her.

“No, we don’t.” He turned to leave.

"James, please. I'm too tired to chase you down. Just hear me out. Tess needs you."

He stopped in the doorway and glanced over his shoulder. Disappointment and pain dimmed his usually bright eyes. "Tess is a big girl."

"Kevin beat her up again."

He stalked angrily into the room but halted halfway and held his hands up. "She's not my responsibility."

"She loves you."

"Then why did she leave with him?" he bit out.

"Because she was scared of her feelings for you."

"Scared of her feelings for me but not of a man who routinely kicks her ass? Please explain how that works. I know this isn't the first time he's hit her." He held his hands out to his sides. "What's wrong with you women?"

"I don't know. Maybe *you* men beat us stupid." Fatigue and missing Gabriel weren't Sweetie's main concern. Tess was. Tess *would* find another man. If Sweetie had anything to do with it, James would be that man.

"You need to talk to Tess," she said. "Ask her what happened."

He ran his hands over his face. "The time to talk is over. I'm through with—"

"Look, I'm tired and irritable. I want to be home with my…" She stopped herself just short of saying husband. *I'm married.*

"What's going on, Sweetie?"

"I'm just tired. I can't take care of Tess anymore. I'm not what she needs."

"And I am?"

"Yes. And what she wants." She wrote her mother's address on a piece of paper, then held it out to him. "Go and speak with her. Ask her what happened with her and Kevin."

He took a step back. "I already know. He dangled a carrot in front of her, and she forgot all about that *love* for me and snatched it. I'm ready to settle down, Sweetie."

"I wanted her to tell her yourself, but you want to play hard headed, so I'm just going to say it. He beat her because she refused to sleep with him."

"What?" he said as he approached.

"She told him she was in love with you."

"She actually told him she loves me," he said slowly.

"Yes. And she's ashamed for leaving here with him. She thinks you'll never forgive her." She held her mother's information out for him to take. "Please, James. You two love each other. Don't miss out because she made a mistake out of fear."

"I want to." He walked over to the window and stared out. "But how long until she gets scared and runs again?"

"You're both letting fear get in your way. I'm in love. I was so afraid…But I love Gabriel more than I fear what *might* happen. I don't want to miss out. I don't want you and Tess to miss out on your chance. Please, James." She held out her mother's information. "Love or fear?"

Be careful what you pray for, Tess thought sadly. Not two minutes ago, she'd sent up a prayer that James would come by and save her from herself. That he'd swoop her up and make love to her until all her self-doubt went away. She touched the bruised area below her eye with her fingertips. She didn't want anyone to see her, especially James. In a way she was proud of herself because her battered appearance wasn't the main reason she'd told Missy—or Mama as she called her—to tell James she wasn't up for company. The main reason was her shame. "Be careful what you pray for," she repeated aloud.

What's wrong with me? Instead of allowing James to love and make love to her, she'd *chosen* to reject all that he offered, and for what? She barely tolerated Kevin. Sweetie often said Tess didn't feel she deserved to be loved by a good man, and that's why she kept seeking out men like Kevin. The way Tess saw it, all she had going for her was her looks, and someday those would fade. James deserved a complete package.

Someone he'd want to spend time with after the pretty package wasn't as pretty.

Someone to grow old with. She wanted to be a complete package. James and Sweetie thought she was a complete package. Man how she wished she thought the same way they did. It didn't matter now anyway. There was no way James would forgive her, especially since she couldn't forgive herself. Why he'd even come by was a mystery. Knowing Sweetie, she'd probably bullied him into checking in on her. How else could he have known her whereabouts?

She bent her bare legs and pulled her oversized T-shirt over them, then leaned back in the plush armchair. She didn't know how long she planned on hiding in the bedroom from the world. The point was moot; Monday she'd have to return to work. Avoiding James would be difficult, but she didn't have a choice. How she'd avoid him was the big question. His kiss had truly claimed her and filled her with dreams of what could be if she were only good enough.

Missy walked into the room. "He's being very insistent."

That news brought a smile to Tess's face. Maybe she should step out on faith and follow her heart. If Sweetie saw something in Tess, there must be something there to see. "Did he sound angry?"

"Where did I go wrong with you two girls?" She stood in front of Tess with her arms folded over her chest. "First you allow a man to beat you, then Monica gets engaged to a total stranger."

"Oh my God," Tess squealed. "Sweetie's getting married! Why didn't she call me?"

"Now some janitor is here for you. What's going on? Please tell me you aren't pregnant by him."

"He's not a janitor. He's a maintenance man." *Oh my God, I sound like Sweetie.* "And no, I'm not pregnant." Though the thought of having babies with James did have potential.

"Umm-hmm. And why didn't your maintenance man protect you from Kevin?" She bounced her finger. "Any man who hits a woman isn't a man or worth your time. The man you *choose* to have in your life should be able to support and protect you."

"I can protect and support Tess if she allows me," James said as he stepped fully into the bedroom.

Both women jumped. Tess wanted to sprint across the room to him, but remained seated. Missy was blocking her view of him, but she was glad. This way he wouldn't see what a mess she'd made of things.

"Sorry, I didn't mean to startle you." James leaned to the side.

Missy moved along with him, still blocking Tess's view of him. "It's rude to enter a lady's room uninvited. And what do you intend to do about Kevin? Look at what he's done to my beautiful baby." She moved out of the way and tilted Tess's face up.

"Mama, please." Shame kept her eyes focused on the floor.

"Could I please have some time alone with Tess?" James asked. The sorrow in his voice almost convinced her to lift her eyes to his.

"You two have business to settle." Missy looked at Tess. "Don't let me down." She kissed Tess's forehead, then smirked at James and left the room.

Tess knew exactly what Missy meant. Missy wanted her to tell James to hit the road. That she didn't want his broke ass, but she did want him. It was scary as hell, but she honestly didn't care about the money—at least not having a lot of money. What had chasing men with money gotten her thus far besides a low self-esteem and beaten? Between her and James's salaries, they could live nicely. And if she went back to college, she'd move up the corporate ladder quickly. She'd be the woman she wanted to be instead of the mess hiding in her best friend's mother's spare bedroom.

As soon as the door closed, James rushed to Tess and knelt before her. "What happened?"

"It's nothing." She finger combed her hair to cover her blackened eye. "I got what I deserved."

He drew in and released a deep breath. "No, you didn't." He carefully stroked her hair behind her ear. Eyes closed, she trapped his hand under hers and held it steady against her cheek. Tears suddenly streamed down her face, but not because of the pain of him touching her cheek. He was right. She didn't deserve to be beat. Sweetie was also right. Seeking men out based on materialism hadn't fulfilled her as she'd needed, so why was she continuing to make the same choices? Even Missy was right. She needed a man who would protect and support her. She needed James. James wouldn't be giving the type of support Missy had meant—financial—but he'd be giving the type of support Tess needed—emotional.

"Tell me when you've had enough, Tess. You have to decide that on your own and do something about it."

"I've had enough," she said softly.

"And what are you going to do about it?"

She opened her eyes and offered a half smile. "A really great friend of mine told me about a degree fair at Navy Pier in a few weeks, but I...well...James...I'm sorry about...please forgive me."

"There's nothing to forgive." He wrapped his arms around her. She was in heaven for a few seconds, then he released her.

"What's wrong?" she asked, worried he'd had time to think about what he was doing.

"I don't want to hurt you."

"I love you," came out before she had time to think about more than what she was feeling. She covered her mouth with her hands and looked down.

He pulled her hands from her face, saying, "I love you, too," leaned forward, then brushed his lips over hers.

She knew Missy was only a few rooms away, but Tess couldn't help herself. Even when she was afraid to admit how she felt, she had still prayed they could be together, could spend night after night in each other's arms.

"Can I make it better?" he whispered and gently kissed her blackened eye.

She pulled back. "I have to make it better myself, but I could use your support."

His face lit up and sent her heart racing. "Perfect answer."

Pride—a feeling she hadn't felt very often—flooded her. "I pull off a good one every now and again." Worried Missy might come in at any time, yet excited that Missy might come in at any time, she glanced at the door.

"You know I want it all, right? I'm an all or nothing type guy."

Concentrating on more than his hands caressing her thighs proved difficult. "I want it all with you." She leaned forward and finished the kiss he'd started. Warmth surrounded her heart and liquid heat pooled between her legs. "Make love to me, James."

He groaned and deepened the kiss, then pulled away. "I'd love to," he said huskily, "but can't. At least not here."

She ran her hands over his chest, wishing his shirt away. "Why not?" She slipped her hand down to his erection and stroked through his work-pants. "It's what we both want."

His eyes rolled back into his head. "You're killing me." He removed her hand and kissed her knuckles. "Ms. Fuller already dislikes me. She'd see me making love to you in her home as disrespecting her. She means too much to you for me to disrespect like that. In time she'll see how good we are together. I'll just have to keep this beast caged a while longer."

She knew he was right, but couldn't stop herself from pouting. She'd been waiting so long. "Can you at least sit with me?" She scooted over. "I don't want to be alone."

He pulled her up, then traded places with her and allowed her to sit across his lap. She rested her head on his shoulder. "When we move in together," she whispered, "we'll make love non-stop. We'll need to go by Sweetie's to get my things."

He embraced her. "I have never shacked up with a woman before and refuse to do it with the woman I love."

"What?" She pulled away. "Now that Sweetie has a man, I can't stay with her."

"You make good money, Tess. Why don't you get an apartment? There are a few in my building."

"This is ridiculous. I'd be spending the night at your place most nights anyway. Why spend money on two places? Plus, I can't afford rent."

"Then marry me."

She gazed into his love-filled eyes. "Marry?"

"I was serious. I want it all, Tess." He fingered her hair behind her ear. "I want it all with you."

"This is all happening so fast," she said nervously. "I want to marry you but...but what if..." She lowered her head. "What if I fail out of school?"

"I'll help you with your classes, and as long as you give your all, you're a success."

"What if you stop loving me?"

"What if you stop loving me?"

"I could never stop loving you."

"I was just thinking the same thing about you. I don't want to pressure you into marriage. This is a big decision to make. Would Ms. Fuller allow you to rent out this room?"

"I'm sure she will, but I won't need it for long. Will you marry me, James?"

CHAPTER ELEVEN

In search of storage space for his shoe shining kit, Gabriel opened the bottom drawer of the corner linen cabinet and discovered Sweetie's "toy box." He wasn't the least bit surprised Sweetie had such an extensive collection of adult toys. Actually, he found it cute and was grateful she was just as bold with her sexuality as she was in other aspects of her life.

He pulled out a triangular box looking thingy that was made of a soft rubber. The corners were rounded and it fit easily in his palm. "What the hell is this for?" He flipped the tiny switch on the side and the contraption gently vibrated. The thing was too wide to stick inside herself, so he was stumped. He flipped it off, then took the drawer into the bedroom where Sweetie was on the bed with her laptop.

She glanced up from her work, and his dick went on instant hard-on. "Umm, I need space for my…How much more work do you have?" If he planned correctly, he could make love with his beautiful wife before their families began arriving.

"About an hour. What's wrong with the drawer?"

"Nothing." He dumped the contents onto the bed. "I'm throwing this stuff out to make room for some of my toiletries. You have me now. You won't need these anymore."

"The hell you are." She set her laptop on the nightstand, then reached for the triangular thingy he'd been curious about.

The V neckline of her red negligee brought his attention to the crevice between her breasts. He licked his lips. "I'll be your toy." The head of his penis was already sticking over the brim of his briefs. He pulled his shorts down low enough to fully expose himself. "Wanna play?"

Brow raised, she teasingly asked, "But what about when you go out on business trips? Then what will I do?" She switched her little toy on, palmed it, then massaged her breasts with it.

The outline of her pert nipples through the silk…her working her hands over her glorious breast…her sultry eyes calling to him…He was sure she asked something, but what had been lost a while ago. "Strip. I want to see you."

"Do I get to keep my massager?"

"If you strip."

She slowly slipped her negligee over her head and tossed it to the side, then ran the massager under her breast.

"Where are your panties?"

"Some crazy man threw them away, talking some mess about easy access." She massaged between her breasts and along her stomach to her inner thighs.

"Umm, spread your legs," he demanded as he wrapped his hand around his engorged length and began stroking.

She traded her massager for a small vibrator, then drew the soles of her feet together.

"What are you going to…?"

Before he could finish, she separated her womanly folds with her fingers and showed him the lush pinkness inside. She moaned as she circled the area around her clit with the vibrator. He wanted to taste the moisture that gathered.

He took off his briefs, then lay on the bed between her legs. Suckling along her thigh, he knew she'd allow him to taste her sweetness, but she stopped him just short of his goal and pointed at a dildo.

"I'm the real thing."

"Yes, you are. Are you jealous of a little toy?"

"Of course not." As he slowly inserted the dildo, he milked her clit with his tongue and lips. She kneaded his scalp with her fingers as she gyrated and cried out.

"That's it, baby," he said.

He definitely couldn't dispose of the massager, vibrator, and dildo. He wanted to find other ways to make her climax with them, but the other items would have to go. Especially that big black dick looking contraption. He pulled the cream covered dildo out of her, then pushed it back inside her.

"I'm not done yet." He helped her lie back, then he straddled her waist as she continued to pump with the dildo deep in her. She ran her fingernails along his thighs, and he inched up further. He settled his hardness between her breasts, then gently pushed them together and stroked as if he were in her vagina. The ecstasy on her face encouraged him to continue. She pressed her breasts together, allowing him to free up his hands for better balance. He'd imagined doing this but had never tried.

He knew he'd blow soon, but didn't want to like this—at least not until he was sure she was pregnant. He reached back and pulled out the dildo, then shoved her legs apart and entered her. Surrounded by her wet warmth, he plunged into her. Stroke after glorious stroke he reaffirmed they'd made the right decision to marry. They had to be meant to be. No way anyone else could this feel so good.

"Harder," she begged.

He rose up on his arms, drove into her with all his might and watched their bodies collide over and over.

"Oh yes!" she called out, her breasts jiggling about from the force.

He felt her tighten around him and pulling him in. "I'm about to…" he trailed off. "Oh, sheeee…" He bit his lip as his seed rushed from his body deep into her. He lowered himself onto her and held her close as she fought for every drop of him as if she were dying from dehydration.

Comfortable silence cradled them for several minutes. He rolled them so she'd be on top, but he didn't exit her body. He could feel himself stiffening again, but knew she had work to complete before they prepared for their guests.

Sweetie knew she was playing with fire, but couldn't help herself. She nibbled on his lips.

"You'd better stop that if you plan on finishing your work."

She'd already come twice, but felt greedy. The third time would be the charm. She pressed her pelvis into him and massaged her breast.

"Allow me." He took one of her breast into his hot mouth and worked wonders with his tongue while gyrating under her.

"Umm..." She could feel each pull of him rush through her body. "I'm addicted to you."

"Good," he said huskily and grabbed onto her hips. "Because I'm addicted to you, too."

A few strokes later, they both cried out, showing just how addicted they'd become.

Gabriel watched Sweetie pace about the living room. "Relax." He patted the cushion beside him. "Come and sit with me."

She pulled her cherry Tootsie Roll Pop out of her mouth. "I wish Tess would change her mind about coming. She could help me deflect some of the drama." She smiled. "Man, she flipped out when I told her about dinner with your mom."

"Are you wearing panties?" He pulled up her thigh-length, jean skirt as she passed by and saw black lace. "Damn."

She rolled her eyes and straightened her clothing. "You have a one-track mind. I'm turning up the heat. Once the house cools from the cooking, it will be chilly."

"Don't touch the thermostat." He whipped the small vibrator out of his khaki's pocket. "Make sure you sit beside me for dinner. I have a special dessert for you that is guaranteed to keep you warm."

She laughed so hard she dropped her sucker. "You're crazy."

"I'm not crazy, and I was serious about the thermostat." He picked the sucker off the floor and set it on the wrapper on the table. "Now come here. I want to kiss my wife."

She timidly went to him. "We don't have time to—"

He pulled her onto his lap and descended on her mouth. Cherry had quickly become his favorite flavor after Sweetie. "Make love with me, baby. Right now." The doorbell rang. He was tempted to yell for whomever to go away, but didn't want to embarrass Sweetie.

She pecked his lips. "You owe me for getting me all hot and bothered when you knew we couldn't do anything about it."

"Who says?" He displayed the vibrator, then stuffed it into his pocket. "Stay close to me, baby. And you'll see what we can do about it." He stood to help greet their first guest.

The doorbell rang a second time. "Coming," Sweetie said. "One second." She ran her fingers through her twists and smoothed out his polo shirt. "I'm afraid."

"Of what?"

"I'm not sure, but I'm scared as hell."

He took her hand into his. "We're in this together, baby."

He opened the door to the most beautiful model-type woman he'd ever seen: flawless skin, tall, slender, light caramel colored skin, hazel eyes, a few strands of gray mixed in with her straight shoulder length auburn hair.

"Mama!" Sweetie hugged her mother and pulled her inside. "This is Gabriel, my fiancé." She took her mother's coat and hung it in the entry closet.

He bowed slightly. "Pleased to meet you, Ms. Fuller." Sweetie was just as beautiful as her mother, but they looked nothing alike. If anything, Missy put him in mind of what he thought Tess's mother would look like.

She graciously shook his hand. "The pleasure is all mine."

"Where is Harold?" Sweetie asked.

He quickly tried to place the name: brother or stepfather?

"I sent him with your brothers for wine."

"So now it takes four grown men to select a bottle of wine?"

Missy laughed with a snort at the end that reminded him of Sweetie.

"Okay, so I wanted a little time alone with my baby girl and her fiancé." She took Gabriel and Sweetie by the hand and led them to the couch, then she sat in the overstuffed armchair and folded her hands over crossed legs.

She was too calm for Gabriel's liking. He didn't know her well enough to know what was wrong, but he did know something was out of sorts. He intertwined his fingers with Sweeties and waited patiently while her mother observed the two.

"I've done my research on you, Gabriel Windahl," Missy finally said. "What do you want with my baby?"

"Mama!"

"Is she pregnant?"

"Mama!"

"Stop Mama-ing me. You don't have to marry because you're pregnant, Monica."

Sweetie smacked her forehead with the palm of her hand and fell onto the couch dramatically. "Kill me. Kill me now."

"I'm in love with your daughter, Ms. Fuller."

"Umm-hmm. Sit up Monica." She snapped her fingers. "You and Tess are up to something, and I want to know what. How can you go from being celibate and avoiding men like HIV to engaged? This doesn't add up." She narrowed her eyes on Gabriel. "You're rich, handsome, can have your pick of any woman. What do you want from my daughter?"

"Ms. Fuller I assure you—"

"Are you saying he couldn't possibly want me?" Sweetie interrupted.

"Of course not. I'm saying he's a playboy and not worthy of you."

"I thought you wanted me to marry a rich man."

"Not any rich man will do. You deserve to be treated like the treasure you are. As I said, I've done my research. Has he ever taken the same woman out twice? I doubt it. And the women I saw hanging off his arm looked nothing like you. You've already had one fiancé take your friend to bed. How long before he's pushing up on Tess? I won't allow anyone to hurt you like that again."

"Gabriel isn't like that." She looked into his eyes, and he didn't see even an ounce of doubt.

"I love you." He leaned forward and kissed her gently.

"I love you, too."

Missy cleared her throat and clapped her hands. "That's enough." Once they separated she said, "If you hurt my baby, I'll have you castrated."

"Mama!"

"What?" Missy took her cell phone out of her purse and speed dialed a number.

Gabriel laughed. "It's alright, baby. We don't have anything to worry about."

"Harold, you can bring the boys up whenever." Missy disconnected.

"No, it's not alright. Mama, I'm marrying Gabriel, and you will not threaten him."

"That was a promise, darling," she said toward Gabriel.

"I can't believe you." Sweetie crossed her arms over her chest and glared at her mother. "You don't even know Gabriel, yet you've condemned him."

"I haven't condemned him yet. I'm just saying that *if* he thinks he can treat you any ol' way…Well, he'd just best think again. I failed you with Robert. I won't fail you again." She pointed a perfectly manicured nail at him. "I have my eye on you."

"Did you at least call Daddy and ask him to come?"

Gabriel blinked. He hadn't seen the change of subject coming. He'd be sure to give Sweetie an extra treat later for deflecting her mother's anger elsewhere.

"Of course not. You called and told him didn't you?"

"Yes, but…I thought if you asked he would actually come."

"No buts, Monica. Stop chasing after that man. He's the one missing out, not you." She fidgeted with her cell phone. "I'm sorry I didn't…I chose poorly when I chose your father. But you haven't let his absence hold you back."

Awkward silence filled the room. Sweetie worried her bottom lip with her teeth. "Are you thirsty, Mama?" Without waiting for an answer, Sweetie rushed toward the kitchen.

Missy connected with Gabriel's eyes. "I won't allow another man hurt my baby. I thought I wanted her to marry, but…Did you know some bastard beat Tess? Men now aday…I shouldn't have pushed those girls to marry. I won't let you hurt her."

"Ms. Fuller, I'm truly, madly, completely in love with your daughter. There's nothing I can say to convince you, but with time you will see."

"I hope so. She deserves nothing less than the best." She held out her hand. "Truce?"

He crossed over and embraced her. "Truce." Just as her body lost its rigidity, the doorbell rang. "Would you mind getting that? I want to check on Sweetie."

"I've got it."

He snatched up the Tootsie Pop and the wrapper on his way out of the room.

He stood in the kitchen doorway and watched as Sweetie poured more glaze over the ham. "You okay?" He tossed the sucker and wrapper in the wastebasket.

"Sure. Could you stir the greens?"

He washed his hands. "What did your father say when you called him?"

"I had to leave a message. I don't want to talk about him. Mama's right. I need to stop chasing after him." Her voice sounded tearful. She crinkled the foil around the pan, then pushed the ham back into the oven. "The sweet potatoes, dressing and macaroni and cheese are done. I think everything is done." She bent and took a cookie sheet out of the lower cabinet. "Maybe I should start the bread."

Instead of stirring the greens, he pulled her up into his arms. "It's alright, baby."

"No, it's not." She rested her tear soaked cheek on his shoulder. "Mama never tricked any man into having children. I just want to understand why he's rejecting me. What did I do?"

"It's not you."

"It sure feels like me. And no matter how much I'm told he's the one missing out, I still want him to love me or I want to stop loving him, stop caring about him. Is that too much to ask?"

"Monica, come out and introduce your fiancé to your stepfather and brothers," Missy called from the living room.

"Do you want me to tell them we'll have to arrange this for another night?" Gabriel asked.

"Nah, I'll be fine. I just want to get this night over with."

He released her, then dampened a paper towel and wiped her face. "As beautiful as ever." He reached into his pocket and pulled out a cherry Tootsie Roll Pop. "I was saving this for later, but..." he unwrapped it, "since you won't let me make love to you until our company leaves," he rolled the sucker on her lips, "you'll just have to pretend this is me."

She laughed with a little snort at the end. "You have a one track mind."

"Let's go in the spare room and—"

"I highly suggest you get your paws off my sister."

Gabriel glanced over his shoulder at Sweetie's brother.

"Stop acting like a jerk, Charles." Sweetie made introductions, then led Gabriel into the living room where she introduced him to Harold and her brothers, Michael and Simon.

Missy had moved to the loveseat where she sat with Harold. Her three sons—each imposing men—stood behind her seat looking like they were ready to pounce.

"Mama has already threatened Gabriel with castration."

"Way to go, Mama," Charles said.

"Don't you guys even think about tripping. Mama was more than enough." The doorbell rang. "That's probably Gabriel's mom. I'm serious. You'd better *act* like you have sense."

Gabriel took Sweetie by the hand and went to open the door. The evening had only begun, yet he could tell she'd already had more than enough. "Are you sure you want to do this?" he whispered. "I can tell everyone I'm not feeling well."

"I'll be fine." She opened the door. "Welcome, Ms. Miller. I hope you didn't have any difficulty finding your way." She took Josephine's coat and stepped to the side.

"Oh no, dear. It was quite simple." She hugged Gabriel, then scrutinized Sweetie from head to toe. "I hope I'm not over dressed." She brushed off her Vera Wang pantsuit.

"Mom, I told you this was a casual affair."

"It's alright, Gabriel. Did you see Mama's Michael Kors dress?"

"Who the hell is Michael Kors?" Gabriel asked as he guided the women into the living area.

"A designer," Missy answered as she stood and held out her hand to his mother. "Hello, Joseph—"

"Melissa Fuller! This can't be. You must be her daughter, niece…The resemblance is…Wow."

Missy's smile beamed bright enough to light all of Chicago.

Gabriel didn't remember telling Missy his mother's name. *She must have seen it when she was researching me.*

"Mama, this is Ms. Josephine Miller. Ms. Miller, this is my mother Melissa Fuller, but everyone calls her Missy."

"B-but that can't be," Josephine stammered. "That would make you…" She stared at Missy.

"Some of us age better than others." Missy winked at Sweetie, then motioned toward her family. "This is my husband Harold, and my sons Michael, Simon and Charles." The men all bowed slightly. "And of course you know my baby, Monica." She pulled Sweetie close and hugged her. "I love you." She took the sucker from Sweetie, then shooed her away.

Josephine stared between the women. "Melissa Fuller is your mother?"

"Did you two model together or something?" Charles asked as he led Josephine to one of the armchairs.

"We did a few jobs together," Missy answered. "Believe it or not, Josephine is actually younger than I am."

Sweetie shot Missy a look that would have killed a lesser being.

"The added weight looks great on you," Missy said. "So how have you been?"

Josephine continued staring at Missy. Neither woman tried to hide her hostility toward the other. There had to be some sort of too-many-divas-in-the-room rule Gabriel didn't know about. But then again, all of Josephine's friends were gorgeous, so why the instant hate between the two? Missy had given up modeling to raise her children years before his mother made it big, so their paths couldn't have crossed too often.

"I'm doing well," Josephine finally replied.

"And how is Johan?"

Gabriel released Sweetie's hand. "You know my father?"

"I knew him many years ago."

Now Missy's dislike of him made more sense. His father, Johan Windahl, was a womanizer of the worse sort. She probably thought, "Like father like son." And the jealousy he saw in his mother's eyes also made sense. With Missy's looks, his father would have definitely pursued her. He cringed, praying none of Sweetie's siblings were actually his siblings. Or even worse yet, what if Sweetie were his sister?

"Are you feeling okay?" Sweetie touched his forehead. "You don't look too well."

A coy smile crossed Missy's lips, and he knew she knew what was on his mind. He looked at each of her sons. None of them resembled her, and only Michael looked anything like his father.

"Which of you is the oldest?" Gabriel asked the brothers.

"Michael's my oldest." Missy reached back for him. "All of my babies look like their father." She settled her hazel gaze on Josephine.

Gabriel choked. Josephine hopped up from her seat, asking, "Where's the restroom?"

Sweetie frowned. "What's going on?"

"I'll show her." Harold led Josephine away.

"Mama, what's going on?" Michael, Simon and Charles asked simultaneously.

"Oh nothing, babies. I was just giving Josephine a hard time. Michael, tell Gabriel your father's name."

"Michael Gibson," he answered. "Why?"

Sweetie sat at the edge of the couch. "Mama, did you used to have a thing with Gabriel's dad?"

"No, but not because he didn't want to. Remember when I said not any rich man would do. Well, he's one that definitely wouldn't do. He'd stick his stuff in any hole that would be still long enough. He wasn't good enough for me. The jury is still out on if his son is good enough for you."

Sweetie held Gabriel's hand close to her heart. "The only jury that counts has decided."

Harold re-entered the room. "Missy, I don't know what game you're playing, but I expect it to stop now. You have these children all upset and have chased Josephine into the restroom."

She waved him off. "I told you what Tess said about how she treated Monica when she went over there for dinner." She looked at Gabriel. "No one hurts my baby and gets away with it. She chased my baby to the bathroom; now it's time for her to spend a little reflective time in the bathroom."

"Okay, Mama, I think she's learned her lesson." Sweetie pinched the brim of her nose. "Please, no more drama. Can we just have dinner? Can we start being a family?"

"Of course, darling."

Gabriel doubted Missy was finished, but couldn't do anything about it. While they waited on Josephine, everyone washed their hands. The brothers brought the kitchen table into the dinning room and set it next to the dinning table to seat more guests. Everything smelled delicious. From what Sweetie had told him, Missy didn't cook, so he wondered where Sweetie learned to cook so well.

Charles and Simon moved to take the seats that flanked Sweetie. "Leave one of those two for me," Gabriel said and set the napkins on the table.

The brothers looked at each other, smirked, then sat in the seats at either side of her.

"You two are so childish," Sweetie said. "Mama, please make them move."

"Stop upsetting your sister," Missy warned. "One of you move."

Simon slid over to the next seat. "If your mother ever comes out of the bathroom, we can eat."

"I'll get her." Gabriel gathered his thoughts as he walked through the spare room to the bathroom. He was upset with Josephine for her treatment of Sweetie, but he didn't want to see her hurt. He tapped on the bathroom door. "Mom, can I come in?"

"I just want to go home."

"Please let me in." After a few seconds, the doorknob turned slowly, and he heard it click unlocked. He entered the bathroom and sat on the tub. Like Sweetie, his mother had set the lid down on the commode and taken a seat. "You women and bathrooms. What is this, the safe zone or something?"

"How could that woman be her mother?"

"*That woman* is about to be your in-law. There's no reason for you two to be at odds."

"No reason! She's flaunting her affair with your father in my face. Did you see her son? His son!"

"She didn't have an affair with Dad. And Michael isn't his son. I'm not saying you two have to be best friends, but this war has to end."

"She started it."

"No, you started it when you disrespected Sweetie. I doubt Ms. Fuller is done with you, but I'm asking you to take the high road. I'm sure Sweetie is out there having basically the same conversation with her mother."

"How do you know they didn't have an affair?"

"Does it matter? If they did have an affair, it was over forty years ago. You divorced him, and she's married to another man. Let it go, Mom. He's not yours to fight for. And I love Dad, but he isn't worth fighting for in this respect."

She wrung her hands. "You're right. It's just so hard, and she's so beautiful. Always has been. Johan used to chase after—"

"You're not in competition with her. She never wanted him. I'm sure you two have a lot in common. You'd probably make great friends." He held his hand out as he stood. "Dinner's getting cold. Please do this for me."

By the time everyone finished eating, Gabriel had decided he liked Sweetie's brothers. They were protective, but knew when to back off. There was still tension between the mothers, but at least they weren't lodging grenades at each other. Harold seemed to be the one most in tune—outside of himself—to Sweetie's low mood. Harold had even snuck her a small package of cherry sourballs.

Sweetie ran her hands over her arms.

"Getting cold?" Gabriel whispered into her ear.

"A little. But some nut wouldn't allow me to turn up the heat."

He wrapped his arms around her, with thoughts of a sure fire way to lift her mood. "I'll keep you warm." Sweetie was sitting in his lap with her legs dangling over the arm of the overstuffed chair across from his mother who was in the armchair. The brothers had commandeered the sofa, and Harold and Missy had staked their claim on the loveseat.

"Mom, hand me the throw."

Josephine took the lightweight blanket off the back of the chair and tossed it to Gabriel. He covered Sweetie and himself, then rested his hand on her thigh. He loved her thick thighs and wished they were wrapped around him at this very moment. But they were stuck planning a wedding ceremony they didn't even want.

"I'm telling them we're married," he whispered into her ear. "I'm ready to start the honeymoon."

"Don't even think about it," she said in hushed tones.

"What?" he asked in all innocence. "I want to make love to my wife."

Harold had brought Josephine into his and Missy's conversation and the brothers were engrossed in their own discussion. The way was clear for him to enjoy his wife. *My wife*...He nibbled along her neck to her earlobe. "I shouldn't have started this," he whispered sweetly. "It's left me in a bad way."

"That makes two of us," she giggled.

"Damn, I'm so hard," he murmured into her ear. "I wish you could wrap your hand around me and squeeze." The urge to pump was so strong..."I'm in serous trouble." He caught himself at the inset of a groan and hushed.

"You alright, man?" Charles asked.

"Yeah, yeah..." Gabriel cleared his throat. "Something was in my throat."

"So when's the date?" Charles asked.

"Date?"

"The wedding."

"Oh, whenever Sweetie wants," Gabriel forced himself to answer easily.

All eyes focused on Sweetie. "Umm," she moaned. "I was thinking Memorial Day weekend."

"Oh no!" both mothers said simultaneously. "That's not enough time."

"What's the hurry?" Josephine asked. "Are you pregnant, Monica?"

He grumbled, thinking he'd had more than enough bonding time with the family.

"For the millionth time, no, I'm not pregnant."

"Not from lack of trying," Gabriel added. "We aren't getting any younger. We love each other and want children. We aren't waiting. So now you need to decide if we have this wedding before she starts showing, while she's changing sizes daily, or after the baby."

"There is no way your father will agree to having a Windahl baby out of wedlock…"

He was sure whatever his mother was talking about was important, but remembering how good it felt to be buried deep inside of Sweetie took his mind to much more interesting places and left him with an engorged dick in serious need of relief. He whispered sweet nothings into her ear of what she had to look forward to. She'd laid her head on his shoulder, and her breathing had become ragged. He could tell she was hot, wet and ready for him. He didn't know how much longer he could wait. He coughed.

"You alright, man?" Charles asked.

"Yeah, yeah, I'm good. Where do we keep the cherry cough drops?" he asked Sweetie, praying she'd catch on to the hint.

"I'll get them." She headed for her room.

"Oh no, baby. I'll get them." He followed her in saying, "You all continue planning. We'll be right back."

He pulled her through their room into the bathroom, closed the door and penned her against the wall. She placed her hands on either side of his face and pulled him into a kiss more passionate than anything he'd imagined.

"I don't want to make love, Gabriel. I want to—"

Frantic with need, he didn't even need her to finish. He yanked down his pants and pulled up her skirt. He couldn't even wait for her to take off her panties. He hooked the crotch of her panties with his finger and tugged it to the side, spread her legs, then thrust his pulsating dick into her.

"Oh God," he bit out. She was so hot, so wet, so his and each of his penetrations into her were so deep, so long, he was practically doing squat thrust.

"Yes," she whimpered and bit her bottom lip. "That's it..."

The walls of her sex clenched and clenched tighter with each stroke. She didn't want to let him go, and he sure as hell didn't want her to. This was where he belonged. Grunts, moan, and the smell of sex filled the bathroom.

"You feel so good, baby."

The support bra she wore was no match for her breasts as they bounced, bobbed, wiggled and jiggled from the force. Imagines of his dick flanked by her lovely breasts filled his mind. He literally wanted to make love to every part of her body.

She grabbed onto him and their lips crashed. Their mouths mated as frantically as their other parts. Soon, soon her body began to quake. He swallowed her cries as his hot seed escaped his body for home where they belonged. He gripped her butt as the orgasm ripped through his body and shook him to his core.

Buried deep in her, he brushed his cheek along hers, his lips on hers. He lowered her to the floor, then held her close as their hearts slowed to normal and he came back to his senses. "I'm sorry, baby. I couldn't wait."

"That makes two of us."

He took a fresh washcloth out of the linen cabinet and ran warm water over it. "Come here. Let me clean you up." He carefully washed between her legs. "I didn't hurt you, did I?"

"I was just about to ask you the same thing." She giggled. "How will we explain our absence?"

He chuckled. "We don't."

A short while later they had returned to their seat in the living room with the rest of the family. The mothers were still fussing about something and the brothers were starting at him as he helped Sweetie get comfortable.

Sweetie laid her head on his shoulder and closed her eyes. He was tired himself. Making love had never been so draining yet satisfying.

"...Monica, wake up," Missy said. "You're keeping your name Fuller, aren't you? And all of your children will be Fullers also, right? There's no guarantee the marriage will last, but your children will always be your children, and they should all have the same last name."

"The only children she has will be with me," Gabriel barked out before Sweetie could get out a word. "And I don't care what last name they have."

"Gabriel! Of course you care."

"No, Mom, I don't."

Sweetie blew out an annoyed breath. "My name and the children's name will be Windahl. End of discussion."

Okay, so he thought he didn't care, but he was wrong. With Sweetie's independent ways, he'd thought she'd fight to the bitter end to keep her last name, so he'd set in his mind to let her have her way.

"I love you." He kissed her lips lightly, then turned to the family. "It's been a great evening. Glad you all came."

Michael laughed and nudged his brothers. "Man, if I didn't know you love my sister, I'd be kicking your ass right now. Let's at least set the date, then you can kick us out to work on making those babies." All of the males in the room chuckled.

"Fine, so what did you decide?" Gabriel asked.

"We'll need at least six months to plan a decent wedding," Missy said. "Can you wait a few months before...? Well, you know."

"No," Gabriel said simply. Sweetie adjusted in his lap, leaving him with a brand new hard-on. He wasn't so tired that he didn't want to take her again. There wasn't that much tired in the world. But this time he'd take his time. "Umph..." He cleared his throat to cover his moan.

"Mama, I probably wouldn't show until five months anyway. I'll just get a gown that flows from below the breast. November is such a beautiful month. Perfect time for a wedding."

"I guess that will have to do." Missy turned to Josephine. "We have our work cut out for us."

"That we do."

"Who is going to give you away?" Simon asked.

Gabriel felt Sweetie stiffen in his arms. He hadn't thought about how her father's absence would mar her wedding day. He nuzzled her neck. "We don't have to have a ceremony if you don't want."

"Oh, yes, she is having a ceremony," Missy snapped. "Her father will walk her down the aisle."

"Mama," Simon sighed more than said, "he's been an absentee father. He'll pay for the wedding, but actually attending…Sorry, but I don't see it."

"This is a media event. He'll be there."

"I don't want him there," Sweetie bit out. "He's not invited. I won't be used as a publicity stunt."

"She's right, Mama," Michael said. "He hasn't earned the right to walk her across the street, let alone down the aisle. I'm the oldest. I'll do it."

"I want Harold to do it."

All three brothers choked out, "Harold?"

Michael nodded toward Harold. "No offense, man, but hell no." He faced Sweetie. "Mama's only been married to him ten years. I've been there for you your whole life. I'm walking you down the aisle."

"Listen up and listen up closely, because I'm only saying this once." The blanket fell from Sweetie's chest into her lap as she leaned forward. "This is *my wedding*, yet I didn't pick the date, and the *mommy brigade* will totally ignore my input for how I want *my wedding*. The only two things I insist on having total control on are whom I'll be marrying and who is giving me away. I want Harold. Unless he turns me down, I will have Harold."

Gabriel observed his mother as the drama unfolded. For a short while, she had this odd look of triumph on her face.

"I'm honored, really." Harold crossed over and hugged Sweetie. "I knew those cherry sour balls were the way to your heart," he teased and returned to his seat. "I'll walk you down the aisle if you'd like, but I want you to reconsider asking your father. I know he hasn't been there for you, but you still love him and want him there."

Missy took Harold by the hand. "You are such a good man." She turned to Sweetie. "I'll make sure your father is there if you want him there."

"I want him to be there because he wants to, not because you are making him or because he wants to use me as a public relations gimmick. We all know why he'd be there, so Harold is my choice." Sweetie laid her head on Gabriel's shoulder and closed her eyes. "I'm so tired."

Gabriel embraced her. "Hush, baby…rest…"

"I'm sorry, but who is her father?" Josephine asked.

"This asshole named Payton Johnson," Michael drawled out.

Gabriel knew the name of one of the few black men to make it into the billion-dollar club.

"*The* Payton Johnson of Payton International?" Josephine asked.

"I think Sweetie has had enough for today," Harold said as he stood and helped Missy up. "Thank you for the lovely dinner."

After their guests left, Gabriel handed Sweetie a large bath towel, told her to strip, then locked himself in the bathroom to prepare to pamper his baby. As the hot water filled the tub, he continued sorting through the bottles of "bath stuff" he'd found in one of the cabinets. Unsure of the correct amounts and too tired to read any instructions, he poured a quarter jar of stress relieving sea salt into the tub. Thought a bit, then poured in the rest of the jar to help counteract the stress filled day she'd had.

One of his ex's was crazy about putting milk into her bath. She claimed it make her skin smooth and soft. He tore open two packets of coconut milk bath soak to keep his Sweetie extra soft. Once every fleck of powder was out of the packets, he added a third packet because he'd be joining her in the oversized tub. He had no desire to be soft, but he knew the coconut milk wouldn't know whom to work on. So he put more than enough for them both.

He wasn't too particular about the coconut smell, but he had an answer for that. He still hadn't put in the moisturizer. He couldn't have his Sweetie walking around all ashy. He poured in the rich blend of fruit and nut oils—peach, pineapple, musk, sandalwood and vanilla. Before he knew it, he'd poured the whole bottle in. He'd have to make a trip to Carol's Daughter to purchase her some more. He turned the label around to see the name—Groove Body and Bath Oil.

"What are you doing in there? I'm tired, Gabriel. If you don't hurry, I'm just going to shower in the spare room."

"Stop being impatient," he said over his shoulder. "Two more minutes and I'm done." He set the foaming bath grains on the edge of the tub and turned off the water. He hoped the grains' citrus scent didn't clash with the other fruit smells when he poured them in. *I have got to invest in some unscented bath supplies.* He would skip the grains all together, but after all the work he'd gone through, he couldn't just use plain soap. For that extra squeaky clean, he set vanilla shower gel and a mess sponge on the edge of the tub.

"Gabriel!"

"Okay, okay." He moved for the door, but his erection was peeking though his robe. He wanted to make love to Sweetie, but not now. That wasn't what she needed. "I'm unlocking the door, but *do not* come in."

"Gabriel," she drawled.

"I'm serious."

"Fine."

He unlocked the door, slipped his robe off and set it on the dressing bench, then stepped into the tub.

Shit! He snatched his foot out of the hot water. His foot hurt like hell, but at least his erection had dwindled. He allowed the cold water to run for a bit, then tested the temperature with his toe to ensure it was all good. He hadn't burned himself on purpose the first time and had learned his lesson.

He sank into the waters of the tub. The floor of the tub was a little grainy from the sea salt that hadn't dissolved. He sloshed the water around, but the sea salt wouldn't dissolve all the way. He wasn't about to re-run water.

"You can come in now."

Sweetie swung the door open. He wanted to laugh at the way she was trying to keep from scrunching up her nose.

"Darling, what have you done?"

"I've drawn a bath for the woman I love."

"Aww, you are too sweet." She tipped in, and her eyes began to water. "I'm sorry. The fumes in here are kind of…strong. I'm shocked there's enough oxygen in here for you."

"That explains why I feel lightheaded." He winked. "Drop the towel and join me. The water is perfect."

She allowed the towel to fall to the floor, and his erection returned full force. *Down, boy, down!*

She peeked into the tub. "Are you sure there's any water in there?"

"Just a touch." Now he was glad he'd added so many things to the water. She couldn't see his erection through the murkiness. Then again, when he drew her into his body, she'd feel his need. He sighed. "Look, baby, I'm harder than a cast-iron skillet, but I don't want to make love to you right now."

She giggled as she stepped into the tub. "Sure you don't."

He frowned. "That didn't come out right. Hell, I want to make love to you 24/7. But I know now isn't the time." He drew her into his body so her back was flush with his chest. "I love this tub."

She shifted uncomfortably. "I'm sorry, but something is sticking to my butt. I mean besides you." She lifted herself slightly and wiped the cheeks of her butt with her hand. "How much sea salt did you use?"

He hunched his shoulders. "A jar."

"That explains it." She kissed him lightly, then retook her seat. "Next time only use a cap full." She relaxed in his arms. "This is great. You are great. Thank you."

He poured the bowl of foaming grains into the water. There was a nice bubbling, but not nearly as much as he'd imagined. The other products he'd put into their bath must have subdued the foam. Next time he'd have to read the instructions.

She rested her head on his shoulder and closed her eyes. "I'm so glad this day is over. Maybe we should just tell them we're already married."

"Oh no you don't. This is too important to our mothers."

"Neither of our mothers wants me to marry you, and then there's my father…"

"When's the last time you spoke with him?"

"When I earned my master's, he came to the graduation."

"See there. He does care." Granted it had been at least ten years since her graduation, but Gabriel was trying to find anything for her to hold onto.

"One of his flunkies had offered me a position at his company, and I turned down his offer. The only reason he came to the graduation was to ask me personally to take the position. I'm sure he thought I'd be so grateful he actually came out I'd jump at the opportunity to work for him."

"Did you tell him why you turned down the position?"

"Nope. I don't owe him any explanations. He owes me a few though." She swirled her foot about the foam. "I don't understand why I'm stuck on stupid where he's concerned. Why can't I stop wanting him in my life? Why do I keep setting myself up to be hurt?"

"Have you two ever sat down and talked? I mean really talked?"

"No…"

"Why not?"

It took a while before she answered, "I guess I'm afraid of him confirming my fears."

"How about we give him a personal invite to our wedding? We can spend a few days in California…His head quarters is in California, isn't it?"

"Yeah."

"Then next weekend let's make that trip. You need answers, baby. No more being stuck in a holding pattern."

"You're right. You're right. I'll make the arrangements tomorrow, but right now…" She looked over her shoulder into his eyes.

"What?"

"I've never made love in a tub before."

CHAPTER TWELVE

Payton Johnson. Sweetie sighed. How many times had she called him over the years, yet the only time he called her was to return her calls. *Stuck on stupid.* The only way she could see to become unstuck was to confront him. Someone honked his horn and knocked her out of her trance.

"Go, Sweetie!" Tess said from the passenger seat.

"Oh sorry." She rushed the Mercedes through the green light and continued down Halstead Ave. Tess wanted to pick up the rest of her things from Sweetie's and move them to Missy's. "I might as well get this call over with."

"Are you sure you want to call him?"

"I keep doing the same thing and ending up with the same results. It's time I took my own advice. It's time for a change." She speed dialed her father's number and turned the corner.

"Hello, Johnson residence."

"Payton Johnson please," Sweetie said and readjusted her earpiece.

"May I ask who is calling?"

"This is his daughter, Monica Fuller."

"Oh, hello, Ms. Fuller. Mr. Johnson just left for a golf date. Would you like to leave a message?"

"No thanks. I'll just call his cell. Thank you. Goodbye." Though she'd had his cell number for years, she could never bring herself to dial it. But Gabriel was right. It was time for her to stop running from what might be.

Sweetie saw a squad car's lights come on and siren blare. She pulled over to allow him to pass, but he pulled in behind her. "Great…" Glad for the reprieve from calling "Daddy," she yanked the earpiece out. "Now what?"

"You weren't speeding." Tess looked over her shoulder into the squad car. "Oh shit. It's that jackass Shaun."

"Shaun?"

"Remember, I told you about the cop that let me out of that speeding ticket last month. That's Shaun. He's been calling ever since. I keep telling him I'm not interested. Damn. What's his problem?"

"Oh lawd. You and your men."

"I'll handle this." She opened the door.

"No, Tess. Let's just see what he wants."

"To ask me out, *again.*" She straightened her huge Jackie O-type sunglasses. "I told his ass off the last time he called, but I guess he needs to hear it personally. It's time for him to be put in his place. He can't abuse his badge like this. You weren't doing anything wrong."

"Oh, but it was okay for him to ignore the ticket he should have given you?"

Tess *tsked.* "This is totally different!"

Shaun opened Tess's door fully. "We need to talk."

"No we don't. I've said all I need to say to you. Stop calling me, you fucking stalker."

"So it's like that?"

Sweetie groaned. All she wanted to do was drop Tess off and call her father.

"Hell, yeah, it's like that. You have no right to stop us."

He tapped his badge. "This here gives me all the rights I need. As a matter of fact, your friend here was driving erratically and is acting suspicious. I'll need to search the car."

"You can't search my car," Sweetie said.

"Oh, but I can. And I thought this was your car, Tess."

"Go to hell."

This had gone too far. No Sweetie didn't have anything in the car to worry about, but that "the man" could actually search her car without probable cause was an abuse of power.

"Get out of the car," Shaun demanded.

Sweetie glared at Tess. "What did you do to make him so angry?"

"Oh, your little friend here likes to play games," he answered for Tess. "I went downtown on her so well tears fell from her eyes."

Sweetie didn't feel it was the appropriate time to point out that any man could do that to Tess. Instead, she got out of the car. Tess had been faking the tears for years. It was her way of boosting a man's ego.

"Then when it was time to reciprocate, she had to rush to an appointment. She told me to call. She said she felt something special between us." He checked under the front seats. "I knew her ass was full of shit about that special thing between us, but damn. When I'd call, her ass was rude as hell. Like I'd forced her to spread her legs for me." He popped the trunk, then rounded the car. Spectators were starting to gather for the show.

"This is ridiculous, Shaun. What do you expect to accomplish?" Tess asked.

"Ruining your day will make mine." He pulled out the spare tire, then froze. He looked over at Tess. "Whose car is this?"

"None of your damn business."

"It's mine," Sweetie answered in hopes of keeping him from slashing the spare tire or vandalizing the car in some other way. As soon as she could make it to the DMV, she was ordering new plates. Too many people—actually men—recognized the HOTNESS plate as Tess's. She couldn't count the number of times she'd told Tess to stop playing games before she played the wrong guy. She watched Shaun—a.k.a. the wrong guy—lean into her trunk and pull out a small vial filled with white stuff. "Now that's not mine!"

"He planted it," Tess yelled. She motioned for the gathering crowd to come closer. "Come on and witness this prime example of police corruption!"

He held the vial between his fingers. "I'm afraid I have to take you in for questioning."

This had to be a bad dream. Sweetie rolled a finger on the electronic inkpad. *This is not happening.* Nine more fingers later, she was still in the nightmare. The flash of the camera for her mug shot didn't wake her either. After they stripped her of her personal effects, the dream continued.

"Ms. Fuller, are you listening," the detective said calmly.

Sweetie lifted her gaze from her lap to the older lady's compassionate eyes. "I'm sorry, I'm still in shock. Never in my wildest imagination did I think something like this could happen to me."

"You didn't know anything about the drugs, did you?" Detective Morning asked softly.

"No. I have no idea how that vial ended up in my car. Hell, I just bought the car, and I know the previous owner. She's not into drugs either. Is this where I get to make my one phone call?"

Morning offered a sorrowful smile. "Yes, you can make a call."

"I know everyone says they are innocent, but I actually am."

"I believe you."

"Great, because I have a humongous favor to ask. You see…I have the numbers saved in my cell phone."

"People don't remember numbers anymore, do they?" Within fifteen minutes, Morning had Sweetie's cell phone. "Do what you need to do."

Sweetie called Gabriel's personal number, but was sent directly to his voicemail. As if her nightmare weren't already bad enough, his message box was full, so she was disconnected. *Unbelievable!*

"I'm sorry, but he's not answering. Can I make another call?"

"Go ahead."

This time Sweetie called Zack. He instructed her not to say another word until he was there—no matter how nice the detective lady was. She ended her call with Zack, then handed her phone over to Detective Morning.

"Thank you very much. I've been instructed not to say another word, but he's acting like I'm guilty of something."

"He's being a lawyer."

"Exactly." The two shared a smile. "Would you keep my phone and keep trying to call my husband? His name is Sexy Voice in the address book, but his real name is Gabriel."

"I'm sorry, honey, but I can't keep your phone." She held out the phone. "Write down his number, and I'll keep trying."

"It's an international call."

"Oh…"

"Or…well…I know I'm in on drug charges, and you have no reason to trust me, but if you make the calls, I will pay your phone bill."

Morning inhaled and exhaled deeply. "I don't know why I believe you, but I do." She wrote down Gabriel's real name and phone number. "I'll keep trying."

Walking off anger, Tess resisted the urge to key every police car in the parking lot. She stopped and allowed a cruiser to pass, then continued about the lot. "This is a bunch of bull!" she bit into her cell phone.

"Does Gabriel know?" James asked.

"I don't have his number, but I called Mama and our brothers." She threw her hand out. "This is all my fault. She'll never forgive me."

"Stay with me for a second, baby. Gabriel needs to be notified. Do you have his work number?"

"Not on me. I'm sure Sweetie used her call to tell him. Oh my God, what have I done?"

"This isn't your fault, Tess."

"But it is. Shaun was mad because I wouldn't date him. And the only way those drugs could have gotten in the car was Kevin. That son-of-a-bitch used my car when I was out of town. I swear I didn't know he did drugs. I swear. She'll never forgive me."

"Stop it with the pity party. Sweetie needs for you to keep it together." He paused. "You'll need to tell her lawyer everything. You didn't tell the cops anything, did you?"

"Of course not. How far away are you?"

"Five minutes tops. Hang in there, baby. I'm on my way."

Hours later, Sweetie swore she'd been in *jail* at least two lifetimes. Zack had arrived shortly after she'd phoned him, listened to her version of what happened, then told her he'd take care of everything. Being Sunday, he wasn't sure if he could ensure her release, but he promised to pull every string he had and find some new ones to pull if those didn't work.

She was so outdone with anger she could barely think straight. All her life she'd respected others, done well in school, was in tune spiritually, worked hard, loved hard and tried to do the right thing, yet now she'd be sent to prison on drug charges.

No one said life was fair, but damn. She lay back on her bunk. At least they were "nice" enough to put her in a cell of her own. *God, please let Detective Morning be able to contact Gabriel. He'll be worried to death.* He was supposed to spend his day with his mother, then meet Sweetie for dinner.

"Hey, beautiful."

Grateful for a familiar voice, she stood to greet Zack. "Welcome to my humble abode."

The corrections officer let him into her cell. "I have good news for you," Zack said and sat on the bunk. "Come, let me explain things."

"The only good news wouldn't be news but someone waking me from this nightmare." She sat beside him.

"Okay, so maybe my news isn't as good, but it's the next best thing. Tess is a real dynamo. She'd taken statements, names, addresses, cell phone numbers and signatures of people who witnessed the incident this morning."

"Incident?" She shook her head. "Is that what they're calling it these days?"

"Got jokes, huh? Well, the search was illegal—"

"Aw, man. That means they can't use the cocaine against me!" she interrupted. "Things are starting to look up." Once she calmed, he went through all the details with her and explained the procedures they'd have to follow for her to go home.

Gabriel's worry quickly transformed to livid outrage when he stepped into the waiting area of the police station. Sweetie's mother, stepfather, brothers, Tess, even James was there. All sitting comfortably, discussing the "atrocity" that had occurred. And that he was only ten minutes away when he received the call…*This shit has to end!* He should have been the one call she made.

"What the hell happened, Tess?"

Everyone jumped or jerked to attention. He folded his arms over his chest.

"Oh, Gabriel," Tess said as she crossed the room to him with James close behind. "I'm so glad you were contacted."

"Yeah, yeah, whatever. Once Sweetie's released, you aren't to call or go near her. I'll give you another job."

Tess backed away as if slapped. The rest of the family began to gather around her.

"Hold up a second." James protectively rested his hand on the small of Tess's back. "Don't come in here talking reckless. I don't give a damn where we are. I will whip your ass if you disrespect my woman."

"Don't let the Armani fool you. Step to me and your ass will be whipped."

Tears dropped from Tess's eyes, and James embraced her, but Gabriel wasn't moved in the slightest.

"You can't lay this at Tess's foot," Missy defended.

"Oh please. Every damn time drama enters Sweetie's life, Tess plays a vital role in the cause. I guess now you're telling me Tess had nothing to do with Sweetie being arrested for drugs found in the car she bought from Tess last week?"

"I'm sorry," Tess whimpered.

"That's enough, Gabriel!" Missy snapped.

"No it isn't. Sweetie spends so much time sticking up for Tess that she doesn't take the time to protect herself from Tess. Sweetie is your daughter, not Tess. Where do your loyalties lie? I'm not confused in the least bit. I know where the hell my heart is." He stepped around Missy. "I'm warning you." He pointed at Tess. "Stay the hell away from Sweetie."

Harold held his hands up slightly. "Emotions are high. Everyone's upset. This is no time to place blame or issue threats. Monica needs all of us."

"Hell, yeah, I'm upset. Someone has to protect Sweetie," Gabriel said.

"We've done a pretty good job without you all these years—" Michael began.

"Yeah, you've done such a bang up job that she's ended up in jail. I'm sorry. I was wrong."

"What's going on?"

Everyone turned toward the doorway.

"Baby!" Missy rushed past Gabriel and hugged her daughter.

He would have beat Missy to Sweetie, but the site of Zack stopped him. *What the...* The rest of the family surrounded Sweetie and Zack.

"So what's the deal?" Michael asked Zack.

"I did it. She's a free woman."

Gabriel locked gazes with Zack. He wanted to knock the smirk off his face but instead held out his hand. "Thanks, man. I'm grateful."

"Anytime Sweetie calls, I'll be there."

So she did use her call on...him. Gabriel withdrew his hand and turned to the family. "May I please get to *my* fiancée?"

Sweetie broke through the family barrier and gripped him so tightly he could barely breathe, but he didn't mind. In his arms is where she belonged. "I was so worried about you," he whispered into her hair.

"I love you so much, Gabriel. I don't ever want to leave your arms."

"Well, I'm never letting you out of my sight again, so I guess I can fill that request."

"I'm so tired. Can we go home?"

"I think you should stay with me a few days," Missy said. "You could use some extra mommy love."

"Thanks, Mama, but no thanks."

Gabriel released a breath he hadn't realized he'd been holding. He'd actually *feared* Sweetie would choose going home with her mother over him.

"But we need to talk about what happened," Missy said.

"You are unbelievable. She's too tired to quell your curiosity tonight." Gabriel nodded at Zack. "He can fill you in on what happened. I'm taking Sweetie home."

CHAPTER THIRTEEN

"I know you didn't just tell me I'm not *allowed* to be friends with Tess anymore." Sweetie stomped into their condo and dropped her purse on the entry table.

Her anger was sexy as hell, but Gabriel had other business to handle before he *handled his business*. "Tess isn't your friend." He slammed the door. "Friends don't get friends arrested on drug charges." He reached to help her out of her jean jacket, but she moved away.

"I explained everything that happened. It wasn't Tess's fault."

"Did you or didn't you say she had some jackass go down on her, then turned around and treated him like crap? A cop jackass at that!"

"And that gave him no reason or right to search *my* car!" She shrugged off her jacket and tossed it at the coat rack, then headed for the bedroom."

"Who told you that, the Boy Wonder?"

She turned, and he bumped into her. "So are you angry because Tess is the nexus of all that is wrong with the universe, or are you angry because Zack is one hell of a lawyer?"

"Yes, Zack is one of the best lawyers there is, but I should have been the one you called. I'm your husband. You have to believe in me."

She stared at him a long while.

"Did you honestly believe I wouldn't move heaven and hell to ensure you didn't spend one nanosecond longer in that hellhole than need be?"

The pain he saw on her face threw him for a second. "What, are you feeling guilty now? I love you with all my heart, but this has to stop. There is absolutely no excuse for every-damn-body knowing you were in trouble before your *husband*."

"You know," she backed away, "I've had one hellacious day. I don't have to explain shit to you. Go to hell." She turned away and walked into the bathroom.

Sweetie's cell phone played Aretha Franklin's "Respect."

"Since you want to be there for me so badly," Sweetie called from the bathroom, "crawl out of hell and get that for me. I'm not in the mood to talk to anyone. And call Mama to let her know we made it home safely. Thanks."

"We're not done."

"So you can't even answer the damn phone? What happened to moving heaven and hell for me?"

"Fine." He stalked into the living room and snatched her phone off the entry table. "Hello," he barked into the phone.

"I'm sorry, but I'm calling for Monica Fuller. Is this her number?"

"Yeah, but she's busy right now. Can I take a message?"

"Is this Gabriel? This is Detective Morning. We spoke earlier today."

"I'm so sorry." He dragged his hand over his face. "Please forgive my rudeness."

"All is forgiven. I understand you've been through a lot also. This won't take long. I was just calling to check on Monica. She's such a sweet girl."

"She's grumpy as hell, but that's to be expected."

"Well tell her not to worry about the phone bill."

"What?"

"After she couldn't get through to your cell phone, she asked me to keep trying—"

"She tried to call me?" He pulled his cell phone off his belt clip. The only time it had rung today was when Detective Morning had called. He scrolled through the missed numbers.

"Of course you were the first person she called. If you ask me, she was more worried about you than her situation." He could hear the smile in her voice. "Young love…I don't want to keep you long. Please tell her not to worry about the bill."

"I will. If you ever need anything, please call me. I'm forever in your debt." They said their goodbyes and disconnected. He set his phone on the entry table, then scrolled through her outgoing calls. Sure enough, Sweetie had attempted to call him around ten this morning. *Shit!*

Sweetie turned the shower on, stripped slowly and tossed each piece of clothing into the trash. She'd been so angry with Gabriel she forgot to bring a fresh set of clothes in with her. *Oh well, I guess he'll get a show when I come out. But he'd better not even think about touching me.* Emotionally exhausted, all she wanted to do was be cared for and cuddled. He'd been so protective at the police station, then on the limo ride home, he morphed into some sort of raving lunatic. She knew she could have easily told him she *had* called him first, but why had he assumed the worse of her. Granted, she hadn't called him when Tess was in trouble, but he already didn't like Tess and…and…she was worried he'd get hurt. He wasn't used to the ghetto-antics she occasionally found herself drawn into.

This was totally different!

She recalled Tess justifying the cop not giving her a ticket. She'd said the situations were totally different. *Am I justifying…?*

She shrugged off her misgivings. No matter how you put it, he was wrong. Why didn't he understand how hard it was for her to ask anyone for help, and to have to ask for help from Zack! They were barely more than acquaintances, and she knew she'd catch heat from Gabriel for calling him. But she was short on time and didn't see a better alternative: Gabriel wasn't answering his phone, her mother would have asked a kajillion-billion questions instead of getting help, if her brothers weren't working, they were most likely out of town, Tess already knew what was going on and Sweetie had no intention on allowing her to hire a lawyer. *I only had one call. Zack was the right decision.*

She stepped into the shower stall without even putting on her shower cap. If the humidity turned her twists into knots, so be it. *I should have gone to Mama's.* But she wanted Gabriel. She'd never trusted a man—actually anyone—to fully have her back. She loved her mother, but with

Missy support was hit and miss. Her brother's wanted to run her life instead of allowing her to live it, her father was out of the picture, and Tess…*Tess is a flake.*

A smile claimed her. The way Tess shot into action at the scene of the "incident" was truly amazing. The woman may be a flake, but she'd had the wherewithal to take names, numbers and statements. Tess performed from confidence instead of insecurity—somewhere Sweetie prayed to see her perform from more often. Now that Tess and James were a couple, hopefully things would change. *I can't believe Gabriel told me we couldn't be friends.* Sweetie loved Gabriel, but there was no way she'd allow him to pick who her friends were. No doubt, Tess had issues, but they weren't deal breakers.

She heard Gabriel rummaging about the bathroom. If she hadn't decided not to speak to him before he realized the errors of his ways, she'd ask him who had called.

He stepped into the shower in all his nude glory with a cherry Tootsie Roll Pop in his hand. She took the sucker from him and popped it into her mouth, then turned her back to him and grabbed the lavender-scented beauty bar. *No sense in letting a perfectly good Tootsie go to waste.*

The not talking to him part was childish—which she knew, but didn't care. She had turned her back to him because her lust for him far outweighed her anger at him. With him standing in front of her, all she could think was to touch, lick, stroke…her husband. *Out of sight, out of mind.* Her plan would have worked, too, except he was standing between her and the water.

"Allow me." He reached around her body and took the beauty bar from her, then wrapped his arms around her and held her close to his body, his erection pressing against her back. "I love you so much, Sweetie."

She believed his love for her was genuine, but that wasn't their issue. She'd needed his support emotionally, and he'd attacked her and tried to take control of her life. He had no right to tell her who could and couldn't be her friends. He'd have to trust her judgment and respect her choices, or they'd be divorced before their wedding.

"I'm an overprotective ass," he whispered.

Liking the direction of this conversation, she reached back and gave his thigh a stroke of encouragement. If he kept this up, she may even give back his sucker.

He took a deep intake of air, then ground his hardness against her gently. The moisture collecting between her legs combined with the waters of the shower. He lathered the beauty bar and turned them to the side so the hot waters would soak them both—her back against his chest.

"You were right. I was jealous of your toys." He chuckled and she stifled a giggle. "I never realized I was the jealous type. But then again, I've never been in love before." He handed her the beauty bar, then cupped her breasts with his sudsy hands and massaged her breasts, leaving her in a state of delirium. The sucker dropped out of her mouth and plopped onto the stall floor and was soon followed by the bar of soap.

The suds quickly dissipated, but his hands remained. "I'm jealous of your family. My jealousy mixed with the craziness of finding out you'd been arrested on drug charges…I was so scared…" He nibbled along her neck, suckled behind her ear and continued to slowly caress, then squeeze…caress, then squeeze…her breasts. The contrast felt so good she could cry out.

"Forgive me…" He planted feather kisses along her shoulder.

Her "forgiven" came out as a lazy *umph*.

He slowly ran his hands to her waist, then held onto her hips as he lowered himself and pressed his shaft between her slightly spread legs. Wanting to feel the tip throb against her heat, she leaned forward ever so slightly. *Umm, that's the spot.* She increased the lean and placed her hands on the tiled wall to brace herself, but began to slip on the slick surface.

"That's not safe, baby." He turned her to face him and backed her against the wall. A flash of their time spent "stuck" in the elevator crossed her mind. Making love standing up was quickly becoming one of her favorite positions.

"I hope whatever thought put that smile on your face has me involved in it somewhere," he said huskily. "Share it with me."

She shook her head no, then suckled water off his chest.

"Not speaking to me…?" He cupped her right breast. "Let's see what I can do to change that." He held onto her hip with one hand and crouched, then taunted her breast with his mouth and free hand.

She felt as if she'd explode in all the right ways. Then he slipped his fingers into her and…"Oh Gabriel…" Her back arched away from the wall as the orgasm flowed through her body. The shower water pelted her face and drenched her hair, but she didn't care. She spread her legs wider, wanting him, needing him. She gyrated against his hands. "You, I want you…"

He gripped her butt with his hands as he gave her exactly what she wanted—harsh, deep, penetration.

"Oh, yes," she cried out as she held on for dear life. Her breast bounced with the force of each thrust. The stall filled with the grunts and moans of their passion and the slurpy sound of their mating. With each stroke she felt herself separating from herself to become one with him, then…then…the waters took a sudden turn to the cold side.

Her yelp mixed with several expletives from him. He lowered her, turned off the water, then took her by the hand and led her into the bedroom, pushed her onto the bed and re-entered her with new vigor.

The water turned out to be a blessing in disguise. Now she matched him stroke for stroke. He reached for one of the legs she'd wrapped around him and trapped it under his arm as he continued to thrust into her.

"Yes, yes," she cried out as he continued to hit her sweet spot. She looked past her jiggling breast to where his length slid in and out, in and out…

"That's it, baby. Let it…umm…"

She felt him swell within her. His mouth covered hers, and they devoured each other.

Tingles spiraled about the sweet spot he'd hit so well, intensified and spread throughout her body. She tightened around him and her back arched to hold on to the second orgasm.

A guttural groan escaped him as he thrust deep into her. His body quaked. She clapped onto his firm butt and held tightly.

"You want all of me," he barely breathed out as his body relaxed.

"And then some."

He brushed his lips over hers, kissed her eyelids. "I can't promise I'll never act like an overprotected, jealous ass, but I do promise to try not to act like one."

Kevin laughed so hard tears fell from his eyes and his stomach knotted into a painful ball.

"This isn't funny, Kevin," Zack snapped.

"The hell it's not!" *I couldn't have planned this better!* "I guess we know where the missing vial is now." Still laughing, he kicked Ronald's foot off the coffee table. "Ron thought you'd taken it. Hell, you paid twenty thousand. If you wanted a vial, take it."

"Do you realize the only reason she got off was because it was an illegal search. She would have gone to jail because of our stupid shit." Zack punched the pimp daddy red sofa as he paced by.

"I know you aren't expecting me to feel sympathy for a fat bitch who got me suspended from my job." He snatched his bottle of beer off the table and glugged it down. If he had anything to do with it, Sweetie would be the next one to be out of a job.

"Your beating your girlfriend's ass is what got you suspended."

"You two really need to stop," Ronald cut in from the opposite end of the sofa. "It's not like I left the shit in there on purpose. You got her off. No harm, no foul. And Kevin's an asshole. Him laughing don't mean shit. Sales are going great! I'll easily be able to move all of the cocaine. We under bought."

"Listen. I was serious. I'm through. I just wanted to let you know how we almost got an *innocent* woman sent to jail." Zack stalked out and slammed the door behind him.

"Good riddance," Kevin mumbled. "We don't need his chicken ass anyway."

"You need to leave him alone. You know how he feels about Sweetie."

"I don't give a fuck."

"Well you should. He knows everything, and we don't have any proof that he came in with us. Stop trippin' and let's take care of business. If you're fired, we'll need to reorganize. Are you looking for another job?"

"What the hell do you mean by reorganize?"

"You can't continue living here if you are unemployed. You drained your savings. According to the government, you don't have a way to support your lavish lifestyle."

"Shit!" He'd been too consumed with thoughts of how to make Sweetie pay for trying to ruin his life to think about anything else. Ronald was right. "I'll start looking tomorrow." *After I ensure Sweetie's ass is fucked.*

CHAPTER FOURTEEN

Sweetie and Tess barely stepped out of the revolving doors when Sam approached them. Usually carefree, the urgency on his face worried Sweetie. He pulled them over to the lounge area.

"I know I give you a hard time, Tess, but you're my friend, so I gotta say this. Don't ever stay with a nigga that would put his hand on you."

Tess's hands flew to her mouth. "Sweetie, how could you tell?" She straightened her sunglasses.

Before Sweetie could say a word, Sam said, "James and I are best friends. He was ready to kill Kevin the other night. I thought we were going to jail for sure. Luckily, I was able to convince him that you needed him."

"Thanks, Sam…And I'm sorry I've been acting like such a…a…"

"Don't worry about it." He nodded at Sweetie. "Something big is going on up in you all's firm."

"What makes you say that?" Sweetie asked.

"Both big wigs are here."

"What?" Sweetie and Tess said simultaneously.

"They came in shortly after my shift started at six. They looked…I don't know…"

Sweetie glanced at her watch. It was almost noon. "When I phoned in and said we'd be late, no one told me anything."

Tess looked around, then quietly said, "I'll bet we're merging with Edgerton Trust. The rumor mill has been pretty accurate lately."

"I pray to God not. I sure as hell don't want to work in the same company as Kevin. Thanks for the heads up, Sam. We'd better get upstairs and find out what's happening."

All eyes were on Sweetie and Tess as they walked into the firm. Tess adjusted her sunglasses.

"Maybe you should take off for a few days," Sweetie whispered into Tess's ear.

"I'll be fine. I'll just stay in our office. Oh, man, how could I forget about the promotion? I'll bet they've decided to have you set up office in Europe. Oh my God! You'll not only be the first black executive president but the first female executive president in the company's history. No wonder they're so hush, hush. You know the ol' boy network is about to come off line." Her pace slowed, and she held to Sweetie's blouse sleeve. "But you'll have to move to Europe."

They entered their office. "I don't want the promotion. I love what I do. The only reason I'd take it is if Gabriel wanted to live in Europe, but he's fine with staying in the states." She set her briefcase under the desk and took her seat. "And what's this talk about me moving to Europe? Don't you mean we? You know that if I took the promotion, I'd hire you as project manager. I don't care about the formal education you don't have. You know the job and are good at it."

"Thanks but..." she took off her shades and set them on her desk, "but I'm in love with James. I don't want to leave him."

"I'm so proud of you, Tess."

"I'm kind of proud of myself. So what's up with you and Gabriel? Did you set a date?"

"November. The moms are arranging everything, so the exact date in November will depend on where and when they can book a hall and such. Maybe we should have a double wedding. Hint. Hint."

"Slip a hint or two to James, and it's on. I can't believe we've fallen in love."

"I've never been so happy in my life! And, Tess, he makes love like...like...there's no word to describe how good he makes me feel." Thoughts of Gabriel had her moistening. He'd packed her vibrator in her purse and promised to call and give her some long distance love in the afternoon. "Shoooooooot, I'm temped to head on back home right now for a little up close and personal noon lovin'."

"I can't wait until the first time James and I—"

"I know you are not about to let that lie come out of your mouth. You have never been ashamed or too shy to tell about your sexcapades before. What gives?"

"We haven't made love—yet. He won't in Mama's house because she can't stand him, and I haven't been to his place. At least she couldn't stand him. After the way he stood up to Gabriel yesterday, I think she's found a new respect for him. At least her snide comments ended..." she trailed off. "Look. I'm sorry about everything."

"It wasn't your fault."

"Not directly, but indirectly it was. It always is. I'm gonna be a better friend. I swear."

"You are the perfect friend." The phone on her desk rang. She answered without looking at the caller ID. "Good afternoon. Jamison and Drake Investments. Monica Fuller speaking. How may I help you?"

"Hello, Monica, this is Trudy." Sweetie's heart began to race. "Once you're settled, please come to Mr. Drake's office. He and Mr. Jamison are waiting for you."

"Sure. I'll be there in a few minutes. Thanks." Heart beating rapidly and hands shaking, she hung up.

"What's wrong?"

"I think you're right about the promotion. They want to see me at Drake's. I've never even seen Mr. Jamison in person before."

Squealing in delight, Tess hopped up from her seat and ran to Sweetie. "I knew it! I knew it! You've got to take this position. You'll be Vice President over European operations. Hell, you'd better take it or I'll kill you."

"I can't believe this is happening." Tears of joy dropped from her eyes. She wanted the position so bad she was afraid to admit—even to herself—she wanted it. In ways, the recognition of her abilities and acceptance by her co-workers eased the pain of her father's rejection. The need for acceptance was another reason she didn't want to work for herself.

Tess embraced her. "You've done it, Sweetie. You've proven to them all that you could make it."

"I'm not trying to prove anything to anyone."

Tess pulled back momentarily. "Sure you weren't. I'm going to miss you."

"We may be jumping the gun a little."

Tess brushed her off and headed back to her seat. "We both know Mr. Jamison wouldn't be here unless they were merging with another company or embarking on something major. European operations definitely falls in the major category. Why would they call *you* in to talk about anything besides promoting you? I don't even know why you're trying to fake the funk now. It's alright to want, Sweetie."

She didn't need Tess's words to convince her what the meeting was about. She was just trying to calm herself.

"You'd best get going. You don't want to keep them waiting."

Sweetie looked across the conference table from Jamison to Drake. The few times she'd seen Drake, his face didn't reveal his emotions. He would nod a lifeless hello and be on his way—this was no different. Reading Jamison was also no different. They'd gone on for at least five minutes about how impressed they were with her work, which she appreciated, but was ready to get to the good part. To hear them say, "We want you to be Vice President of European operations."

She could hardly wait to tell Gabriel. *Oh shoot, the wedding.* The wedding was still on, but so were their attempts at her getting pregnant. Once she took the position, her move to Europe would probably be immediate, and she wasn't comfortable about flying back if she were six months pregnant. *The wedding will just have to be sooner.*

Now that she thought about it. She didn't even know where in Europe they'd be based. She knew she'd do her best to convince them Sweden. Stockholm to be exact.

"…which is why it pains us to have to let you go," Drake said.

"Excuse me?" Sweetie had spaced out for a minute, but she was pert near sure Drake had just fired her.

"We've received word and verified that you were arrested on drug charges," Drake continued. "I'm disappointed. I thought better of you."

"But I didn't!" She drew her hands to her chest. "I'm innocent."

"Ms. Fuller," Jamison said, "you were not found innocent. You were released because the police department did not follow proper procedures. I'm sorry, but our clients will not trust their finances in your hands. We're asking you not to fight us on this. I understand that drug use is ramped. You obviously haven't let it interfere with your work, but…"

"But we're asking you to put the team first," Drake finished.

"But I didn't do it."

"Do you think our clients will believe that? Like Mr. Jamison said, you've been an excellent worker, which is why we're looking for another position for you in another company. A less visual position."

"But I didn't do it. Do you hear me? I didn't do it."

"That doesn't matter. If word leaks out that we have drug addicts handling our client's finances…" Jamison sighed. "I know we have no right to ask this favor of you, but please. Do this for the team. You have my word that we'll find you other employment."

She gazed into Drake's eyes and actually saw pity.

"You've been an excellent worker, Monica. I've had Trudy draw up a letter of resignation for you, and I've already called in a few favors. By end of business today, you'll have offers pouring in."

"What's wrong with Sweetie?" Gabriel asked as he rushed into the condo. The second he heard Tess's voice on the line, he knew something was drastically wrong. Tess had refused to tell him anything over the phone besides Sweetie needing him, which infuriated him. Helpless, all he could do was hold on to her words to meet him at Sweetie's condo instead of the hospital or prison.

Tess grabbed him by the arm and tried to lead him into the living area, but he didn't move. Instead, he stared at the closed bedroom door.

"What's going on?" He stepped toward the bedroom door, but Tess yanked him back.

"Stop and listen to me." She pointed at the sofa.

He forced himself into the living room, but couldn't force his mind from Sweetie. "What happened, Tess?"

She swallowed hard. He didn't know if whatever she was about to tell him was so difficult to say because it was bad or because he'd scared her yesterday.

She drew in a deep breath and squared her shoulders. "Those assholes fired Sweetie."

"What the…what?"

"Keep your voice down," she snapped under her breath.

"How could this happen? She's the best thing that will ever happen to that company."

"Someone contacted Mr. Jamison and Drake and told them about Sweetie's arrest. Whoever it was gave full details."

"But she was cleared. And who knew besides family?"

Tess stared at her lap. "I think it was Kevin. He's been following me since I first broke up with him. He confronted me in the parking garage, then he showed up at my office. He was probably following us yesterday and saw the whole thing."

"I'll kill him," he bit out. Too angry to sit still, he paced about. "They still can't fire her."

"Oh they're slick. The bastards asked her to resign for the good of the company and even found her other employment."

"She didn't sign anything did she?"

"I don't think so, but it doesn't matter because—"

"The hell it doesn't. They aren't firing her." He snatched his phone off his belt clip. Tess took the phone from him. "What the hell are you doing?"

"Gabriel, sit down and listen to me. I've known Sweetie my whole life. This isn't something you can or should fix."

"I'm not about to let them railroad her out of her job. Hell no!"

Tess stood toe-to-toe with him. "Do you realize the only place Sweetie has received true support—approval—besides you is from work? Even I get on her about her weight and lifestyle. All through school the teachers deemed her 'difficult' because she'd ask the tough questions and demand answers. They called her the know-it-all, but she wasn't. She wanted to know it all. You've seen Mama. Hell, Sweetie can't even eat a sucker in peace around that woman. And what do you think about me calling Missy Mama? As kids, I didn't realize…okay, I realized but liked the attention from Mama trying to show Sweetie what the ideal daughter should be." She rested her hands on her chest. "I'm a constant reminder of what Mama wants. And to tell you the truth, I'm just realizing I haven't been a real friend to Sweetie at all."

Every time Gabriel tried to speak, Tess would launch another barrage at him. He finally gave up and just listened. Tess wasn't telling him new information, but she had given more depth to his knowledge.

"…And her father. Don't even get me started on him. Then there's work. She was appreciated. Her inquisitive nature was an asset. She was needed. She was accepted." She returned to her seat. "Even those assholes who were jealous of her had to admit she was the best. We all have our limit, Gabriel. Sweetie has reached hers. She didn't get to choose her family, and I come along with the deal. But her career…She doesn't want to work for someone who would so easily turn their back on her after all she's done for them."

Wind knocked out of him, he settled on the couch. "Shit…"

"She worked her ass off for them, and they should have shown more loyalty to her. I'm not stupid. The only reason they offered to find her other employment was so she wouldn't make a stink."

"So what do I do to help her?"

"You can be the shoulder Sweetie cries on. You can try to understand what she's going through and that you can't fix it. You can allow Sweetie to be Sweetie."

"But I love her."

"Then give her what she needs instead of what you want her to need." She stood. "Can I borrow Sweetie's truck? I'm headed home. Don't worry, I'm taking the scenic route. I'll drop by the office first and see if there is any more news. You do realize that once I get home you only have about thirty minutes alone with Sweetie. I wish I didn't have to tell Mama. She'll already be furious I didn't call her immediately."

"Why didn't you call her?"

"Because Sweetie asked for you, and I love Mama, but once she gets here, this will flip from being a mess to a chaotic mess. There's no way to stop Mama. But you can help lessen the impact of whatever Mama does." She backed away. "Let me get going. James and Sam said they'd help me get our things out of the office."

"Did they fire you also?"

"No, I quit." She turned to leave.

"Tess..."

"Yes?"

"I wanted to apologize for my behavior yesterday. I was out of line and wrong about you. You are good people."

Her light cheeks reddened. "Thanks." She hugged him. "Now go take care of Sweetie. I'll call when I get to Mama's." She snatched up the keys on her way out.

It was barely two o'clock in the afternoon, yet the bedroom looked as if it were the middle of the night, a power outage had claimed the city, and someone had kidnapped the moon and all other sources of light. *The calm before the storm...* He left the door closed and timidly crossed over to where he remembered the bed being, praying he didn't trip on his way.

He bumped softly into the bed. He couldn't even hear Sweetie breathing, yet he knew she was there. He could feel her presence. He stripped down to his T-shirt and boxers, then slipped between the sheets and lightweight blanket. He'd barely had time to touch flesh to sateen when Sweetie clung to him.

He wrapped his arms around her, wanting to make things better, yet admitting Tess was right—he couldn't. At least he couldn't at the moment. He'd have to give more thought into how to proceed.

His T-shirt quickly became saturated with her tears. *How could they do this to you?* Outraged, he could barely hold it together. He weaved his fingers through her Afro to her scalp and massaged lightly. This morning she'd allowed him to take down her twists and wash her hair. They'd ended up making love again. He hadn't truly understood what making love was until Sweetie. Before her making love was just a synonym for sex women liked to use. He slowly ran his hand along her spine.

Tess had bought them a few hours of peace before all hell would break loose. Missy *would* go on the warpath, and he'd do his best to protect Sweetie from the fallout.

CHAPTER FIFTEEN

Blinding light flooded the room and storm troopers crashed in.

"Shit!" Gabriel shot up in the bed and quickly discovered he wasn't in the midst of an intergalactic raid, but something far worse—Missy!

Sweetie rolled her eyes and covered her head with a pillow. A small chuckle escaped him. She was entirely too cute.

"Mama!" Tess rushed into the room. "You can't just barge into a couple's room."

"I've had more than enough out of you for one day, young lady. Zip it!"

Tess opened her mouth as if to say something, then closed it.

"Get up, Monica." Missy snapped her fingers.

"I love you, but go away, Mama. I'm not in the mood." She peeked from under the pillow at Gabriel. "This would be an excellent time for your over-protectiveness to kick in. Hint, hint, hint…"

Before Gabriel could get a word out, Missy snatched the pillow off Sweetie. "No daughter of mine will hide like some damn ostrich with its head in the sand. They can't fire you. I'll show them."

"Please, Mama, just let it be."

"Humph…" Missy paced about the room. "Who the hell do they think they are?"

Gabriel could see James in the living room, wandering about like a lost soul. He could only imagine the hell Missy was putting him though. "You might as well come in, man."

James nodded at Gabriel as he entered.

"Did you call your father?" Missy asked.

"Of course not. Why on earth would I tell him I was fired?"

"Oh, no, he will be told, and he will clean up this mess. The only worthwhile thing he's ever done was make you. It's time for him to contribute again. Hand me your phone, Monica."

Sweetie signed and massaged the bridge of her nose with her thumb and index finger. "Gabriel. If you loved me, you'd kill me."

"I do love you." He kissed her forehead. "Hang in there, baby."

"The phone, Monica!" Missy impatiently tapped her stiletto-covered foot on the wood floor.

"No, Mama. I don't want you to call him."

"He'll get your job back."

"I don't want it back! Could you please just do things my way for once and leave well enough alone?"

"Tess, go get my purse out of the entry."

Tess would have deleted Payton Johnson's number from Missy's address book, but she knew that would only make matters worse. She watched Gabriel wrap his arm around Sweetie, and her own heart sighed—just like in Sweetie's romance books. The obvious love and admiration she saw between the two was what she wanted with James. And the passion…Oh yes, she'd like a double dose of passion.

"Hello, this is Melissa Fuller. May I speak with Payton Johnson, please?"

James took her hand into his. An energy passed through them that shocked the mess out of her. Not a painful shock, but an amazed shock.

Missy sucked air through her teeth. "Excuse me, young lady, but I don't care what he's doing. Please check his list of who is to be placed through to him immediately. I haven't phoned in over a decade, but I guarantee I'm still on the list."

"Mama, please leave this alone," Sweetie begged. "I don't want or need him to fix anything for me."

James's brows drew in. "You okay?" he asked Tess and kissed the back of her hand, which was sweet.

He'd insisted on changing his clothes before they could go to Missy's. She had thought—prayed—this was his way to get her alone so they could consummate their relationship. But when they arrived at his place, he left her alone in the living room while he changed out of his work clothes into khaki's and a cream Polo shirt. She'd asked if he needed help, but he'd just laughed and told her he thought he could manage. The man's willpower was driving her insane. Yes Sweetie was having a crisis, but Tess was having a crisis of her own and knew Gabriel would ensure Sweetie landed on her feet. Maybe once James became more comfortable with their relationship, he'd be more adventuresome.

Tess had told James he didn't have to impress Missy, but he said if something as simple as changing out of his dark blues would help ease the tension, it was worth the change of clothes. Then his sexy lips had curled into a rakish grin as he said, "Besides, a quickie won't do it for me." Then he'd nibbled on her lips. "Will you come home with me tonight?"

She interlaced her fingers with his. Tonight couldn't come quick enough for her.

"Hello, Payton…" Missy used her hands as she spoke. "Would I be calling you if there weren't something wrong with her? She was fired from her job today, and I expect you to do something about it."

"Mama! This is ridiculous." Sweetie hopped out of bed and reached for the phone. Her mother put up a hand, stopping Sweetie in her tracks.

Gabriel quickly grabbed Sweetie's robe and covered her with it. Tess didn't see anything wrong with the T-shirt. It wasn't any shorter than a miniskirt would be. Since the circus had come into town, Tess figured her work was done.

"It's time for us to say our goodbyes," she said to James.

"Tess." Missy snapped her fingers. "Come here and tell Payton what happened. Start with yesterday."

"You are unbelievable!" Sweetie stomped toward her walk-in closet.

Missy handed Tess the phone and followed Sweetie. "Where do you think you're going?"

"To a hotel. My place has been infested." She yanked the door open, then disappeared into the closet.

"That child is entirely too dramatic," Missy said.

Tess shook her head. Missy was "The Ultimate Drama Queen." She closed her eyes and tried to focus. This was Sweetie's father. She felt James's strong hands on her shoulders, massaging.

"You don't have to do this."

"If I don't, Mama will tell her version." She rested her free hand on his in thanks, then explained the events of the past two days to Payton. It saddened her that she'd probably spoken more with the man in these few minutes than Sweetie had over a lifetime. Halfway through the call, Sweetie exited the closet fully dressed, said her goodbyes and left with Gabriel, who had also dressed.

This is a tragedy.

When Payton made comments or asked questions, he was straight and to the point, but she heard the concern behind his words. The concern he'd tried to hide. Why he wouldn't want people to know he cared for his daughter was beyond her. After she explained what had happened, he said he'd take care of everything, then hung up on her.

"This is not good." She closed the phone and handed it over to Missy. Even if she told Sweetie that she thought her father cared for her, Sweetie wouldn't believe it. "Mama, I know you're tying to help. But you're making things worse. I'm begging you, please call him back and tell him not to interfere."

"I know what I'm doing, Tess."

Bored, Tess let the seat back as far as it would go, so she could stretch her legs out and take a nap. They'd been stuck in construction traffic so long, Tess could literally describe every detail of the cars that surrounded them on the Dan Ryan expressway. James merged the car with the right lane of traffic. His exit was a few blocks away, but she'd bet Missy would call James son before they actually made it.

She stole a quick glance at James. *Damn.* He caught her, nodded politely, then faced the non-moving traffic ahead of them. Yeah, it was illegal, but she wished he'd take the shoulder around the traffic so they could get home.

Uuuurrgh, she groaned internally. Before they left Sweetie's, she'd removed her panties to give him easy access. *What in the hell was I thinking?* Instead of gripping the wheel with those big fingers of his, she wanted them plunging into her heat. The mere though of him separating her folds and delving in had her dripping wet. But no…He was too damn proper. She was so horny she was getting pissed off. If she could move fast enough, she'd unzip his pants and suck his dick just to shock the proper out of him. No man could resist a hot, moist mouth around his dick.

The thought of his reaction sent giggles bubbling out of her.

"What's so funny?"

She covered her mouth. "Oh nothing." He'd probably crash into the van in front of them.

He studied her suspiciously, then returned to watching the parking lot of a road.

This was a definite "area of improvement," as Sweetie would say. *And I'm just the instructor he needs.* Within a month, she'd have him sexing her up right in the middle of a stadium full of people. More giggles escaped her.

"You'll have me paranoid if you don't let me in on what's tickled you."

"Trust me, you don't want to know." She shook her head. "The things that cross my mind…Whew! Ignore me. I've been cooped up in this car too long."

She looked out the passenger window to keep him from seeing the stupid grin that must be on her face. But it would be nice. She could see it all…The crowded stadium. The weather would be rainy, so he'd bring a trench coat. She'd lean on the balcony railing as if she could hear better from it. Still wearing his trench coat, he'd come from behind and lift her miniskirt. Of course she wouldn't be wearing panties. In her opinion, panties kept her kitty from breathing properly. Then he'd hold her hips still as he sank his hardness into her. People would want to know what was going on under the trench. They'd suspect, but not say anything. Some would point. Whisper. Many would stare. *Damn that would be sweet.*

Wetness pooled between her legs. She needed release so badly she was ready to stick her fingers in and hump like there was no tomorrow. And she would have, but…but she loved James and didn't want to scare him off. He'd think she was some sort of sex-crazed lunatic.

"You know what I want?" he asked.

"What," she said lazily. Just as she turned to face him, one of his fingers slipped into her heat.

"James!"

He began to remove his hand, but she clamped her legs closed and held onto his hand to keep him from withdrawing. "Don't you dare." Her eyes fluttered closed and head lulled back against the headrest as he fondled her. "Ummm, James…" She gyrated on his fingers. This felt so good the shock from his actions were a distant memory. She overlapped his hand with hers and reached across to his crotch with her free hand, then wrapped her hand around his engorged dick.

"Umm, girl. You're gonna make me wreck the car."

"You've been holding out on me," she purred and stroked him. "You've been very, very naughty."

"Not holding out," he said through tight lips, "trying to hold on until the right time."

"No better time than the present is what I was taught." She pumped his fingers a few more times to hold her over, then unsnapped her seat-belt. "You know I can't let you be naughtier me."

"You are crazy." He inched the car forward.

"You started it." She unzipped his pants, and he surprised her yet again. "Oh my, James. Someone stole your underwear." She wrapped one hand around his length and slowly stoked from the tip to the base…tip to base…and massaged his balls with her other hand.

"Damn." He drew in a sharp intake of air. "I'm a…a quick learner…" he trailed off as she took him into her mouth. She would have teased him longer, but she couldn't wait to have his thick, pulsating dick in her mouth.

She rarely went down on a man, and when she did, it was out of obligation. Well, actually, because she thought whoever would quit going down on her if she didn't occasionally return the favor. She swirled the pre-cum about the bulb with her tongue, then suckled along the shaft to his balls back to the bulb.

James was different. She actually craved to have him in her mouth—among other places. Couldn't get enough of his salty taste.

He gripped the steering wheel with one hand and weaved his fingers of his other hand through her hair to her scalp and guided her head as she took him in. Soon he was gyrating under her. "Don't stop…Whatever you do, don't stop."

She watched his face contort as she continued to suck him off and slip her fingers in and out of her own slick, wet, heat.

Breathing heavily, she pulled back. "James, please." Still on the floor, she leaned her back against the passenger door and spread her legs. "I need you." She separated her folds and inserted two fingers, then circled her clit with her thumb.

He maneuvered the car onto the shoulder and sped along. Before she knew it, he'd parked and was hopping out of the car, zipping his pants. In the blur of making it to his apartment, they'd somehow disrobed. Still disoriented by lust and need, she looked down to see him spreading her legs. She rested her back against the arm of the couch.

The bedroom was only a few steps away, but she was grateful he hadn't taken the extra seconds to go into it. She couldn't wait any longer. He feather kissed along her inner thighs and sunk his thumbs into her heat. Her vaginal walls gripped at his fingers.

"More, James, I want more." She loved to have oral sex performed on her more than she enjoyed the act of intercourse, but today, right now, she wanted him to take her and take her hard. She grabbed at his shoulders. Oral sex would be just a tease, and she was tired of games.

His eyes connected with hers, and she saw a mischievous glint she'd never noticed before. He held her by the hips and gently sucked her clit.

"Oh God…" she moaned and gripped the cushions. The sensations shooting through her were more intense than she'd ever felt.

His tongue dipped between her folds, and he made love to her with his mouth. She wrapped her hands around his head and rode his tongue as if it were the best dick she'd ever had. "Oh yes…yes…," she whimpered.

He returned to her clit, blowing gently, then licked and nibbled.

Her back arched and orgasmic bombs detonated, but he held her steady and delved his tongue into her depths. Tears, genuine tears, fell from her eyes.

He lifted himself, then pulled her to him so she'd be lying on the couch. Her vision had blurred, but she could see he'd already protected them both. With one powerful thrust, he penetrated her.

The walls of her vagina expanded to take in his girth. She wrapped her legs around his thighs and met him stroke for glorious stroke. She clutched his butt as she hit another climax. Two times. Two! No one had ever made her come twice. He took her mouth as he continued to pound into her. She bit on his shoulder to keep from crying out, for she knew if she did, she'd shatter his eardrums.

He threw his head back and cried out, pushing her over yet another edge. She'd never cursed condoms until today. She wanted to feel his seed rush into her.

He lowered his lips to hers and gently kissed her.

"When are you going to make me an honest woman?" she whispered before she could catch herself.

"How about tomorrow?" He rolled them over so she'd be on top.

"I'm not trying to pressure you into marrying me. I shouldn't have said that."

"Tess, I love you. Will you marry me?"

She felt her smile spread from ear to ear. "Oh my God. You're serious. You want to marry me!"

"I'm free tomorrow."

"Yes," she kissed him, "yes," she kissed him, "yes," she kissed him. "But not tomorrow. You think Mama doesn't like you know…I'm afraid to even think what she'd do if we got married tomorrow. I'll see if Sweetie minds having a double wedding."

"Whatever you want." He pressed her head onto his shoulder.

"This is so crazy. I'm in heaven. I mean...Wow. Married." Suddenly, Sweetie's situation darkened her mood. "You know the wedding might be a single wedding after all. Sweetie's so...so...funny when it comes to what she perceives as being a kept woman. She won't marry Gabriel as long as she's unemployed."

"Don't worry. Sweetie is the best at what she does. She'll find another job in no time."

"No," she sighed, "she won't."

"What's going on, Tess."

"I know Sweetie. She won't accept employment at any agency Drake and Jamison made recommendations to her on their behalf. She has to feel she's made it in on her own. She won't marry Gabriel if she can't support herself."

"He's going to take that personally. I know I would."

"Like I said. There may not be a double wedding in November after all. I just wish there was something I could do. Something to fully clear her name." She strummed her fingers on his chest.

"He's going to take it personally."

She propped herself up on her elbow. "Kevin is the only other person who has been in that car. The cocaine must have been his, but he doesn't use."

"What are you up to?"

"Why did he have cocaine in the trunk of my car? Why was he snooping around my car?"

"You think he's selling, don't you?"

"He is. And I'm going to prove it!" She thumped his chest with her fist.

"Hold on, lil' bit. There's no way in hell I'm letting you go after Kevin." He gently touched below her bruised eye. "I don't even want that bastard on the same planet as you. No."

"But I have to help Sweetie. I know he's selling. I just have to prove it."

"No."

"Yes. Sweetie is my best friend. She's stuck her neck out for me more times than I can count. I love you, but don't try to stop me."

He blew out an exasperated breath. "Then we'll do this together."

"No. I don't want you involved."

"It's this simple. Either I'm in this with you and running the show, or I tie your ass up and keep you locked up until this whole thing blows over."

Her clit perked up. "Umm, will you tie me up even if I say yes?" He hardened within her instantly.

"You are a mess in the best way, Tess."

CHAPTER SIXTEEN

Sweetie liked the feel of Gabriel's hand on her lower back. He opened the door to their condo complex and guided her inside. His touch made her feel more secure, yet not completely secure. Everything in her told her he'd be there, that he wouldn't let her down…everything except a tiny morsel of insecurity. The morsel screamed not to give Gabriel the chance to let her down. She'd been let down too many times in her life, and the pain of his failure would be too great for her to bear…She couldn't even think about it.

"How ya doin' today, Gabriel, Sweetie," the security guard asked as he reached behind the front desk.

Gabriel nodded a greeting.

"I'm okay, Matt," Sweetie said.

"I have something for ya." Matt handed a large manila envelope to her. "A courier dropped it by early this morning."

"Wow." She'd never received a message from a courier before. Her name and address were front and center but no from information was given. Suddenly, she felt dread. "Thanks," she mumbled. "Catch you later."

They headed on to their unit. Gabriel set their overnight bag to the side. "You planning on opening that?"

"I don't think so." She set it down on the entry table, then went into her bedroom. They'd spent all night cuddling and sleeping, yet she was still exhausted. She'd lost her appetite. She didn't even crave a cherry Tootsie Roll Pop. She stripped down to her panties and bra, then crawled into bed.

Gabriel entered with the envelope. "This must be something important."

"With my luck, someone has probably died."

"So how long do you plan on staying in bed?" He set the envelope on the nightstand and began taking off his clothes.

"Forever is sounding pretty good about now."

He chuckled. "What about when you need to go to the pot?"

"I haven't worked that part out yet." She lifted the covers for him. "Want to join me?"

Stripped down to his boxers, he slipped between the sheets with her. "So I guess we'll have to postpone the wedding or have it in our bedroom."

"So you plan on encouraging my lunacy? I think I'll keep you."

"Hold that thought." He reached over to the nightstand and grabbed the envelope. "You need to open this. People don't just send a courier to deliver packages for no reason. What are you afraid of?"

She propped the pillow under her chin. "It has to be from my dad. All my life I've fought for his acceptance, then I finally accepted myself, but…but I still want him. Now that I'm a failure…"

"You're not a failure."

"I feel like one."

He tenderly stroked her cheek with his knuckles. "You have been failed. You are not a failure."

"I know you're trying to help. I appreciate you being here, holding me all night. I wish I could just snap out of this funk, but…But I think I'm in shock." She rested her hand over his on her cheek. "I love you. Without you, I'd be in a lot worse shape than a funky mood. Just give me time to sulk, then I can think about my next move."

"And what about this?" He tapped the envelope. "

She nibbled her bottom lip. She wanted to know what her father had said, but she didn't want to know. "I'm not sure. Yeah, I guess so. But you open it."

"Baby," he began to tear the seal, "the torture you're putting yourself through is much worse than anything in this envelope. What's your greatest fear?"

She sighed. "I'm just so sick of being let down by him. I'm afraid to expect anything from him, because I can't take him letting me down again. But no matter how much I don't want to expect, still I do."

He pulled out a handwritten letter. "I'll read it to you."

"Monica,

I tried to call your cell. After what you've been through, I guess you don't feel like taking calls. I know you are innocent, but we both know the business world doesn't care about that. They care about image.

I don't blame you for not wanting to work for me. At first I was angry, hurt. Thinking back, I didn't want to work for my father either. But you are still my child. My responsibility. I've deposited three million in your savings account, enough for you to start your own company and grow larger than Drake and Jamison can imagine. And yes, Melissa gave me your account information.

Please call me when you are up to it.

I love you, Monica.

Payton Johnson."

He set the letter on the nightstand, then faced her and rested his hand on her waist. He didn't say anything, for which she was glad. She needed time to process what she'd heard. She just about had it when he interrupted, saying, "He loves you."

"He's just trying to uphold his image. Like he said, image is everything. What would it look like if he left his daughter destitute?"

"That's not what he said, and you aren't destitute. Trust me on this. Men sit and handwrite letters for only two reasons: love or in a fit of rage. And he's right. You should start your own business and show those assholes what they were too stupid to hold onto. My network is yours, and I'm sure your father's is also at your disposal. This gift is the answer…"

While he rambled on, she closed her eyes and thought. According to Michael, Missy had been in love once before Harold came along—with Payton Johnson. She did care about the other fathers of her children, but Payton was the first one to capture her heart. They'd even been married and should have lived happily ever after. Soon after their nuptials, Missy became pregnant with Monica and things changed. Payton became controlling. He thought because he paid the bills Missy should do as he said, no questions asked. They were divorced before Monica was born.

She rubbed her belly. What if she were pregnant? Would Gabriel change? He was already talking about how he was going to set up *her* business. "I don't want to use your connections. I don't want you planning *my* company. I want to do whatever on my own."

His brows knitted together. "Fine."

"Please try to understand. If I start a company, I want it to be my company."

"I understand." He watched her for a while. "Thinking about Junior?" He placed his hand over hers, which was still rubbing her stomach. "Originally, I didn't say anything about us living in the states because this is where your job was, but now..." he scooted so close their noses almost touched, "now there's no reason for you to stay here. I want to move back to Stockholm before the baby is born."

"What do you mean, 'no reason?' My whole family living in Chicago is more than enough reason." She backed away and sat up, thinking she'd only been unemployed one day, and he was already taking over.

"I misspoke." He sat up also. "Of course your family is very important, but *our* family is most important. I think we need time to come into ourselves away from our families. They can visit anytime they want. I'll even pay for the flights."

"Your father's family lives in Sweden."

"But we aren't close. Not like your family."

Head tilted to the side, she asked, "So is this your way of separating me from my family?"

"Stop twisting my words. You're upset about everything that's happened the last few days. I shouldn't have brought this up now."

"You're damn skippy, I'm upset. And when the baby comes, I don't want to be halfway around the world. I want my family to know *her*. And if I'm not pregnant now, I'm not getting pregnant. I'm unemployed. I can't have a baby now. I can't afford it."

"Sweetie, we're married. The baby is *ours*. And, yes, *we* can afford a baby. Hell, *we* can afford a hundred babies. I can understand your apprehension about my interfering with your career, but our children are a totally different matter. There is no you or I. With them and our marriage, it is we."

She dragged her hand over her face. "I love you to death, but I want a divorce."

"What? You're not serious."

"Yes, I am. Until I can support myself, I don't feel comfortable—"

"No."

"I refuse to be a kept woman."

"The only thing you refuse to do is put your faith in me. The man you supposedly love. I'm not your father. I'm not your mother. I'm not Tess, your brothers or your ex-fiancé. I'm here to support you, but you won't let me. You won't trust me. Without trust, there is no love."

"I do love you." She lowered her gaze to her lap. "I do love you."

"Then how can you talk divorce?" He cupped her cheeks in his hands and lifted her face. He leaned forward and gently kissed her lips. "I love you, baby. Let me love you."

Tears spilled from her eyes. "I'm scared, Gabriel," she said slowly. "I'm so confused and scared."

He pulled her into an embrace. "It's okay, baby."

"They arrested me…" She sniffed. "And fired me."

He rocked them slowly. "You're going to make it. We're going to make it." He Eskimo-kissed her, then ran his nose along her cheek to her ear. "We're going to make it," he whispered.

"But Mama told…she told him they fired me…He'll never love me now." Her tears did nothing to cool her burning eyes. "He'll never love me."

"Oh, baby, he does love you. I could tell."

"Then why isn't he here?"

"I wish I knew the answer." He wiped the tears from under her eyes with the pads of his thumbs. "We'll find the answers. We're in this together."

"Together—I like the sound of that."

He nibbled on her bottom lip until she opened freely. All worries disappeared, leaving only her and the man she loved. He released her breasts from her front-fastening bra and cupped one in his hand, massaged, then pinched its hardened peak.

Moaning, she broke from the kiss and pressed her breast into his hand.

"That's my girl," he murmured into the hollow of her neck as he feather kissed a trail to the tip of her breast. The moment he took her breast into his mouth, she knew she'd died and gone to heaven. Wetness pooled at her center as he licked, flicked and nibbled from the nipple to the base, all the while fondling her second breast.

She ran her hand along the ripples of his chest down his abdomen to the throbbing head of his dick, which had topped the bridge of his boxers.

He glanced up from his suckling. "You may wish to leave that beast caged for a bit longer."

She slid her hand into his boxers and gripped his hardness.

"Umm," he groaned, "I love that stubborn streak of yours."

The feel of him pulsating in her hand as she stroked him from bulb to base combined with the tender loving care he was lavishing on her breast sent sensual tremors throughout her body.

He showed her other breast due consideration, then pressed them together and handled both simultaneously. The hum and sensations flowing through her didn't want him to stop, but she ached in other places—hot, moist places that contracted with need.

"Gabriel," she said breathlessly.

"I know, baby." He tasted her stomach…waist as he made his descent. He stopped at her heat and suckled through the cloth barrier. Her legs spread of their own volition, giving him better access.

She cupped, squeezed and massaged one of her breasts as she guided his head with her free hand. Soon, she trembled as an orgasm rocked through her.

He pulled her panties off and his boxers, then licked and gently suckled the wetness along her inner thighs as his hands returned to her breast. Tiny, tingly chards circled about her center.

"Gabriel," she panted.

He blew over her lust-swollen clit, sending the chards spiraling out of control. He held her hips still as he sucked, licked and blew her to the edge of another orgasm. She knew she should have had enough, but she wanted—needed—to feel him deep within her.

"Please, Gabriel…"

He rose from the depths and took her mouth hungrily. She tasted herself on him as they devoured each other. He penetrated, then moved slowly in and out of her. Matching his pace, she looped her arms under his and over his shoulders. His slow in and out was a most beautiful death—at least she thought she'd die. She'd never been on the edge of a climax this long before. Never appreciated how sweet the view was as she climbed higher and higher. Never experience how exhilarating holding off before a longer jump could be.

Then it happened. She freefell happily over the edge into ecstasy. The greater height plunged her deeper into the pool than she'd imagined. Vision and hearing distorted, she felt Gabriel there with her. His seed filling her. She grasped onto him.

"I've got you, baby." He continued to pump though his shakes. "I've got you." He gently kissed her lips. "I'm never letting you go."

The morsel of insecurity she'd had dissipated. "I love you, Gabriel."

Tess and James spent the day following Kevin. He'd spent most of his time at a batting cage. Tess would have made a crack about him needing to be out finding a job if she weren't in need of a job herself.

James was a doll and took the rest of the week off from work to play detective with her. If they didn't find evidence within the week, she had to give up. Agreeing to his terms was difficult, but she understood. While in the car waiting for Kevin to go to and fro, they'd updated her resume on James's laptop. The unforeseen bonus of the day was when there was a lull in activity. They'd finished her resume and scanning the newspaper for positions and were just waiting, shooting the breeze when he'd asked her to join him in the back seat.

Within minutes, they'd forgotten Kevin and were making love. By the time they finished, Kevin's SUV was gone. They'd lost him.

"We'll get him tomorrow." Tess entered James's apartment.

"It's been a long day."

She wrapped her arms around James's neck and stood on her tiptoes to kiss him. "Tonight you're mine."

CHAPTER SEVENTEEN

"Are you sure you want me to leave?" Gabriel sat on the edge of the bed next to Sweetie. She'd eaten the breakfast he'd prepared, and then told him she loved him and knew he was there for her, but she needed a day alone to figure out her next move. He could tell she was still depressed and had just eaten to satisfy him.

"I'll be fine."

"How about we do lunch together?"

She raised a teasing brow. "No thanks. I can scrounge something up."

"How about I do you for lunch?"

Her lips curled into a sexy grin. "I can scrounge a little something up for that, too. Now get." She waved him on. "I need time to regroup."

Gabriel set his briefcase in the passenger seat of Sweetie's truck, then broke out his cell phone, scrolled down to Payton's private number and dialed. He'd programmed the number while Sweetie was napping.

"Hello."

"Hello, Mr. Johnson." He sent a silent prayer to God for Payton not to hang up on him. "My name is Gabriel Windahl—"

"How did you get this number?"

"Monica, she's my…my fiancée."

"Her what!"

"I'm her fiancé. We were planning to give you an invitation to our wedding personally this weekend," he added quickly, "but then everything went haywire. Sir…" he trailed off. He'd never been nervous about speaking to anyone in his life, but this was different. This was too important to Sweetie to mess up. "I need to speak with you in person about Monica. It's very important."

"Monica's engaged?" He sounded more hurt than confused. "I've…I've missed so much."

"Are you in California? I can catch a flight first thing in the morning."

"No, no, that won't be necessary. I arrived in Chicago yesterday—"

"You're here?" Gabriel cut in. "I'm sorry, I mean…why?"

"Monica didn't return my call or say anything about the package I sent. I thought it was time for me to make an appearance."

"So you're actually here to see Monica?"

"She'll be twice as stunned as you are, which is why I'm glad you called. Yes, we need to talk about my daughter."

Gabriel drove downtown in a daze. He hadn't decided if Payton showing up was a good or a bad thing. *It doesn't matter.* He pulled into the parking garage. The man was here and Gabriel would do whatever it took to help Sweetie though whatever came her way. He walked into the building and to the elevator bank with Payton still on his mind. Before he knew it, he was standing in front of the receptionist desk.

"May I help you, sir?"

"I'm Gabriel Windahn and have a nine o'clock with Mr. Drake and Mr. Jamison." He checked his watch. "I'm a little early."

"Oh, Mr. Windahl, they said to send you on back whenever you arrived."

"Thank you."

"I'll let them know you're here. One moment please."

Between the time Gabriel stepped from Trudy's desk to stand in front of Drake and Jamison, he'd regained control. Payton being in town had thrown him for a major loop.

"Mr. Windahl, please have a seat," Drake said as he motioned to the large leather armchairs in the sitting area. "It's such a pleasure to finally meet you in person."

Gabriel shook hands with both men, then took a seat. He didn't like either man. The only reason he originally brought his business to the firm was because his father pressured him into it. Jamison was some sort of distant relative. He was about to move his business elsewhere when Sweetie called him with an update on a project. From the first time he heard her voice, he wanted to know everything about her. Then the more he learned the more he wanted of her.

He didn't know what he was thinking when he *suggested* they move to Stockholm—yes he did. Chicago was her family's territory, and he was the underdog. In Stockholm, the table would turn. He could protect her.

"How's your father, Gabriel?" Jamison asked. "I'm headed back home in another month. I can hardly wait."

Gabriel was uncomfortable with Jamison being so familiar with him. Just because the man had a relationship with his father didn't mean Gabriel considered him a friend. "Just how are we related?"

Jamison blinked and turned red. "Excuse me?"

"I asked how we are related. My father said we are distant relatives."

"Oh, we're related by marriage. My sister married your cousin, but Johan and I grew up together, attended all the same schools."

Disgusted with himself for veering off the path, Gabriel returned to his purpose for being there. "I'd like to discuss Monica Fuller."

"Oh, such a sad situation," Drake said. "But don't worry, Mr. Windahl, the situation has been handled."

"Handled? You call firing my w…fiancée over a bunch of bull, handled?"

"What?" Both men gasped simultaneously.

"Yes fiancée. But even if she weren't, I'd be taking my business elsewhere."

"Ahh n-now, Mr. Windahl," Drake said from the edge of his seat, "let's not make any rash decisions. I'm sure something can be worked out."

"Rash? Let me tell you what rash is. Rash is firing your best employee because some coward called you anonymously."

"Gabriel," Jamison said evenly, "you're an excellent businessman. This was a business decision. What the caller said was true, and he threatened to tell our customers."

"First, stop calling me Gabriel. I don't ever recall giving you permission to be so informal with me." Jamison's mouth fell open, then snapped closed. "Secondly, didn't it strike you suspicious that someone would just call you out of the blue with such blackmail? How did this person get his information and what was his motive? And you have absolutely no loyalty to your employees. I know how many hours she worked for you. She went well beyond the call of duty. But how did you repay her—?"

"I assure you, we didn't want to lose her, Mr. Windahl," Drake interrupted. "I know how hard she worked for us, and I appreciated it. That's why we made arrangements for her."

"You turned your backs on her and gave her a flimsy offer so she wouldn't bring attention to the situation when you should have stood by her. Shown the world that you would not bow down to such tactics. Had her take a drug test. Fully investigated and discovered that she'd just purchased the car. Known it was one vial in the trunk. It would have been obvious to most the drugs were not hers." He stood. "All of my business dealings with Drake and Jamison end today. And I will be telling my associates why I'm taking my business elsewhere." He nodded a goodbye, then walked out of the room.

Gabriel's father would be upset with him for taking such action, but he didn't care. Sweetie had never been able to count on anyone to help fight battles. No longer.

Sweetie used the remote to turn off the television, then rolled over in bed and continued crying into her pillow—crying for the lost lives, for the unfairness of it all. After spending the morning watching infomercials and news about starving children and war-torn countries, shame overcame her. She always gave large amounts to charity and was active politically, but that wasn't the point. The point was she had been ungrateful for the many blessings she had in her life. There were people out there with real problems, and she was pouting because her father wanted to give her millions of dollars and she had a rich husband. The absurdity of her behavior sickened her.

Growing up, she'd hung with her cousins on the wrong side of town quite often. When they called her a spoiled little princess, she would deny it with everything she was. But looking at what her life had become, she agreed.

No more feeling sorry for yourself. She wiped the tears from her eyes and switched out her pillowcase for a dry one. She had plans to make for her business, but first she needed to call her father and thank him for the gift, though she couldn't accept it for the purposes he wanted. She'd be donating the money to charity.

All her life she'd wanted someone to truly be in her corner. She inhaled Gabriel's scent from the pillow, and her body warmed. Gabriel was that someone. An ironic laugh tugged at her. Here she was unemployed and willingly dependent on a man—a way she swore to never be—yet this felt more right than just about anything she'd done in her life.

She took a Tootsie off the nightstand, unwrapped it and popped it into her mouth. She still intended on calling her father, but she wanted Gabriel with her when she did.

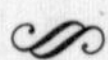

Tess clicked picture after picture of Kevin with shifty looking people she didn't know through the shaded, back-passenger side window of the rental SUV. When she told Sweetie her plan, Sweetie told her to drop it, but Tess couldn't. Kevin needed to be stopped. James wasn't happy about "playing sleuth" either. "I told you he had to be dealing," she said to James.

They'd parked diagonally from the hand carwash where Kevin was yucking it up with the fellas outside. All the times she'd driven past this shop, she'd never seen any vehicles actually being washed, yet the six-car parking lot was always busy.

James wrapped his arms around her waist and pulled her into his chest. "This isn't proof, but it's enough to take to Detective Morning. It's time to leave."

"Just a little longer. We can get more on him. I can feel it."

"Talk about feeling." He stroked her hair over one of her shoulders, and suckled along her neck. "There's plenty of room back here." He ground his erection into her butt.

"Room for what?" she cooed.

He slipped his hand into her panties and fingered her clit. "I don't know. I'm sure we can think of something.

Just as her eyes fluttered closed, she saw a car drive through the intersection where the "carwash" sat on the corner. Shots rang out from the car. Tess screamed. James shoved her onto the floor, wedging himself between her and the side of the SUV. She heard cars screeching and a few more shots. Then everything went silent, and James's arm began to relax on her.

Shivering from fear, she removed her hands from her face. "I don't want to play detective anymore. W-we can tell Detective Morning what we know."

James rasped into her ear, "I love you." He grimaced and drew in a ragged breath.

"James…James!" Afraid of hurting him, she carefully crawled from under him. "No, no, no, no…" The back of his shirt was slowly darkening with his blood.

He wheezed something incoherent.

Tears blurred her vision. "Hold on, baby." She hopped into the driver's seat. "You're gonna be fine." She drove toward the nearby hospital.

A smile tipped Gabriel's lips. Things were extremely awkward when he first arrived at Payton's hotel suite, but the more they spoke about what they didn't want to speak about, the more comfortable they became with each other. "Sweetie…I mean Monica has your eyes," Gabriel said to veer the conversation toward his real reason for visiting.

"Humph, you mean evil?" Payton said from the couch with cheer in his voice. "People have always said I look possessed."

"Oh yeah, she can throw a mean assed look at you." They shared a laugh.

Elbows on his knees, Payton lowered his face into his massive hands. His graying locs tumbled over his shoulders.

"You miss her, don't you?" Gabriel asked from the armchair.

Payton scrubbed his oval face with his dark hands. "I don't even know my child. People look at me and think I'm this great success story." He leaned back and stretched his long legs out. "But I'm a failure. A lonely, miserable failure."

"I know we just met, but I need to ask some very personal questions. I need to ask things she wants to know, but won't ask. You can be completely honest with me, and I'll soften whatever blows there may be, but she needs to know the truth. The whole truth. Sweet…Monica needs your help."

"You keep calling her Sweetie." He slowly bounced his head. "When she was a baby, I used to call her Sweetie. I'm shocked it held." He shook his head. "I should have never allowed Missy to move back to Chicago with my baby."

"Everyone except you and Mrs. Fuller call her Sweetie. She has this sweet tooth you wouldn't believe."

"You don't say," Payton said with his brows raised high, then reached into his inner suit pocket and pulled out a few pieces of hard candy. "Don't leave home without it." He chuckled. "I firmly believe that all sugar-free and fat-free products should be outlawed. Of course that is if they aren't naturally sugar or fat-free."

"Sweetie is definitely your child!" Gabriel slapped his knee and chuckled lightly. Sweetie had a few choice words for him when he'd mistakenly bought sugar-free whipped cream. As soon as her tongue touched the cream she'd sprayed on the tip of his penis, she'd pulled back, saying, "This does not taste right. I think it's spoiled." She then checked the can for a freshness date and noticed it was sugar-free. She flew into a tirade about the sins of sugar-free products. And her passion had turned him on even more.

His dick jerked to life. Sweetie said not to disturb her, but if he came home with the correct whipped cream, he bet he could change her mind. He shook the thought out of his mind. Sweetie needed time alone. "You two have a lot in common."

Payton seemed to sink into the couch. "Yeah, I wanted nothing to do with my father, and now my child wants nothing to do with me. Things weren't supposed to turn out this way. I wanted to be nothing like my father." He momentarily held up his hands. "Don't get me wrong. I know he loved us, but…But he was always into some get-rich-quick scheme. My mother literally worked herself to death trying to keep us from drowning in debt. I was only fifteen. Instead of staying home with me, my father went off in search of riches and left me with my uncle. I didn't see him again until I graduated from high school."

"Did you hear from him at all?"

"Oh yeah, he'd send cards on my birthday and Christmas. When he came to my graduation, he was a rich man. He'd done it." He broke out in a full-fledged smile. "By way of lotto. After Uncle Sam took his chunk, my old man had a little over twenty million left"

"Wow."

"Yep. Wow. He bought a car dealership and wanted me to work for him, but I wanted nothing to do with him. My uncle told me I was being a hardheaded fool and eventually convinced me to accept a million dollars of guilt money from my father."

"So what you gave Sweetie is guilt money?"

"No," he said simply. "I don't have enough money to pay for how much guilt I feel."

"So what happened with her mother?"

"I had good money when I met Missy, but I didn't have as much money as her previous men, so my male ego got the best of me. She loved me. And when she agreed to be my wife…" He smiled. "What more can I say?"

"I know exactly how you feel."

"After we married, I wanted to adopt her sons, but she wouldn't ask the fathers to sign away their rights. Looking back, I can now see how wrong I was, but at the time I didn't want to compete with those men. I wanted to be all she needed—all she wanted." He held his hand flat to his chest. "I could provide for her and her children. I'd be their father."

He gazed out the window, then back to Gabriel. "I've always admired how Missy puts her children first. She's not the most conventional, but she's a fantastic mother. I kept pressuring her and gave her an ultimatum I shouldn't have, and she made the choice she should have."

"You told her if she didn't ask the fathers of her sons to sign away their rights, you'd divorce her, didn't you?"

He nodded. "That's about the size of it. She had told me a million times she couldn't take those children's fathers from them. That they were good men and her sons deserved to have their fathers in their lives. Plus these men loved their sons. She was right, but I was too immature and arrogant to hear it. What I heard was these men have more money than you, so there's no way I'm cutting all ties with them.

"When I put in for the divorce, I didn't think she'd actually go through with it. I thought she'd see I meant business and change her mind. Missy's a strong woman."

"Sweetie would never admit this, but she takes a lot after her mother also. Both are very strong, independent-thinking women. They know what they want and will not settle for anything else, and damn what the world wants."

Payton's shoulders bounced as he chuckled. "Yep, you know Missy. She actually divorced me! I had to get her back. I poured myself into my business, thinking she'd take me back once she saw what a success I became. I sent Monica gifts for her birthday and Christmas, but I honestly didn't realize how fast time flew by. Next thing I know, my baby girl is graduating from high school and wants nothing to do with me, just like I hadn't wanted anything to do with my dad. All of the intentions I'd had to make her events over the years meant nothing. There was nothing my father could have said to win me over, so I knew my apologies would mean as much as my intentions. So I waited and prayed she'd forgive me someday."

"When she earned her masters degree, you offered her a position in your company."

"I'd gotten tired of waiting. I wanted to offer another olive branch. I hadn't realized she'd been recruited by my company and offered a position. I had no way of knowing her grades and didn't investigate because I didn't care. I just wanted my daughter." He hunched his shoulders. "I mean, what were the chances..."

"She took your offer of a job the wrong way. She thought you didn't want her until she'd graduated number one. That's why she turned down your offer. It was her way of rejecting you for all the times she felt rejected by you."

"I don't know how or if I can fix things between me and Monica...Sweetie."

"You both want the same thing."

"Mama, no! Don't call Sweetie. She's already going through more than enough."

Missy's heels clicked on the floor as she approached Tess. "What has this...this janitor gotten you mixed up in? That could be you in there!" She bounced an accusing finger in Tess's face. "I expect you to break things off with him before he gets you killed. He's not good enough—"

"Just stop!"

Brows raised, Missy slowly said, "Oh, no, you didn't."

"I'm scared, Mama." Tess rested her hand on her chest. "That's the man I love in there, and it's my fault he's hurt. He was protecting me!" She wiped at the flood of tears falling from her eyes. "I always hurt the ones I love. He might die because of me."

Compassion quickly replaced the shock on Missy's face. She grabbed Tess into a loving embrace. "It's okay, baby."

"But it's not." She sniffed. "It's not. I've got to stop this. I've got to make some changes. I love Sweetie and James."

"What happened with Sweetie wasn't your fault."

"I'm taking responsibility for my part in what happened. It's time to set things straight. Mama, I love you. When my mother died, you stepped up and were the perfect role model for me, but I'm not your child. Sweetie is. Sweetie's needs should have always come before mine with you."

"I have enough room in my heart for you both. Yes, Sweetie is my baby, but I still love you as a child."

Tess backed away. "And I've taken that love and run with it, but I can't any longer. Not at Sweetie's expense. Not if you're going to make James feel inferior. I'm in love with a good man."

"What are you talking about? Sweetie loves you." Missy took Tess's hands into her own. "You two are best friends. You're upset about this boy. It has you talking crazy."

"He's not a boy, and I'm more sane now than I've ever been, Mama. I'm not the same person I was even two days ago. How do you think it makes Sweetie feel every time you tell her she's not good enough because she's not like me?"

"I've never said that!"

"The hell you don't. You use different words, but the meaning is clear, and you've said it countless times. It stops today. You will not compare us again. And James…" She could hear him whispering his love to her. "I love him and will marry him, if he'll still have me." She proceeded to tell Missy what had happened.

"What in the hell were you thinking, Tess?"

"Sweetie was fired because of my drama. I wanted to set things right."

"This is unbelievable." Eyes closed, Missy slowly shook her head. "You're right, Tess." She sat on the nearby leather-like loveseat. "I hadn't meant to put Monica down, but…" She blew out a long breath and lowered her face into her palms. "It's her father…"

Tess's brows knitted together. "How is your putting down Sweetie her father's fault?"

"No, not his fault. I loved him so much…He's the first man I gave my heart to, and he broke it." She straightened her posture. "Sweetie's so much like him. She looks like him, acts like him."

"So, she was a constant reminder of you're pain."

Missy nodded slowly. "Yes, but I didn't realize what I was doing until I spoke with him on the phone. Heard his voice again." She smiled sadly.

"He about swallowed a piece of hard candy when I told him about Monica."

"Well, at least she comes by it honestly," Tess said with a smile of her own as she sat beside Missy.

"I'm sorry I've been using you. Please don't distance yourself from me. Sweetie walking out of her own home was an eye-opener for me. I don't want to push her away." She placed her hand on top of Tess's. "I guess we've made some miraculous changes lately."

"For the better."

"Yes, baby, for the better…And James…I'm sorry about everything. He's a strong man. I'm sure he'll be fine."

Tess wished she were as confident as Missy.

"I'll go in first. She'd kill me if I brought you in and her hair was all over the place," Gabriel said to Payton. He actually wanted to ensure Sweetie was dressed. She sounded awfully frisky during their phone conversation, which was a good thing in his opinion. Slipping the key into the lock, he grinned. After the reconciliation, he could make love to her. "I'll be right back."

Payton nodded and popped a piece of butterscotch candy into his mouth. "Take your time. I need to gather myself."

Gabriel followed the soft jazz playing on the stereo into the bedroom. At the site of Sweetie lying naked on the bed seductively rolling a cherry Tootsie Roll Pop over her lips, his dick pressed hard against his zipper.

"Welcome home," she cooed.

"Oh God," he stroked himself, "you're trying to kill me."

She giggled lightly. "Can you think of a better way to die?"

Debating if he should keep Payton waiting in the hallway until he made love to the most beautiful woman in the world, he glanced over his shoulder toward the door. Once Sweetie found out her father was waiting and he'd kept the man in the hall while he—he smiled—made her come until her hair straightened, she'd be rightfully upset.

"I can't believe I'm doing this, but I need for you to get dressed."

She laughed. "You're joking, right?"

"I wish I were. I brought a guest for dinner."

"What were you thinking?" She snatched her robe off the end of the bed. "I'm in no mood for guests."

"I'm sorry, baby. I'll make it up to you."

"Who is it anyway?" she asked on her way into the bathroom.

Ignoring her question, he headed out. "You have five minutes."

Gabriel returned to the hallway.

"That didn't take long," Payton said.

"I just needed to tell her we had a guest. She was still dressed in night clothes." His favorite night clothes—nothing. *Damn, I had time to at least taste her.*

"Did you tell her who her guest is?"

"No. She asked, but I acted like I didn't hear. Let's go on in."

"Wait a second." Payton inhaled and exhaled several large breaths, squared off his shoulders and became stone faced. "Okay, I'm ready."

"She doesn't need to see the businessman Payton. She needs to see the father who loves and misses her. Let down your protective shields. Let her see you're hurting without her in your life."

"You're right." He patted Gabriel on the shoulder. "You're a good man."

Gabriel and Payton were just taking a seat in the living room when Sweetie came out of the bedroom.

"Hello..." she trailed off upon seeing Payton standing there. "Wha...what?" Her confused gaze traveled from Payton to Gabriel. "You brought him here?" she asked, tears filling her eyes.

"No, baby," Gabriel said softly. He wanted to be the one to comfort her, but it wasn't his place. He wasn't the one she needed. "He was already in town to see you." He saw a spark of hope in her eyes.

"But why?" she asked her father.

"Because I love and miss my little Sweetie." He wiped the tears from his own eyes, then crossed the room and embraced her. "Please forgive me."

Gabriel stood back and watched as Sweetie broke down in her father's arms. His cell phone rang. He went into the kitchen to answer and give father and daughter some much needed alone time. He checked the caller ID, frowned.

"Hello, Mrs. Fuller."

"Hello, Gabriel, and please call me Missy or Mama. We're going to be family."

He knew he should be elated, but something in her tone worried him. "Yes, ma'am. Is something wrong?"

"Is Monica near?"

"She's occupied in the other room."

"Good, because I need a few minutes."

"This sounds serious." He sat at the kitchen table.

"It is. First, allow me to apologize for my behavior. There is no excuse."

"No problem. What's wrong?"

"I'll let you decide what and when to tell Monica." She proceeded to tell him everything that had happened with Tess and James. "The doctors say James will recover fully, but Tess is still a mess. She needs Monica here but doesn't want her to know what's going on. She's afraid of overwhelming her."

"I'll take care of everything."

Sweetie burst into the hospital room. Visitation hours were over, but Missy had already called in favors so Tess could stay at James's bedside. She pulled Tess out of the chair and embraced her. "Girl, if you ever hold out on me again, you'll need a hospital bed when I'm done with you."

"Oh, Sweetie, I was so scared. I almost lost him. I don't know what I'd do without him." She returned to her seat and retook James's hand.

"But you didn't lose him. Don't focus on what could have gone wrong. Focus on what went right."

A half-hour or so later, Gabriel came in and wrapped his arms around Sweetie. "Detective Morning is in the waiting area. She says Kevin was arrested at the scene. They found drugs on him, then got a warrant and searched his home. And guess what they found?"

"Vials of cocaine," Sweetie and Tess said simultaneously.

"Exactly." He nibbled along Sweetie's earlobe.

"You two need to head on home," Tess said with a devilish smile on her face. "I'll be fine."

"Are you sure?" Sweetie asked.

"I'm with the man I love. I can't help but be fine."

Sweetie cupped Gabriel's hand to her chest. "I know what you mean."

EPILOGUE

Nine months later

Sweetie watched as her son suckled gently from her breast.

Just as Sweetie had suspected, her input for the wedding had been mostly ignored by the mother brigade. Instead of the colors of fall; green, blue and yellow pastels brought the cathedral to life. The two hundred person guest list Sweetie and Tess had compiled of friends and family grew to over two thousand in attendance—most of whom Sweetie nor Tess knew. The Moroccan and Mexican menu they'd strongly recommended was tossed for a French buffet—never mind that French food was one of the few Sweetie didn't particularly like. There was no electric slide because the string quartet didn't know the "Electric Boogaloo" or anything else appropriate. The bridesmaids' dresses were the most hideous things Sweetie had ever seen…All in all, it was the best day of her life.

Payton had walked Sweetie down the aisle and Harold had stood in for Tess's father who had passed a few years ago. When Payton offered Sweetie to Gabriel, tears had fallen from her eyes. She'd never been so happy.

"You okay, baby?" Gabriel asked, breaking into her thoughts.

"I was just thinking about how beautiful our wedding was. I can't believe I wanted to skip the ceremony."

"It was nice, wasn't it?" He fingered the tiny black curls that covered the baby's head. "He's so precious. Thank you, baby."

Someone knocked at the door. Gabriel covered the baby with a light receiving blanket, but the baby shoved it away. The person knocked again.

"It's okay, Gabriel, we're all family now."

"You can come in, but the baby's feeding, so, well, you know…"

Tess waddled into the room with James close behind. "Oh, my!" She rushed to the bedside. "He's so handsome." She tugged at James. "Look at our Godson," she said excitedly.

"He is adorable." He scooted a chair close to the bed for Tess.

"Wait until my Godbaby is born." Sweetie placed her hand on Tess's belly. "Oh, she's pushing at my hand. She's ready to come out. Maybe she'll make an early appearance."

"I wish she would come on," Tess drawled out. "I don't know if I can wait another month."

Josephine rushed into the room and went to the ever-crowding bedside. "He's so darling."

Ever since she'd found out Payton Johnson was Sweetie's father, her attitude toward Sweetie changed. Now she couldn't get enough of showing off her daughter-in-law and saying whose child she was. At first Sweetie was put off by the sudden change, but she decided to let it go. Some battles just weren't worth fighting.

The baby finished feeding and was quickly falling asleep. Sweetie covered herself and handed him over to Gabriel to do his part. He gently placed the baby against his shoulder and patted his back until he belched.

"Oh, that was a good belch," Missy said as she fully entered the room with Harold at her side. "That has to be my grandson."

"None other but," Sweetie said proudly.

A few minutes later, Payton arrived. He worked out of Chicago now.

"Daddy!" She opened her arms wide.

He kissed her forehead. "You done good, baby." Beaming, he took his grandson from Gabriel. "He looks like you, Gabriel." Everyone in the room nodded in agreement.

The grandmother's held their hands out for the baby. Payton reluctantly handed him to Missy, then turned to Sweetie. "So what are you naming him?"

"I wanted to wait until those knuckle head brothers of mine arrived, but I guess we can tell everyone now."

Gabriel took Sweetie by the hand. "We are proud to introduce Payton Johan Windahl."

Group Discussion Questions:

Please explain your answers.

1. In the opening of the book, Sweetie suspected Kevin had beaten Tess a few times over the past few months. Do you think Sweetie should have said something to Tess sooner? What do you think she should have done? What would you have done if you suspected your best friend were being abused?

2. Abused women go back to their abusers every day of the week, just as Tess did in this novel, why do you think that is?

3. Were Zack's feelings for Sweetie genuine?

4. Was Tess a gold digger? What about Missy and Josephine?

5. Do you believe that Tess was as good a friend to Sweetie as Sweetie was to Tess?

6. Sweetie's father met his financial responsibilities toward her, but Sweetie still felt neglected. Do you think daughters—children—need their fathers in their lives or can the mother fill both roles? Or can the father fill both roles if the mother is not in the picture?

7. Why was Sweetie so upset after she'd been asked to resign? Why didn't she immediately accept money from her family to start her own business?

8. Was Sweetie's company right in asking her to resign?

9. Throughout the novel Sweetie wore the façade of a strong, black woman. What is your definition of a strong black woman?

A Note From The Author:

Physical and emotional abuse are two very serious issues. If you or someone you love is suffering at the hands of an abuser, please do something. The National Coalition Against Domestic Violence website is an excellent place to start figuring out what that “something” is to do. http://www.ncadv.org/ or you may phone their hotline at: 1-800-799-SAFE (7233).

Also, I took a little artistic license with Sweetie’s marriage to Gabriel. There is a waiting period in Illinois, so don’t y’all think you’ll run off for a quick wedding!

Much Joy, Peace and Love,
Deatri King-Bey

About the Author

Currently a Chicago-area resident, Deatri King-Bey works as an editor. Three children, two dogs, and one husband keep her days pretty full. An avid reader since childhood, Deatri's idea of a great afternoon is a trip to the bookstore, followed by hours curled up on the sofa with her newly purchased novel. For more information about Deatri and her upcoming titles, you may visit her Website at http://www.deewrites.com or http://www.myspace.com/deewrites. She also loves to hear from her readers and can be contacted at deatri@deewrites.com.

Parker Publishing, LLC

Celebrating Black
Love Life Literature

Mail or fax orders to:

12523 Limonite Avenue
Suite #220-438
Mira Loma, CA 91752
(866) 205-7902
(951) 685-8036 fax

or order from our Web site:

www.parker-publishing.com
orders@parker-publishing.com

Ship to:
Name: ____________________
Address: ____________________
____
City: ____________________
State: __________ Zip: __________
Phone: ____________________

Qty	Title	Price	Total

Shipping and handling is $3.50, Priority Mail shipping is $6.00
FREE standard shipping for orders over $30
Alaska, Hawaii, and international orders – call for rates
See Website for special discounts and promotions

Add S&H
CA residents add 7.75% sales tax
Total

Payment methods: We accept Visa, MasterCard, Discovery, or money orders. NO PERSONAL CHECKS.

Payment Method: (circle one): VISA MC DISC Money Order

Name on Card: ____________________
Card Number: ____________________ Exp Date: __________
Billing Address: ____________________
____
City: ____________________
State: __________ Zip: __________